He was no business of baring Gis His loving fingers lifted the brief sk of her gymslip up over her back. His eyes gloated on the sight revealed as those same wanton fingers peeled her knickers slowly down. He rolled and nudged them all the way to her knees, where gravity did the rest. He seemed mesmerized at the sight of her slim young buttocks, squirming on the pillow on his lap; and, as Véronique saw, there was something appealing in the way her body bent and tapered inward from the width of her hips to the narrowness of her tightly clenched knees.

Also by Faye Rossignol

Sweet Fanny
Sweet Fanny's Diary
Lord Hornington's Academy of Love
A Victorian Lover of Women
ffrench Pleasures
The ffrench House
Pearl of the Hareem
Peal of the Courtesans
The Girls of Lazy Daisy's
Nude Rising
The Call of the Flesh
The Hôtel Nymphomania
Beginners Please
Willing Girls
Sporting Girls

Véronique

Faye Rossignol

Delta

Publisher's message:

This novel creates an imaginary sexual world.
In the real world readers are advised to practise safe sex.

Copyright © 1998 Faye Rossignol

The right of Faye Rossignol to be identified as the Author of
the work has been asserted her her in accordance with
the Copyright Designs and Patents Act 1988

First published in 1998
by HEADLINE BOOK PUBLISHING

A HEADLINE DELTA paperback

10 9 8 7 6 5 4 5 3 2 1

All rights reserved. No part of this publication may be
reproduced, stored in a retreival system, or transmitted,
in any form or by any means without prior written
permission of the publisher, nor be otherwise circulated
in any form of binding or cover other than that in which
it is published and without a similar condition being
imposed on the subsequent purchaser.

All characters in this publication are fictitious
and any resemblance to real persons, living or dead,
is purely coincidental.

ISBN 0 7472 5939 9

Printed and bound in Great Britain by
Mackays of Chatham plc, Chatham, Kent

HEADLINE BOOK PUBLISHING
A division of Hodder Headline PLC
338 Euton Road
London NW1 3BH

Véronique

Véronique

With trembling fingers Veronica took the packet from the dapper, manicured hands of Sheridan McLaren. If only his eyes weren't so hypnotic! He hadn't taken them off her ever since the clerk had shown her into the office.

"I presume you already knew your aunt had died?" he asked her.

"She was not much talked about in my family, sir," she replied.

Actually, that wasn't quite true. In Veronica's childhood Aunt Connie's name had been mentioned often. Aunt Connie was the rich member of the family. Aunt Connie had no children. Aunt Connie had to leave her money to someone. And Veronica had been made to suck up to her (no other word for it) shamelessly. It hadn't been too difficult. Aunt Connie was funny. And tolerant. And generous. And she had been (or seemed) sincerely fond of her little niece. But then something had happened and Aunt Connie's name had never been mentioned again. No one had ever explained the sudden silence, but Veronica was used to that. Her family home had always been rather dull and silence was its usual climate.

"I knew her when she was your age," McLaren said.

His eyes brimmed with amusement but the girl was not to know that it was the biblical use of the word 'know' that tickled him. Connie had been the first lady of the night he ever enjoyed. She had only just started then, in a house in Wych Street off the Strand, before they pulled down all the brothels and dirty bookshops there to make way for Aldwych and Southampton Row. Oh, those were the days — when his prick could stand for hours and he could enjoy five or six girls in an evening! But darling Connie had been the first and she'd awakened such an appetite that many hundreds of girls had not been able to satisfy it since.

It was rampant even now — at eleven in the morning! A pretty little thing like this Veronica girl could have no idea what she had done to him down there. Ten minutes ago it had been a limp, warm sausage between his legs; now it was trying to burst out of his flies or climb out over his waistband. He leaned forward on his desk, partly to accommodate its massive growth, but mainly to bring it closer to her in secret, to relish the thought of her sweet innocence so close to that gnarled old ruffian, who had taken the innocence of so many girls like her down the years.

"To come to the point," he said, "I am the executor of her will and it directs me to pass you that package now in your hands. I am to draw your attention to her seal." He reached across to show it to her. "And to the fact that it is unbroken. No one knows what is inside — nor ever will unless you choose to tell them."

Veronica rubbed the sealing wax daintily, trembling slightly. It was all so exciting.

His fingers 'accidentally' brushed hers; he longed to caress them but held himself in check. There might be time enough yet. He loved girls' fingers. He loved to think of all the secret places they had been.

"D'you want to take it home and read it?" he asked. "Or ... the room next to this office happens to be empty. I could see that you were not disturbed there."

While the girl turned the package over and over, considering the offer, he tried to think of something else to say about old Connie. He could see her quite clearly in his mind's eye, as she had been when she handed him the package. And, of course, he knew what was in it. He was almost desperate to know how the girl would react.

A fine sporting girl • 3

"She's got the makings of a fine sporting girl, Sheridan," Connie had said. "I look to you to rescue her from my sister and that ghastly husband and let her discover the heights to which she can rise."

She had it all planned out, too — every stage. First he was to hand her the package, containing the gold watch and the letter. No more than that. If the girl took the bait and went to work for the Hegels, or at any other sporting house, and stuck it for a year, she was to be told of the rest of her inheritance: until then she was to know nothing about it.

When dear Connie had written that will back in 1919, it was as a mere precaution, of course. Her niece was then a toothy, squat little fourteen-year-old and the old aunt intended putting her plan into operation in person when the girl came of age and her parents could not sue. That would have been in 1926. But this was only 1922, when the girl was …

"May I ask how old you are, my dear?" he said.

"Sixteen, sir," she replied meekly. "I shall be seventeen in two months time — in August."

Sixteen! The lawyer broke out into a light sweat. Sixteen — and a virgin for sure! He *had* to have her — and, after all, he would only be carrying out the old aunt's wishes. Such a gem of a girl could not possibly be allowed to go straight to Nymphenburg, the Hegels' rather grand sporting house down in Little Venice. They'd spoil her …

"May I go to the next room and read it, sir?" she asked shyly.

With a practised flick of his pelvis he got his erection safely tucked up against his belly and secure behind his waistband. He ushered her across the room, appraising her figure from behind. She'd be about 5ft 4in in her stockinged feet — his prick leaped an inch at the thought of her in fishnet stockings ... and lace suspenders ... and ... stop! She'd be about 36in round her bust. He'd already admired their firmness and rounded shape, their palm-itching protrusion. She'd be slightly less about the hips, 35in, say, but oh what a delicious derrière she wagged before his eyes in that brief crossing of the room! Round the waist she was hardly more than a delicate 21in. His fingers and thumbs would almost meet around her there. As she fiddled with the doorknob he imagined grasping her corseted body round that wasp waist and bending her there, arching her back to bring her delightful bottom closer, closer ...

"I'll see you're not disturbed," he assured her again. "Just come back to me when you're done."

When you're *done!* Down at Nymphenburg she'd be *done* six or more times a day — if Connie's letter proved persuasive enough. It was not the sort of life a sweet little sixteen-year-old virgin should be thrown into, willy nilly. She should be introduced to it gently, over a couple of months — for instance, as the mistress of a handsome, virile, and above all experienced professional man of taste and refinement.

As soon as the door had closed behind her he ran tiptoe to the bookcase and took out five volumes of law reports — Chancery Division. This revealed a gap in the bookcase, and in the panelling on the other side, through which he could observe her unseen; the lighting was such that, even if she stared directly at him, she would see nothing but what looked like a heavier bit of wooden moulding that cast a deeper shadow than the others.

She had broken the seal and taken out the gold wristwatch — an elegant little specimen given to Connie by the Hegels after twenty years in service, two down in Wych Street and the rest at Nymphenburg. During that time she reckoned she'd been done by more than 30,000 men — or more than

30,000 times, anyway, because, of course, she'd had lots of regulars down the years, Sheridan McLaren among them.

He noticed that the girl smiled at the inscription. Good. That meant she understood. And was not shocked. She tried it on her wrist, liked it, wound it up, and left it there. She turned to the letter. The lawyer watched her long enough to be sure she wasn't going to throw it aside in disgust, then returned the books to their place and himself to his work. He glanced at his own pocket watch for he was now impatient for the hour of 12:30 to come around.

Ten minutes before that time the girl finished reading Connie's letter. Either she was a slow reader or — much more likely in the lawyer's opinion — she had been given much to think over. There was already a slightly different air about her. She was still respectful but the mousey submissiveness had gone.

"I'd be grateful if you'd look after this watch for me for a few more days, Mister McLaren," she said, handing it to him. "My aunt's letter ... did she show it you, by the way?"

"No, of course not," he replied. Strictly speaking it was true. Connie had not shown him the actual wording but she had left him in no doubt of its contents in general.

"Well, she makes a number of suggestions as to how I should conduct my life — suggestions that need some careful thought. Meanwhile, it would be tactless if my parents were to find the watch. I shall return in a week or less to collect it."

"By which time you will also know whether to take up your aunt's suggestions?"

"Yes."

"Then may I respectfully ask you to take no irrevocable step without consulting me? I shall not charge for it. Your aunt was a dear, close friend and I should like to help you in any way I can."

Now there was suspicion in her eyes. "I think you *do* know what is in this letter," she said.

He dipped his head in acknowledgement. "I have not seen its actual wording but, yes, she did discuss its general tenor with me. However, let us not speak of it now." He consulted his watch again. "I have an urgent appointment, which I fear I cannot ..."

"In Maida Vale?" she asked teasingly.

He froze. Then, recovering swiftly, he said, "Clearly there are things in that letter which she did *not* discuss with me." He eyed her speculatively. "You are not shocked?"

She shook her head. Then, after a moment's hesitation, she threw the letter down beside the watch. "Read it yourself, if you like," she said. "I think I shall have made my decision by tomorrow. May I return then?"

"Of course ..."

Before he could say more she had turned on her heel and gone.

He longed to read the letter at once but he longed even more to do what he did every weekday lunchtime and on as many other occasions as he could manage, in a house he owned in Maida Vale — the sort of House that was not a home. Besides, he belonged to that generation which always left the jelly and ice-cream to last.

The girl was hopping onto a bus, northbound on the Edgware Road, as he emerged from his office. His regular taxi was waiting for him. It was only a short drive but every minute was precious. He would arrive at 12:40, eat a light luncheon until 12:50, pass an hour in happy copulation with Giselle, his current mistress, and arrive back at the office on the dot of 2:00.

Such had been his lunchtime routine for the past eighteen years, since 1902, when his wife had finally told him to make

You're not shocked?

other arrangements. 'Find some little tart to leave your sticky muck inside,' had been her way of putting it. He'd had over a hundred mistresses during that time; some lasted a week, some half a year; the average was two months.

Curiously enough, it had all started for him on a visit to Nymphenburg to see Connie, shortly after his wife had made that elegant suggestion. Then as now, every single house in that particular street in Little Venice had been a small brothel, each with three or four girls to play with. Nymphenburg, the house in the middle of the terrace, was the largest with eight; it was really two houses *knocked* together (lots of jokes about that, of course). As he'd approached the house on that particular day, he'd noticed this young girl walking up and down in an obvious state of agitation. When he had asked if he could assist her, she had started crying — and asking him what it was like for a girl to work in 'a place like that'?

Her name was Leonore. She was the daughter of a respectable shopkeeper who had died, leaving his family in debt. Her mother had gone to pieces and she was their sole support. She was starving, of course, and had felt a lot better once she had a square meal inside her — which was when he had taken her up to this house in Maida Vale, which he now owned but which he was then looking after for a friend on an overseas posting. And there he had shown her 'what it was like for a girl to work in a place like that'! Six times on that first night — he still remembered it with proud affection. The things one could do in one's early thirties! Not that he was a dullard at fifty, mind, but twice a day was all he could now sustain.

Six months Leonore had stayed. He paid her what she would have earned at Nymphenburg — less the Hegels' cut, of course — so he'd got the exclusive use of a first-class sporting girl for half the price and, in passing, had taught her all he knew, which was most of what she needed to know to get a good position there — a good *horizontal* position, as they liked to joke. The Hegels were so impressed that, instead of turning away such hopeless, tearful little starvelings as Leonore had been, they started sending them to him for breaking in and training. About half his hundred-odd mistresses had come to him in that way. The rest he had found for himself in various ways. Some were sisters of girls he had helped. Some applied for a place as housemaid at the house or typist at the office. One delightful young thing had been about to get married and wanted two weeks' schooling in the conjugal arts; she had applied at Nymphenburg and the Hegels had sent her on to him. He thought all wives — and husbands — should work in houses of pleasure for two or three weeks before marriage. At present more than two percent of marriages ended in divorce — a shocking rate that could be cut to virtually nil if his scheme were followed.

Such musings and memories carried him all the way to his love nest. Giselle was waiting for him. She had already had her lunch. Gerty, the maid, was upstairs, turning down the bed, drawing the curtains, and putting out the biscuits and fruit cordial. Giselle's job was to fire him up. She had made a good start, being obviously naked beneath her thin, floral housecoat.

Two months ago she had been another frightened little waif, dithering around outside one of the brothels in Little Venice. Madame Hegel had seen her and sent her on to him with a note. She was one of the most scared, jumpy young creatures he'd ever handled. Three days it took before she'd let him deflower her. But oh it had been worth the wait! And now she was one of the raunchiest, randiest, dirtiest-minded

A good horizontal position • 9

girls he'd ever known. She could not wait to start working in Little Venice — which was all to the good because Sheridan McLaren now had plans to replace her with young Veronica.

Giselle's way of firing him up was crude and direct — and, needless to say, effective. "Today, Sheridan darling," she murmured, "I want you to fuck me in my mouth, then in my cunt, and then in my arse. Have you got three shots for me in your locker, today? I've been trembling with desire all morning just thinking about it ..."

The erotic litany went on and on while Sheridan McLaren calmly ate his cheese and celery and sorbet and sipped an excellent Montrachet '14.

He never schooled the girls he was given for breaking into the profession. This particular house — let us admit it now — had been the most celebrated sporting house in northwest London back in Edwardian times. Sheridan McLaren's overseas friend had inherited it after it closed and, finding it amusing for a while to entertain ladies there, had kept it until McLaren had, in turn, offered to buy it for his daily pleasure. All its original fantasy chambers were intact and it was crammed to the rafters with erotic clothing, books, pictures ... even erotic comics for those whose tastes lay in that direction. It always amazed him how girls, once their inhibitions were removed, would develop their erotic natures in such varied ways. He believed that although a man's libido might be stronger than a woman's — that is, his desire to 'pot the red,' as they say, might be stronger than a girl's desire to have the 'red' in her particular 'pocket' — her erotic nature, her fantasy, her stamina far outweighed his. Giselle, for instance, had not been able to say penis or vagina without blushing when he first knew her. And now here she was saying, "I don't want you to squirt your sticky in my mouth, though. I want it all over my face. I want to feel it like hot, wet pellets on my eyelids, on my cheeks, up my nostrils ... And d'you think if I bit it, like this" — she took his thumb and nipped it between her teeth — "wouldn't that be nice? Would you like that, too? Come on!"

He had finished his light repast by now so, as he downed the last drops of his wine, she played one of her favourite tricks. She popped his buttons and flipped his organ out through his flies. And what a gnarled old veteran it was! Seven inches long, thicker at the top than at its root, curved like a banana with a skew to the right (because of 'massive self-abuse' in puberty, he always proudly claimed), stiff as a poker, and with a big, weepy eye gleaming in the centre of its hot red head.

Giselle bit her lip like a naughty schoolgirl and, gripping it tight, right down at the root in her eager hand, she set off up the stairs, leading him as any man would adore to be led. The housecoat opened as she walked and the movement made it slip off her shoulders. She left it where it fell, changing hands to get it off the arm that held him so delightfully. The girlish figure that wiggled and swayed in front of him could hardly have been more different from the one he had slavered over in his office an hour earlier. For Giselle was gamine, boyish, with a long, slender body and slim thighs that could not meet in her fork even when her knees were tight together. The first time she began to loosen up, she pointed out this feature. "Look!" she said delightedly. "Even with my thighs pressed tight together a man could still get himself inside me — don't you think that proves I'm just *made* to be a *fille-de-joie?*"

Her long blonde hair, tied into a single, loose ponytail, streamed out behind her. And when she turned to grin at him her big violet eyes twinkled and her high, round breasts jiggled. And she was, all in all, such an enticing dish that he automatically to the top of her fork and were rewarded with the glorious vision of her slim, frilly labia hanging in the gold of her bush. Her breasts hung down too and jiggled invitingly.

It was too much for him. He leaped from the bed and waddled across to her with his erection swinging like an eccentric metronome in front of him. When his hands clamped round her hips she pretended to squeal out in surprise.

"I was the first that ever burst," he intoned as he slipped the length of it along her furrow, feeling for her hole, "into that silent c."

She giggled and swept her buttocks aside as she reached for her towel, leaving him out in the open again. "Well your Ancient Mariner will just have to wait a minute longer, until I've made myself comfortable."

She dried her face and then returned to the bed. He got out a jar of Vaseline while she made a breast-high pile of all the pillows and cushions so that when she bent forward her body sank into them and she did not have to bend at the knees. In fact, she made two piles, one for her head and shoulders, the other for her tummy and hips. Her breasts had no support and had to dangle free in the space between, where any randy man's hands could get at them.

She did not test any of these arrangements, for it was not the first time she had made them. When all was to her satisfaction she leaned forward with a sigh and snuggled her lithe young body to the most comfortable position, spreading her legs a little. "How's that?" she asked, wagging her tail at him.

He thrust his erection down until it was near-horizontal and touched it against her labia. "One cushion short of absolute perfection," he replied as he went to fetch it from the chaise longue.

She stood upright again briefly as he slipped it in front of her, just where it would lift her bottom a tiny bit higher and make her arch her back a bit more, which would bring into perfect alignment the two delightful holes she had asked him to exercise today.

When she was settled he took up the Vaseline jar and smeared the lubricant all over his tool, making sure to wipe an excess into the groove just under his peeled-back foreskin, between the head and the column. She had a tight little bumhole squeezed in there between her slim, boyish buttocks. He wiped the excess off on the puckered ring and worked a little of it just inside her. The sphincter went into spasm and a shiver passed all down her.

"Fleur says I'm the kind men like to poke there," she said with a giggle.

"Fleur says, eh? Have you been talking with the girls at Nymphenburg, little one?"

"I met her in Harrods."

"And recognized her?"

She giggled again. "Recognized her type. We got talking. It didn't take long. She says men will tip well for the privilege of enjoying a girl's back passage."

First it was 'arse' then 'back passage'! Her fickleness was part of her charm, to be sure. He grabbed his erection and began sliding it up and down her furrow, moving in and out slightly to match its curve. "Oh, that's good!" he murmured.

"M-m-m!" She wiggled slightly from side to side to make it more interesting. "Don't you like it? You never said."

"I don't *dis*like it, but I prefer the proper place. However, I'm more than willing to assist you in your preparation for the Gay Life at Nymphenburg — especially if you can earn goos tips for it." He slowed down and halted with his knob pressed tight against her sphincter. "Ready?"

She swallowed hard. "Go gently."

He pressed with controlled firmness until he felt the muscle yield and her rectum swallowed the tip of it.

She let out a sigh and closed her eyes. Her right hand stole toward her mouth and, a moment later, her thumb disappeared between her lips. She sucked it like a happy little baby. "Tell me what it feels like," she murmured round the comforting digit.

"It feels much less tight than previously," he replied. "It's responding well to our training."

She smiled and continued to suck her thumb. He did not know that both his sons, on their secret visits to her, had been assisting in that 'training' — or did he? Like her, they — Terence, the barrister, and Rory, the army captain — weren't sure whether their father knew they had been visiting his mistresses for some years past, always at times when they knew he wouldn't catch them at it. They told her they never spoke to him about it, nor he to them; and she, too, kept not only her silence but also the fivers they left behind them from time to time. "I'm a quick learner," she said, "and so is my body. Tell me more what it's like. How is it different from my vagina? I need to know these things from the man's point of view."

"Well, petal, to *me* it feels like those rubber vaginas you can buy in the back rooms of certain shops in Paris — tight at the entry, looser inside. Also it's more rough. I don't mean abrasive-rough but ... well, it's like the difference between driving over asphalt and over cobblestones."

He pushed his erection farther in, but not yet all the way. She let out a gasp and shivered.

"That was good," he said. "Just a little gasp like that, not too exaggerated. Can you do it again?"

She obliged.

"And again?"

She did it a third time. "I meant it, you know. It feels delicious to me."

"Yes, but the time will come when it no longer does. That's when you've got to remember how you once ..."

"Never!" she exclaimed vehemently. "I'm going to enjoy doing it with every man who ever takes me upstairs — well, maybe not *every* man, but as many as I can." She almost told him about last Wednesday, when she'd done it twice with him at lunchtime, followed by Rory, also twice, at teatime, and then Terence for two heavenly hours in the evening when she stopped counting. Terence could do it three times, straight off, without even going soft. So that was at least ten goes, and she'd come each time. And ten goes, according to Fleur, was more than most girls at Nymphenburg did in a typical day. Six was their average. So why shouldn't she get as much fun as she could — *and* get paid?

She was starting to come now. The first little ripples of pleasure were stirring in the small of her back and down the backs of her thighs; soon they'd spread. Sherry's breathing was starting to be erratic, too, she noticed. He might claim to find anal distasteful — and perhaps his fastidious, polished self did so truly — but deep inside him a more primitive animal was starting to respond.

Sheridan had never confessed it to any of his mistresses, nor ever would, but he actually found a girl's backgammon as tasty as her filet mignon. In fact, he considered that every hole that a kindly Mother Nature had provided in the female body was equally delightful — including those temporary cavities furnished by her armpits, her hands, her breasts, the fork of her tight-clenched thighs, the backs of her knees, her folded elbows ... and anywhere else his erotic fantasy and her acrobatic dexterity could conjure for his of his knob, just underneath the glans. She squeezed between squirts and let go as they spouted out. And he cried, "Oh!" and "Ah!" and watched in heavy-lidded fascination as the sticky little packets of his milt flung themselves into the void and landed on her brow, her cheeks, her eyelids ...

When the first gushing rapture was waning she prolonged it by leaving off her squeezing and, grabbing his tool like some giant lipstick, rubbed it side-to-side across her half-open mouth ... and round her mouth, and over her cheeks and brow until there was not one part of her adorably gamine face that was not smeared with his sticky.

To end with she popped it back in her mouth and sucked gently, feeling for the last little tremor. It stayed stiff. It was a matter of pride to Sheridan McLaren that he could still keep it stiff for at least two, and sometimes three goes with a girl. It was a far cry from the six or more of his youth but these days he could make up in quality what he could no longer have in quantity.

"Naughty cocky! Naughty pricky!" Giselle slapped it playfully as she pushed him away. "Still got an appetite has he, eh?"

"I don't think he's the only one," Sheridan said. "I think there's a silent glutton hidden between your thighs that's weeping for want of attention. Isn't that so?"

Giggling she slipped from the bed and crossed the room to the wash basin, which she filled with warm water. He lay back on the bed, admiring her slim, almost boyish form, which made the slight swelling of her hips seem as feminine as — well, as Veronica's, say. Yes, Veronica was going to make a nice, voluptuous change after slim, svelte young Giselle.

She bent over the basin to dip her face in the water. To steady herself she spread her feet apart. His eyes went began to wonder if he could really part with her to make way for young Veronica. However, he always felt like that before a change-over; he knew that when he set eyes on Veronica tomorrow, she would captivate him all over again.

By the time they reached the bedroom the maid — a big-boned, middle-aged countrywoman who could go a whole week without speaking — had withdrawn. Giselle turned into a little she-animal, tearing the clothes off him — but being careful, of course, not to damage them in the slightest — and panting hard with her impatient desire. The moment he was naked she bore him back on the bed, flung herself between his thighs, and, grasping his erection in both hands, began to suck at it as if it would provide the elixir of life.

She licked all around the base and then up the sperm-spouter tube, all the way to the glowing red helmet at the top. There she sucked and swallowed and bit, and licked again, and sucked again ... until she felt those stirrings of his body which, she knew by now, were the first stages on his unstoppable progress to a mighty gusher. He stirred. He groaned. He tensed the muscles of his buttocks to thrust his plaything up for more, more, more of those teasing lips, those infuriating teeth, that deliciously hot, wet mouth.

At last, just before the inevitable happened, she grabbed it tight and rolled over on her side, then onward, onto her back, pulling him on top of her. Hastily, in a stupor of sexual passion, he scrabbled himself to his knees, struggling not to take his pride and joy beyond reach of her mouth. She made it easy for him by gripping it tight. Then she gripped and squeezed and sucked and bit and licked ... and squeezed and squeezed again until she felt the old hydraulic ram pumping away inside the gristle she held in her hands.

With an expertise gained from his masterful training, she slipped her fingers up the shaft of it and squeezed and let go

And again? And again? • 17

delight. He had enjoyed them all. (Also, of course — to clear up this point now — he *did* know that his sons were rogering his mistresses. And they knew that he knew — indeed, they often met at his club to talk about it. But, like the poet of ancient times, he knew that 'women be full of raggery, and swinken not sans secrecie.' So he got his sons to *swink* with the girls in apparent *secrecie*, which made the girls feel even naughtier, which, in turn, increased everyone's pleasure all round.)

"If I do this ...?" she asked, opening her eyes and grinning naughtily as she squeezed her rectum tight around him.

He gasped with delight, unable to stop himself.

"And again? And again? And ... again!" She squeezed at each repetition.

He just stood there, eyes closed, and shivered.

She stopped because it was pushing her too swiftly toward her own climax. She wanted to savour each little increase in its intensity and push the glow of it farther and farther out into her limbs until she was alight all over.

He began to withdraw and then to push into her again slowly, in and out, doing a little savouring of his own. But in his case it was not the gradual spread of erotic pleasure throughout his body but its ever-mounting concentration in the hot, throbbing knob of his tool. He moved slowly so as to feel every one of those soft wrinkles and muscular knots which made this hole so delightfully different from the one nature intended a man to enjoy.

"Deeper!" she pleaded with a little moan.

"All the way?"

"M-m-m!"

"Sure?"

"Yes! Yes!"

He rose on tiptoe and thrust himself inside her to the hilt.

Her buttocks quivered and tightened but he inserted his thumbs into their cleavage and pulled them apart to gain an extra half-inch. Then he folded himself down over her and, resting his head on hers, slipped his hands into the space she had left for her breasts, found them, and began to fondle them in ways he knew would drive her wild. When they were dangling like this, she loved him to place the flat of his palms beneath them, to lift them slightly, and then to rub them round and round — the way you'd move a ping-pong bat while trying to keep a ball balanced on it. And every now and then she enjoyed it when he made his thumbs and fingers like spider-legs and raked their nails as gently as possible down, down, down until they met at her nipples, which were by now hugely swollen and excited. Then, to crown it for her, he took them each between thumb and two fingers and furled them over on themselves, upwards, downward, and from side to side, as he — equally slowly — withdrew from her, almost all the way, and then — with a sudden ferocity — rammed himself back in to the hilt.

It was all she needed to brim her over. She collapsed completely beneath him. Her thumb fell from her mouth. Her lips hung slackly open as gasp followed moan followed whimper followed sigh. He watched in fascination, marvelling for the millionth time at the astonishing difference between the male and the female orgasm. How the whole of her body relaxed, as if little valves in every vessel were opening to let the thrill flood out and irrigate her every extremity.

The thought that the fires of orgasm were at that moment consuming every part of her limp, defenceless body brought him within an ace of his own climax. Hastily he withdrew all the way and tried to think of the points of the brief he would be preparing that afternoon. It was, he had found, his best way of avoiding premature ejaculation. But all he could

Grin and bare it • 21

She came over and soaped his prick for him. "Bloody hell!" she exclaimed admiringly as it started pulsing back to life in her hands. "More?" She stared eagerly into his eyes.

"No time," he replied. "Busy afternoon, too. When's your next period due?"

"Two weeks."

He frowned. "But I don't recall …"

She grinned. "I found a way of using a sponge. The doctor says it's all right if I boil it once a day and keep it in salt water in between. You didn't feel it up me, did you!"

He laughed. "To put it another way — I never knew you *had it in you!* Can you show my next girl?"

"Oh? Am I allowed to know her name?"

"I'll tell you as soon as I'm sure of her. If all goes to plan, I'll bring her here tomorrow and leave you to hand over everything and tell her all about my funny little ways …"

"You don't have any funny *little* ways."

"Ha ha! And then I'll take you down to Nymphenburg … or wherever."

"Nymphenburg," she insisted again.

"Till lunchtime tomorrow, petal. You won't get lonely now?"

Not with your two sons sniffing round my honeypot! she thought. "I'll grin and bare it," she replied.

Back at the office Sheridan McLaren took out the letter darling Connie had written to her niece. It read:

Darling Veronica,
 So I've gone before my time. What I'm going to tell you in this letter is something I had hoped to tell you in person when you came of age. You were always my own darling girl and I've never wished anything but the best

for you. You may still be puzzled at the way your mum and dad broke off our friendship. I'm sure they never breathed a word of explanation but you may have worked it out for yourself by now. The awful truth is that your dear old Aunt Connie was 'no better than she ought to be,' as they say. If you're in any doubt, look at the inscription on the back of my gold wristwatch (which is now yours, my pet): TO CONNIE WHO FOR TWENTY YEARS TOOK ALL COMERS IN HER STRIDE — *In gratitude — Wolf and Josie Hegel.*

I never called them Wolfgang and Josie, of course. He was always *Mister* Hegel and she was never anything other than *Madame* to me. The Hegels owned and still own a top-class sporting house called Nymphenburg. (Never call it *the* Nymphenburg, by the way. That's as bad as calling Albany, where the swell young bachelors have their apartments, or 'sets,' *the* Albany, or calling the Coldstream the Coldstream *Guards*. People in the know don't make such mistakes.)

Anyway, I was one of the most popular sporting girls who ever spread the gentleman's relish at Nymphenburg. There now! When I started with them, it was *Old* Nymphenburg, down off Wych Street. The Aldwych is there now. Even then it was one of the top-notch sporting houses in London and it still is though now it's moved to Little Venice. If ever you're in trouble, short of money, and don't know where to turn, go to Nymphenburg and show the Hegels my old watch. They'll see you right.

In fact, and this is what I would have wished to tell you myself in person, you could do worse even if you're not in trouble or short of money. Well, everyone's short of money, even the king, but you know what I mean — really flat-out broke. The reason why your mum stopped you seeing me, though she's my sister, is that she was afraid you'd start making comparisons between her and me. You'd see her struggling over money, what little your dad can earn, and you'd see me, never short of a bob or two, always in nice clothes, driving my Lanchester and eating out in swell places and going on cruises and things like that. And you'd begin to think I was the clever one to do what I did and she (your mum) was the mug.

Well, I think that's exactly right. I did do the right thing and she was the mug, slaving for your father, who doesn't hate her but he doesn't exactly love her, either, be honest. And what did I do that your mum thought so wicked? I took to the life of a sporting girl. And I really did take to it, let me say. A sporting girl sleeps in late. She pampers her body, looks after her health, keeps herself in top form. She works an eight-hour day like other lucky people — which is about half what a domestic slavey does. Or most wives. And during those eight hours she rents the use of her body to half a dozen gentlemen for their pleasure (and, be honest, her own pleasure, too, sometimes).

"Ooh, disgusting!" say the respectable women like your mum. But is it? How many wives just lie in their respectable marital beds and let their husbands enjoy their conjugal rights while they, the wives, get on with planning tomorrow's meals or a bit of redecoration or a knitting pattern? If the men didn't object, those women would probably prefer to be knitting while their husbands got on with it! Thousands of men, yes, literally thousands, have told me their wives say things like, "Must you?" or "Hurry up, then!" or "I s'pose you have your rights," or "Don't you never think of nothing else?" So it's obvious the wives aren't in the marital bed for their own fun, isn't it! They're in it for the housekeeping and their own bit of pocket money out of his wages.

Well, I ask, where's the difference?

Actually, I'll tell you where the difference is. I reckon I hired myself out to about 1,650 gentlemen each year I was on the Game. Or rather to about 800 actual partners, because many of them were regulars who came back to me week after week, some of them twice a week, year after year. I earned five bob a go at the beginning, but money has about halved in value since the Great War so that's really like ten bob a go today. And ten bob a go is what the girls earn in the best class of sporting house today. What they get to keep, I should say. The way it works is the gentleman pays a quid and the house keeps half. So I've always been earning at least £825 a year in today's money values. Which is enough for four or five round-the-world cruises in the first class. More to the point, it's over five times what your dad earns today! And that's leaving out my tips, which can easily bring it up to a thousand. I worked on the Game for thirty years, from 1882 when I turned sixteen until 1911, when I was forty-five.

I banked my earnings every week, never had a pimp to take it off of me, never spent extravagantly like some girls did, never got on the booze or dope. I lived frugally because I always knew I'd enjoy the money more after I left the Game. And so I am doing. Or did. Because if you're reading this, I'm not doing it any more, I'm pushing up daisies, instead. Shed a little tear for me, darling, but consider seriously what I say.

And what I say is you should have a good long think about going on the Game yourself. You're a very pretty girl with the sort of figure that makes men go weak at the think of was Connie's letter, which Veronica had left behind. It served the purpose just as well but it also made him less reluctant to finish this, one of his last lunchtime sessions with Giselle.

So, instead of letting his pleasure fade completely, he slipped his meat back inside her, into her vagina this time, while he was still throbbing with the last few pulses of a just-thwarted orgasm. He went all the way in at once and then stood up so that he could take a tight grip on her hips and move her this way and that, arching her back or flattening it or turning it at an angle, side-to-side, to increase the delightful friction between her soft flesh and his hard.

She did not resist for she was now on that plateau where one orgasm could melt and flow into the next, and anything that enhanced his pleasure could only add to hers, as well.

He closed his eyes now, not because he found the view unstimulating — far from it — but because, as he rose to the peaks of his own climax, his mind's eye could offer one more stimulating still. He liked to imagine his sons' two pricks thrusting in and out of that same divine canal — and of all the other pricks that would, soon enough now, be doing the same. He assembled a sort of composite view of all those stiff rods of male gristle, plump or slim, long or short, gnarled or smooth, curved or straight ... all going in and out like pistons.

A 'view' of something that is completely buried inside something else is hard to imagine and even harder to describe. It was a view of an *idea* as much as of anything physical. He did not see the situation as if it were an anatomical diagram, with half a vagina, half a penis, cross-sections of bone, and so forth. Instead it was as if the girl's body became translucent to the point where the man's rutting gristle just became visible — and then the *idea* of the rutting gristle took over and sharpened the image up. A further leap of the same erotic imagination then superimposed all those other male ramrods, all rutting away, not side by side but magically occupying the same space. He could imagine them getting more and more excited and finally gushing like wildcat oilwells — his own among them — filling the top of her vagina with a hot, slippery ocean of semen in which his erection bathed luxuriously.

He continued to hold her slender hips in his hands, soaking it in her warmth. It would be a nice change to have a mistress like Veronica, with her wasp waist and generously swelling hips. All the same, he would miss Giselle's slim, almost boyish hips and buttocks. He even toyed briefly with the idea of having them both at the same time. But memories of past experiments in that direction made him wary. Still, he did not consider it utterly impossible. Time would tell. Veronica might even decide to ignore her aunt's letter and stay a 'good' girl.

His prick fell limp at last and dropped out of her like a filleted finger.

"Oh, poor thing!" she murmured dreamily and wiggled her bottom this way and that, trying to grab it up with her pussy-lips again.

"So," he said, waddling over to the wash basin to wash away the reek and stain of his debauchery, "do you think you're ready for one of the houses down in Little Venice?"

"Nymphenburg!" she replied at once.

"I didn't promise you'd rise as high as that, all in one leap." He held up a warning finger. "I only said I'd do my best." In fact, he knew very well that the Hegels were eager to have her after all the praises he'd sung; but he didn't want her to think it was *fait accompli* already. "And so I shall," he added. "I'll do my very best. More I cannot say."

knees. You're much too good to waste on some spotty bank clerk or small shopkeeper, which, face it, is about the best you're going to get, barring miracles. Look at your mum. She was as pretty as what you are once, much prettier than me. And what has she got for it? Even her beauty has gone now. So that's your choice.

After my nest egg in the building society built up to about £5,000, I began to put half my earnings into more speculative investments. £5,000 will yield an income of £200 a year, on which a single woman could live in modest comfort. Very modest, I agree, but she wouldn't have to work ever again. So it was always my basic nest egg. And that was where Mister Sheridan McLaren was so helpful. He knows about stocks and shares and things like that. So do I, now, but he's the one what taught me. And, if you follow my advice and make the most of your assets on the Game, he'll help you, too. Thanks to him, my speculations mean that I retired worth £45,000. Not bad for a sixteen-year-old nobody whose sole assets got squashed every time she sat down, eh! (Don't ask what's happened to the rest of the money because it's gone. I've left every last penny to a home for broken-down whores who never had my luck. You won't need it, anyway, if you follow my advice. And money you earn yourself is always enjoyed more when you spend it.)

Old McLaren knows I'm writing this letter — well, he's got to because he's going to be looking after it until he hands it to you along of the watch. And he knows in general what I'm going to advise you about going on the Game yourself. But I shan't let him read it and he's a man of honour who'll pass it on to you with my seal unbroken. So what I'm also going to tell you is that, if you do follow my advice, he will give you every assistance.

And I do mean *every*.

I'll tell you a little story about him. He was one of my earliest customers back in the Wych Street days. He could take five girls up to bed, one after the other, and give each a really good poking. So he was a very regular regular down at Old Nymphenburg. Well, one day he notices a young girl hanging about outside, hungry and scared half to death. Needs to earn money. Can't get a character. At her wit's end. So he takes her home — not to his home but a house up in Maida Vale which used to be a sporting house and which he's looking after for a friend who's gone abroad. And very slowly, very gently, over the next week or so he takes her virginity and, in return, gives her the feeling she could lead the life of a sporting girl quite nicely, thank you. But he keeps her on as his mistress for another two months. And when he takes her back to Old Nymphenburg, the Hegels are delighted with the way he's broken her in to the Game. So much so that they offer him another girl who's just come to them looking for a place and who they think could be quite good except she's so raw and scared.

And that, really, is all he's done ever since. The Hegels, and other Madames now, ring him up when they've got fresh fillies that need a bit of breaking in and schooling. Of course, not all of them go on to work in a sporting house. And maybe you wouldn't either. Maida Vale is where a lot of the upper-class gentlemen keep their mistresses, so quite a lot of old McLaren's young fillies go on into the mistress line. And some even get married well above anything they might have expected.

He generally keeps a girl for a couple of months. A few only last the one night, when they discover they can't go through with it. And he never forces them or tries to argue them out of it. Some, at the other extreme, last as much as half a year. But, like I say, two months is the average. So, darling girl, take your time. And if you do finally decide to follow me on the Game, you could do a lot worse than turn to my old friend Sheridan McLaren for advice. He'd probably take you to his place in Maida Vale — he owns it now — and give you the finest, gentlest, most enjoyable schooling a girl could wish for.

And in that case, you should know he has other letters from me to you, waiting to hand them over as you reach the appropriate stage in the Game. If not, at least you've got the watch to remember me by — and don't think of me too badly. I did what I thought was right, and that's what I'll say at the Last Judgement, too.

God will forgive me. I know he will, because it's his trade, after all. Everyone must have their trade and mine was one of the best.

Your loving Aunt Connie

Sheridan McLaren smiled to himself as he folded the letter back into its cover. Given her money to a home for broken-down whores, indeed! It was all still in the bank and the building society and the stock market. *After* Veronica had made her choice, her mum and dad would be getting just enough to rub their noses in it, and the rest was to be put in trust — in the GAG TRUST, whose mysterious name was intended to thwart inquirers. In fact, the initials GAG stood for 'Get Above the Garter' (for 'The Gag Club' had been the name of a group of rakes in Connie's young days). Like the letters he was to hand out to Veronica at various stages of her progress, the existence and purpose of this trust was also to be made clear to her in due course.

He wondered what the dear young girl was going to decide tomorrow. He had a good idea which way she'd jump but there was just enough doubt to make him fear he'd never enjoy her — and just enough certainty to make him start drooling and shaking at the prospect right now.

Veronica lay in her bed at home, studying for the millionth time the cracks in the ceilings and the lacy pattern of light superimposed upon it by the lamps outside. Two drunks were arguing again, right beneath her window. The mad trumpeter opposite was at it again. The drain had blocked again and its sad, sour smell overlaid the cooked cabbage that had always pervaded this house — probably even before her mother and father first rented it.

Funny — she had never before imagined them moving in. She had been born here and so it seemed *they* had always been here. In fact, they moved in the day they got married. Aha! *That* was why her thoughts were running along these unaccustomed lines: newlyweds. Another thing she had never before imagined was mum and dad *doing it*. Now, briefly, she did — and it was not a pretty sight. Judging by their wedding photo, it had probably not been a pretty sight then, either. Her dad was a dear, kind, ineffectual man but he'd never set a woman's heart aglow — not even mum's. He was 'the best one available,' as she had once told her daughter.

Veronica faced the thought that she, too, would probably have to settle for 'the best one available' in her turn. Especially as so many young men — more than a million — had been killed in the Great War. She dared to face the thought now that Aunt Connie had challenged her with an alternative. *The* alternative. The one every pretty girl faces. And now Veronica turned to face it, too.

What would it be like to go upstairs with a strange man, a totally strange man you'd only met a minute earlier, and let him undress you, and undress him maybe, and then, in Aunt Connie's words, rent your body to him for half an hour or so? What did they do to you, those men, for their pleasure? Of course they gloated over your body ... Well, she could live with that. She had to. Men did it all the time for free, anyway. Like that solicitor today — his eyes could be arrested for soliciting!

And they'd touch you, of course. Here, for instance. She moved her hands up to her breasts and caressed them through the flannelette of her nightie. She could certainly live with that! Even with a stranger? Well, that would be a bit icky — but they wouldn't *all* be strangers. Aunt Connie said half her gentlemen were regulars or something like that. A lot of them, anyway.

Of course, you'd be naked when they fondled you there.

Her heart beat double as she reached down toward the foot of the bed and pulled her nightie up to under her armpits; this was definitely getting a bit naughty now. When she was fourteen and didn't understand anything she used to do this every night and fondle her breasts when they were starting to bud, and tickle her nipples, and then lie on her back and bend her knees and part her thighs and let her fingernails rake all over her skin, down over her tummy, down to *that place* where the hair was just beginning to grow ... and she'd slip her finger into the groove there and tickle herself and play stinky-finger until she almost passed out with the lovely feelings it sent all through her. But then Monica at school had told her she'd go blind and her hair would fall out and they'd cart her off to the looney bin if she overdid it. The looney bins were full of women tied to chairs so they couldn't feel themselves up.

Monica said it was called *mastrupation* and it drove girls mad. So now Veronica only did mastrupation on Saturday nights and only if she could get through the seven-, nine-, and eleven-times tables in under one minute, as a proof she wasn't losing her mind. But this was only Thursday night, so it was very naughty. Still, she did it — because she was going back to that solicitor tomorrow and she'd have to give him an answer.

She tried to imagine a man, a stranger but a gentleman, doing these things to her ... touching her here, and here, and here ... and it didn't seem too bad, either. So ogling her body *and* fondling it were both okay. But then they'd want to stick their *things* into her ... *down there*. Into her *hole*. Go on — use the word and be damned! And it's not their 'things' but their *pizzles*. Men would want to stick their pizzles into her hole. There now — she'd said it all!

But saying wasn't doing.

Of course, she knew what it was like to stick her long finger in there and wiggle it about. It was absolutely scrumptious — so scrumptious she could easily believe it drove some girls mad and they had to have their hands tied to stop them. She did it now, and felt the old familiar melting in her belly and thighs. But she stopped before it took hold of her. This wasn't a Saturday-night mastrupation. It was a serious investigation of certain stark choices that now faced her.

A man's pizzle wasn't like a finger. She knew that even though she'd never seen one. Monica said it was like a carrot. She said her big sister used to chew the ends off a couple of carrots until they were about six inches long and then she'd take one of her girl friends out to the bushes on Mill Hill golf course and they'd diddle each other with them and take turns to pretend to be men.

It could drive girls mad • 31

There were carrots in the scullery downstairs but Veronica knew her mother would notice if one went missing. She rose up on one elbow and surveyed the room. Of course, a girl's room at this Nymphenburg place would be a million times better than this. Silks on the walls. And silk sheets, she wouldn't wonder. And carpets six inches thick. And a fire burning all night in the winter, not just when you were gravely ill. She sighed. Aunt Connie's letter had really opened her eyes to how drab her life was here!

And at that moment those same newly opened eyes fell upon the candle at her bedside. How odd that she hadn't noticed it before. It just showed how preoccupied she must be. Her mother *never* left a candle in her room at night — just a little nightlight half an inch high. When she'd been eight or nine and could be trusted with matches she'd always had a candle. But when she grew up some more, about fourteen, her mother had read an article about how dangerous it was when young people tried to read in bed with candles, and so it had been a nightlight from then on — *and* no reading in bed, anyway.

And I swallowed the story, hook, line, and sinker! Veronica thought. *What a naïve little innocent I must have been!* Now that she looked at the thing with new eyes, she saw at once why her mother had removed such a suggestive and tempting object!

With trembling hands she reached for it, touched it, lost her nerve, retreated, got angry with herself, grabbed it, and yanked it out of its holder before she could get cold feet once more. She lay on her back, wriggled completely out of her nightie, drew up her knees again, let her thighs fall apart, and slipped the candle down into her groove.

Brrr! It was icy cold. Well, not *icy* cold, perhaps, but pretty chill. She clamped it under one armpit and, while she waited for it to warm up, began pleasuring herself as before, to get back in the mood again. Soon her breath was coming in shivers and catches. She moved the candle to the other armpit and kept it there until it felt as warm as herself. Now she was trembling all over and could hardly hold the thing, but somehow she steered it down into her fork and got the tip of it resting against the mouth of her hole.

She knew what it looked like down there because once, when she was alone in the house, she'd looked at it in the mirror. So she could just imagine what it looked like, poised there, ready to plunge inside her. Now all she had to do was imagine it not as a smooth, waxy-white cylinder but as a gnarled, lumpy sort of carrot, only flesh-coloured and not yellowy-red. When she had that image firmly in her mind she started to slip it inside.

How *wet* she was down there! The game of stinky-finger often got her quite moist but never as wet as this.

And what a delicious melting sensation seemed to fill all her body and radiate out into the very tips of her fingers and toes! If being on the Game meant getting into this situation half a dozen times each evening and ending up with £1,000 a year, she'd say yes now. Especially if half the time she'd be *doing it* with a regular gentleman, who'd be like a familiar friend to her. And the rest of the time it'd be with a gentleman she might never see again, who might be awful but who might just as easily be quite exciting. And even if he was awful — so what? He'd be gone in half an hour or so, probably forever.

Slowly, cautiously, ready to jerk it out again at the first hint of discomfort (or madness), she slipped the candle into her vagina and tried to imagine it was the first pizzle of half a dozen that she'd be letting inside her this night. It was so agreeable, this all-over melting, that her fingers lost their grip and she had to stuff her nightie across her mouth to stop her little moans and whimpers from alerting her mother, who slept like a cat and could come awake instantly.

Her fingers took a new grip on the bottom end of the candle and she pushed it in again. In and in and in. It was about seven inches long and all of it went in without any feeling of discomfort. That was more than twice the length of her long finger! And yet she'd always thought her hole finished just a little way beyond where she could reach. So that was all right! She didn't see how a man's pizzle could be anything like as long as that — not if the vine leaves that covered them up in the statues down in the art gallery were anything to go by. Therefore she was going to be able to accommodate them. She could 'take all comers in her stride,' as the inscription on Connie's watch said.

'In her *stride*'! Oh ha-ha — she saw the joke now.

So what would men *do* once they were inside her like this? Just lie there and kiss her until their time was up? It didn't seem very exciting. If her own feelings were anything to go by, they'd want a bit of movement, too. Would she do the moving, or them? She tried wriggling her hips but, of course, the candle moved with her. So then she jiggled it around a bit. And that was utterly heavenly. She had to hold her nightie over her mouth again to stifle the noises she could hardly help uttering. She went on wiggling it about inside her, getting more and more excited, until in the end she had to roll over on her tummy and bury her face in her pillow, like when she wanted to weep without anyone hearing.

That was even more divine because she could stretch one hand under her breasts and tickle one nipple with her thumb and the other with her middle finger, and she could reach the other hand round behind her and wiggle the candle in her hole that way. And at the same time she could rub her bush against the bed and pump her bottom up and down — all of which produced such a riot of thrills in her flesh that she almost passed out.

At last she had to force herself to stop, because if she was going to do this thing properly, she'd have to try it five more times that night to see if she could stand it.

She awoke next morning feeling on top of the world without knowing why. Then she remembered last night and she knew why. And she knew why Aunt Connie had always been such a lively, cheerful, happy soul. And she knew she was going to go to that solicitor and say yes to everything. So she got up, put the candle carefully back in its stand, washed herself all over with a flannel (which she did every day, anyway), dressed, and went downstairs, singing a little song, to make her own breakfast.

Two minutes later her mother stormed into the kitchen and plonked the candle down on the table. "You filthy, dirty, disgusting, degraded bitch!" she yelled. "I know what you've been doing!"

Veronica was so taken aback she could only stare.

"Oh yes — you're all innocence *now!* But I know! Why d'you think I left the candle there, eh? Did you think I just forgot it? I've had my suspicions about you for some time, my girl. And you've fallen right into the trap!"

"You mean you put it there ..."

A stinging slap across the face halted her words.

"Don't you try and justify yourself to me! You've been polluting yourself with your filthy habits. Well from now on you're going to sleep in handcuffs, you little bitch ..." The words trailed off as she saw her daughter rise and make for the hall door. "And where d'you think you're going? Answer when I'm talking to you!"

"To my room." Veronica ran up the stairs and slammed her door and turned the key in the lock.

Her mother, tit for tat, shot the bolt on the outside, something she had not done in years. "I'll get Father Mulcahy to come and talk to you," she shouted.

Veronica took a battered cardboard suitcase down from the top of her wardrobe and looked around for things to pack. After two minutes she had assembled two pairs of knickers, an art-silk scarf, her rabbit's-fur slippers, her Teddy, and a copy of *Little Women* with the title page missing. And that was it. Nothing else was worth taking! If ever she needed an argument to leave, that was it.

She opened the window and got out — onto the roof of the wash-house, which she had done often enough as a child. A minute later she was out in the back lane and two minutes after that she was in a bus on her way to Edgware Road and the offices of Sheridan McLaren, attorney-at-law.

She told him nothing of the argument with her mother, only that she had run away from home and they were unlikely to come looking for her. And even if they did, there was nothing to connect her with him or Nymphenburg or any of her likely future haunts. He, of course, was over the moon to hear of her decision.

"Have you ever been with a man before?" was the first thing he asked.

She shook her head, amazed that she could be so cool in the face of such a question.

"Have you ever seen a man naked and in a state of excitement?"

Again she shook her head and this time whispered, "No, sir."

"So! You know what your aunt said was likely — that I'd offer to take you in as my mistress and gently introduce you to the mysteries of her profession? D'you want to do that? Or would you rather jump in at the deep end? I could take you down to Nymphenburg at lunchtime and, by midnight tonight, you will have seen at least half a dozen naked men in a state of excitement — great excitement in your case — and you will have pleasured them all ..."

"Taken them all in my stride, sir." She smiled shyly and his heart somersaulted.

"You learn fast," he said. "Yes. Is that what you would prefer?" He hung on tenterhooks for her reply.

She shook her head. "I have thought only of you, sir, and that house in Maida Vale, all night."

He ran a finger around the inside of his collar. "I'll put you in a taxi now," he said huskily. "I cannot get away until twelve-thirty. But my present mistress is there — a charming young girl, a little older than you — called Giselle. She knows about you — at least, she knows of your existence, but no more than that. But she's now dying to start working on the Game at Nymphenburg, so she'll be very happy to see you. You can talk with her much more freely than you could with me. Ask her any question you like. I'll come along at lunchtime for an hour of fun and frolics — with her. My last, perhaps. It'll give you time to adjust and settle in ... buy a new wardrobe and some nice frilly underwear, make up, toiletries ... things like that. Giselle can take you out shopping this afternoon. Two pretty girls out on a shopping spree! Would you like that?"

Veronica was too happy to reply.

"Just before you go," he said.

"Yes, sir?" She turned again to face him.

"Undo your blouse and show me your breasts — there's a good girl."

She swallowed heavily and did as he asked.

He stared at them in adoration. For the first time she had the merest inkling of the power her sex could exert over men, even over sophisticated men of the world like McLaren. It brought a strange, tickly feeling to those parts of her she had fondled and pleasured last night. Things began to connect and as they fell into place something within her just said, "Yes!" as if it had always known it was so.

"You may touch them if you like, sir," she told him. "I think I should quite like that."

His hands reached out greedily and then he plucked them back. "No," he said, taking out his handkerchief and mopping his brow. "If I started I might not know when to stop." He breathed deeply and braced himself. "All in good time, eh, Véronique?"

"Veronica, sir."

"If you are going to be professional about this business, petal, you will need a professional name. Like actresses, you know. It *is* part of the acting business, too, after all. Giselle is really Gillian, or Jilly. Will you accept Véronique? Think of it as a present from me."

She licked her lips and replied, "I think I will accept a great many things from you, sir."

After she had gone, he picked up the phone and had a long talk with Giselle or Jilly. She only just put the phone down as the taxi drew up outside. "Okay, hen," she called out to Gerty, the housekeeper and maid-of-all-work. "I'll answer the knock."

She opened the door just as the girl was lifting a hand to the bell-pull. "You must be Véronique," she said. "Welcome, love. Come in."

"I must be Véronique," the girl replied as she stepped across the threshold. She set down her cardboard suitcase, closed her eyes briefly, and thought, *Now it begins!*

"I'm Giselle." She held out her hand. "Not my real name, either. It's really Gillian, or Jilly you can call me." They shook hands.

"I'm really Veronica but friends call me Rom. So many names!" She took off her shabby coat and hung it up. How drab her dress was beside Jilly's!

"Names for us to hide our real selves behind," Jilly said as she picked up Véronique's suitcase. "I'll take you to your room."

They passed the maid on the landing. "That's Gerty, the housekeeper and maid-of-all-work," Jilly said. "She doesn't say much but she sees everything, don't you, Gerty!"

Gerty sniffed and mumbled, "I'm sure."

"I say 'your room'," Jilly went on as they resumed their climb. "In fact, for the next two nights it'll be *our* room. I don't leave until Sunday evening."

"Oh ... nice," Véronique said. "Listen, Jilly — I hope your leaving has nothing to do with ... you know."

"You coming?" Jilly laughed. "Of course it has, you goose! But don't worry. I'm more than ready to start on the Game proper, believe me!" She saw the look of consternation in Véronique's eyes and added, "Not that I've grown unhappy here. Far from it. A girl could live this life for ever — except there's so much more money to be made down at ... well, other places."

"Nymphenburg?"

"Oh, you know about that? Did *he* tell you — darling Sherry? He just rang me and told me — it's definite I'm going to the Hegels at Nymphenburg. I'm so thrilled at the thought, I can't tell you."

Véronique explained about Aunt Connie having been at Nymphenburg as they walked along the landing. She showed her the watch, which Sheridan had just returned to her.

"Oh well, then," Jilly said, "you're already in the family — as long as you're not in the family *way!*" She laughed and touched wood. "I've been lucky so far."

She threw open the door on a room more luxurious than any Véronique had ever seen — with a huge four-poster bed, a chaise longue upholstered in crimson velvet, carpets that swallowed your feet, and, in front of a large, ornate fireplace, a bearskin rug with a real bear's head. The wallpaper was dark red with gold stripes and purple leaves. Everything in the room whispered to her of sensual indulgence, luxury, and sin. Her friend's next words came as no surprise, therefore.

"Fifty years ago this house was a brothel," Jilly said as she put the suitcase into a wardrobe. Véronique caught a glimpse of many elegant clothes. "Its glories are a bit faded now but Sherry won't change a thing."

"Is this where you and he ... you know — *do it?*" she asked hesitantly.

Jilly laughed. "We *do it* in every room in the house — of which there are plenty. Wherever his fancy takes him, there he takes me." She eyed the girl shrewdly. "Have you ever *done it*, Rom?"

Véronique shook her head and wished her heart wasn't leaping about all over the place.

"Ever seen people *doing it?* In the parks or up the cemetery?"

Another shake of the head; her mouth gaped at the very thought.

Jilly came closer and lowered her voice. "Would you like to? You could watch me and Sherry when he comes here this lunchtime."

"Oh, I don't really think so ..." Véronique, all confusion now, sat down and fanned her face.

"Bless you, pet! I don't mean sit in the room and watch. No — Sherry won't even know you're there." She crossed her fingers secretly as she made this promise.

"How?" Véronique's mouth was dry. She had to admit that the prospect of watching a couple *doing it* was very exciting. It would clear up so many of her doubts. She glanced at the wardrobe, which was certainly big enough to conceal her.

Jilly, following her gaze, shook her head. "I told you this place was once a brothel. Well, every brothel has a room where people can watch the loving couple, or any other sport that's going on inside it. Come on, I'll show you."

She led her out of the room again and right round the landing to the room on the farther side of the stairwell. As they passed various doors, some of them hidden behind heavy drapes, she said, "The Ecclesiastical Room ... the Oriental Harem ... the Railway Room ... the *Belle Époque* Room ... to name but a few!"

Since the house was symmetrical, the room to which she led Véronique ought to have been the same size as the room they had just left — and so it would have been but for a long, narrow room or wide passage that had been cut off at one end. Access to this was by way of a door concealed in a section of panelling out on the landing, which swung inward at the touch of a button. Véronique giggled with amazement when Jilly demonstrated the feature.

Beyond the secret door was a row of chairs, all facing the wall that divided it from the bedroom. The whole of this long, narrow room was painted black.

"Sit in any one and you'll see," Jilly advised.

Véronique did so. Now that her eyes were growing dark-accustomed she could make out a strip of light all along the wall at just about eye-height to a seated onlooker. Leaning forward she saw that it was, in fact, a long, narrow window of glass — ten feet long but only two inches high — through which she could see every part of the bedroom next door. There was a chaise longue, this one in blue satin, near the peep-window at the farther end and a bed with dark blue sheets right against the wall at the near end.

"A viewer would certainly get an eyeful from here," she said.

"Voyeur." Jilly corrected her. "They call them voyeurs. Some men come to sporting houses just to be voyeurs. They pay as much as any other clients, so the girl gets double. Of course, she has to put on an extra good show with the paying partner."

"How d'you know, Jilly? Did you work in one of those places before ..."

"No, but I've spoken to lots of girls in those houses. Is that what you're hoping to do — go on to Nymphenburg? Wouldn't it be fun if we met up there again!"

"I'll say! Do the men know — the paying partners — do they know they're being watched?"

"Not as a rule. Some do and they don't mind. They like showing off, see. Men with big sexual organs are very proud of them."

Véronique had another peep at the room; she felt very visible, despite the dark. "Are you sure I won't be seen?"

Jilly shook her head. "Come and have a look from the other side. It's called the Blue Room, by the way."

"And surely Mister McLaren knows about this voyeurs' room? I mean, it's his house, after all."

"He knows," Jilly agreed. "But he doesn't know that *I* know." Again she crossed her fingers out of sight. "So when I tell him I feel like doing it on the dark blue sheets today — which I've done often enough in the past — he won't suspect a

thing. In fact, I think he enjoys that room because he likes to *imagine* he's being watched and admired by the ghosts of randy Edwardian rakes outside there." She relaxed when she saw that Véronique had swallowed this improbable tale.

"See!" she said, pointing out the strip of half-silvered mirror just below the dado. It was part of an intricate mosaic based on obscene murals from Pompeii, all framed in strips of mirror. Only the top strip was semi-transparent, of course, but it looked like the rest. "Because it's so light in here and so dark in there, you can't see anything from this side. And anyway, who's going to look at a strip of mirror when there's a whole painted scene like *that* to enjoy!"

Véronique's jaw had dropped again as certain details in the picture registered. "Are men's ... you know ... pizzles — are they *that* long?" She was looking at one so big that the man had to carry it before him in a wheelbarrow.

Jilly laughed. "They all fondly *think* they are, of course! My eyes nearly popped out of my head when I first saw the size of Sherry's, because ..."

"Was he the first man who ever ... you know ..."

"Fucked me? Yes. But he ..."

"What was that word?"

"Fucked. That's what *doing it* is called — fucking. There are a million others. They're all written down in a book, which I'd show you, except there's no time now. Anyway, Sherry told me his prick has measured the insides of over five hundred girls and none of them had any trouble fitting it inside them. Five hundred! You can just imagine how small that made *me* feel! I'd have done *anything* to please him after that. I'd have drilled an extra hole if he'd asked! Of course, that's what he wanted, cunning old devil! What were we talking about? Oh yes — size of men's pricks. The way I look at it is — how big is a baby, eh?" She held her hand about a foot apart. "And how big is its head?" She shaped a sphere too large to hold in both hands. "And all that has to come out that way when the baby's born, right? So, there's no prick in the world that's even half the size of a baby. So it's san-fairy-ann as far as I'm concerned. Mind you, Rory McLaren — Sherry's younger son ... no, there's no time to tell you that now. We've got to plan this lunchtime show."

Sheridan McLaren turned up, eager and trembling, before his usual time and he bolted his lunch even faster than was his habit. Then Véronique, following Jilly's advice, stretched and said she'd like to take a bath if that was all right. Then have a bit of a lie-down, perhaps.

After she'd gone, McLaren said, "All according to plan?"

Giselle (as she now was for him) nodded. "I'll go up and change."

He rose. "Me, too. Oh, I *do* like being watched by my *next* mistress!"

"I remember." She tweaked his nose. "You wicked man!"

"What d'you think of her?"

Giselle paused. "I think she's going to amaze you, Sherry. She told me something of her Aunt Connie. You knew her?"

"Often!" He laughed.

"She's got that blood in her — so you watch out!"

The bathroom was at the end of the landing, just beyond the secret opening in the panels. Véronique (as she was now determined to think of herself, both on and off duty) knew she had ten minutes while they changed — ten minutes to take her bath, dry herself, and slip into the big towelling dressing gown Jilly had given her. She timed it so perfectly that, as she knotted the cord she heard them come down the landing and close the door of the Blue Room. Stealthy as a cat she tiptoed back along the landing, pressed the button in the panelling, and slipped into the voyeurs' gallery. A quick peep showed her they were standing at the far end, by the chaise longue. They had their arms around each other and were kissing. McLaren was wearing a dressing gown like hers and Giselle was in something skimpy, pink, and silky. Her fingers were raking passionately up and down his back and he was caressing bits of her nakedness with tender sweeps of his hands.

Véronique stood again and picked her way carefully among the chairs until she reached one in front of the chaise longue. When she next peeped through the narrow window she saw that McLaren, standing, was arranging Giselle in a sitting pose with her legs stretched out along the seat of the chaise longue; she could have reached out and touched them both if the wall had not been there. And now she could see that Giselle was wearing a harem-girl outfit — a pair of baggy silk pantaloons that started below her navel and finished just beneath her knee and a peignoir of fine gauze, gathered in one ribbon around her neck and another, of elastic, just under her breasts. It darkened her skin somewhat but concealed nothing of her charms.

McLaren pushed her gently until she was leaning against the backrest, almost at a forty-five-degree angle. Then he went to stand behind her, behind the backrest, where he could bend forward over her body, which was now utterly relaxed and stretched out beneath him.

He clasped her shoulders, touched her ribs, handled her waist like a man taking an inventory. Then he slipped his fingers under the elastic band beneath her breasts and lifted the gauze up over her nipples. She, meanwhile, closed her eyes and raised her arms behind her head, throwing her

Breasts like two firm melons 45

breasts out and up at him like two firm melons. McLaren licked his lips and stared at them with popping eyes. He eased his gown slightly and Véronique saw that his prick was thrusting the material forward like a spinnaker on a yacht. She could not see the *thing* itself yet, though.

Giselle opened one eye and reached her right hand farther back to touch it. She fondled it through the material. He half closed his eyes and his jaw dropped as he thrust it toward her for more. At the same moment he cupped his hands round her breasts and caressed her nipples. Véronique saw them harden and swell between his fingers. She slipped her hand inside her dressing gown and began caressing her own breasts in sympathy.

Giselle let out a little sigh, inserted her fingers between the folds of his dressing gown, and toyed with his prick, naked fingers on bare skin. Véronique could see his pulse shaking the whole of his body, though she still could not see that one bit of him which *pricked* her curiosity most of all. She smiled at her own wit. They stayed like that for a minute or two, kissing and caressing each other, each seemingly lost in the other's erotic pleasure. Véronique felt alone and jealous, despite the delectable feelings radiating from her own nipples by now.

McLaren bent right down and started to suckle Giselle's nipples. Her right hand was still toying with his prick but she raised her other hand behind his head and scratched gently in his hair. They kept it up for several minutes, not hurrying in the slightest. Then he raised his head from his feast and slipped around the chaise longue to stand beside her. With gentle hands he made her part her legs and sit astride the seat, with her body still leaning against the backrest. He sat astride it, too, facing her. He edged forward, moving his knees under her legs as he drew near. This made her thighs spread wide open, and now Véronique saw that her pantaloons had an open gusset right down into her fork. Her pale auburn bush and the firm swelling at the front of her cleft were clearly visible.

Grinning wickedly, eyeball to eyeball, Giselle lowered her hands and took hold of the edges of his dressing gown so that his prick sprang out into the open at last. And what a prick it was! Véronique thought. She could quite understand why it had scared Giselle witless the first time she saw it, especially as she, too, had never fucked a man before.

Fucked a man?

Or been fucked *by* a man?

She must remember to ask.

She continued to stare at it as Giselle squeezed and caressed it with gentle fingers. It was about seven inches long, she guessed (so the three-inch fig-leaves in the art galleries were a blatant lie!). And it curved upward like a banana. It looked as if it were thinner at the bottom, where it sprouted out of his bush, and got gradually thicker toward the top. The curved shaft of it was white and a bit lumpy. Gnarled-looking. She could easily believe it had 'measured the insides' of over five hundred girls down the years, but not that it had all happened without complaint. She wondered how her own insides would 'measure up' to it. A little twinge of fear — and fascination — stirred down there between her thighs.

The shaft of it was pale, almost white, and hair grew halfway up its sides, a bit like a dog's; and the sort of knob part on the end of it, shaped like a Prussian helmet — from the side, anyway — was as fiery-looking and as gleaming wet and red as a dog's, too. She almost expected to see him panting at Giselle with his tongue hanging out. He had the correct soppy-dreamy look in his eyes, anyway. Giselle, she

The sexual organs of these two people certainly had a hearty appetite, anyway!

Giselle lifted her other leg and clasped that around him, too, resting her bottom on the very top of the backrest. He stood close and tucked his hip right in under her, getting himself inside to the very hilt of him.

At this point Véronique remembered that, only last night, she had wondered what men did with their pricks once they got them inside you. And she had assumed they just left them there, moving around a bit every now and then, until they'd had enough! She almost gave herself away by laughing out loud. And then, just as she was wondering what on earth these two could find to do next, McLaren stood up straight and waddled to the other end of the chaise longue — with her still impaled on him. When he arrived there he sat down heavily on the very end of it, which, naturally, pulled his prick out of her and left her standing, facing him. His prick gleamed brightly with her juices.

He turned her around and reached up his hands to loosen the drawstring of her harem pants. They fell to her knees and when she stooped to take them off altogether she gave him a fine show of her petals; he could not resist leaning forward and kissing them. Then he undid the hooks that fastened her gauze peignoir, which floated like gossamer to the ground. He turned her to face him again, to admire and gloat over her nakedness.

Véronique felt a pang of jealousy at Giselle's slender, almost boyish figure — which made her large, round breasts look even more feminine and inviting. She wanted to touch them herself. In fact — and the thought made the hair suddenly prickle on the back of her neck — she wanted to press the whole of her body against Giselle's. Such a thought had never even entered her mind before.

McLaren ran his hands up and down that same glorious body, watching Giselle shiver. Her face now had a dreamy stillness. He caught her nipples between his thumbs and fingers and began to roll them gently; she stretched her arms right up as far as she could, throwing back her head and thrusting her breasts toward him. He caressed her with a gentleness that must be driving the girl wild, Véronique thought. Down over her body they went next, feeling their way down to her waist, where they turned her slowly round until her pale bottom was before him again. Now he devoted all his caresses to the two slender moons of her buttocks, slowly, ever so slowly, bringing her nearer him. He slipped his knees in between hers so that, as she moved backwards, her legs were forced farther and farther apart. At last the knob of his prick vanished between her parted thighs, but from the way he arched his back Véronique could tell he was deliberately not touching that part of her which must now be craving for the feel of him once again.

Sweat beaded Giselle's skin and she struggled to breathe. At last his hands went up to her waist and gripped it firmly; simultaneously he spread his thighs wide apart, forcing hers to go even wider — and then *wham!* He pulled her down on him with a vigour that almost amounted to violence. She gave out one great sigh of ecstasy and collapsed against him.

He pulled her body tight to his. One hand went down to fondle that little jellybean in her split and play among her petals, the other went up to her breasts, spread wide so that his thumb and little finger could work on both her nipples at once. She arched her back, which, Véronique guessed, would bend her hole to fit the beautiful banana-curve of his prick quite perfectly.

And there she sat, wriggling her hips and buttocks as if to escape the gentle, exquisite probings of his fingers down

Come, my darling man! • 55

there, while he, for his part, closed his eyes, leaned his head against the back of hers, and surrendered utterly to the sensual excitement of her skill.

Véronique wriggled her own derrière on her chair and thought, *I can do that.* Then she thought, *I will do that, too, the first chance I get.*

Something was happening out there. His whole body was growing rigid. His jaw was wide open. His eyes, too — and they were glazed-looking. And he was gasping, "Oh!" and "Ah!" and little cries that weren't words at all. And Giselle was jiggling her bottom around more and more energetically, crying out, "Yes! Yes!" and "Come! Oh, my darling man, fill me with your come!"

And then he clasped her tight and held her absolutely still while his entire body, from head to toe, experienced a convulsive kind of fit, shuddering and rigid by turns. It lasted about half a minute, slowly fading in intensity, and when it was quite over he just collapsed. He went completely limp and fell back on the seat of the chaise longue, panting for breath as if he'd just run a marathon.

Giselle, still sitting there impaled on his prick, started gently wriggling her bottom again. But he groaned and reached a trembling hand to her hip and murmured, "No, please have pity, Giselle."

She leaned forward, put her hands to her knes, levered herself upright, and ... what on earth was *that*? Véronique wondered. That limp, shrunken little ... surely not? But it was — and the fig-leaves in the art galleries had not lied after all. This was more exciting yet, Véronique thought. It was suddenly clear to her that, most of the time, men went around with something like *that* little thing hidden inside their trousers, about the size of a finger. But then, when they got excited — when a girl got them all excited — they could not help it growing to the size of the great stiff prick she'd seen on McLaren earlier. Talk about the tail wagging the dog! The thought that just by *being* a girl you could take that bit of a man's body out of his control and make it grow and stiffen in your honour, ready to pleasure you as his had just pleasured Giselle … it was quite giddy-making.

Suddenly her heart dropped a beat. She was forgetting herself and the fact that she wasn't supposed to be there. McLaren would expect to find her resting in the bedroom. She almost ruined it all by overbalancing her chair in her haste; she only just caught it before the back of it hit the floor with a thump. She raced tiptoe along the passage, back to the room with the four-poster bed. There she took off her dressing gown, slipped between the silken sheets and started caressing her body all over while her mind relived the wonders she had just witnessed.

"There she goes," Giselle's sharp ears heard the farther bedroom door close. "You really don't want another?"

He shook his head lazily. "That was perfect. One of our best sessions, I think."

"Absolutely our best," she said. "I never knew it was so thrilling being watched."

"And I'd forgotten."

"I wonder," she asked casually, "if it would be just as thrilling if the dear girl were in the bed with us?"

He chuckled. "Are you suggesting a threesome, angel?"

"I've always wondered what it'd be like."

"You'll find out soon enough. It's a popular extra down at Nymphenburg."

"And so don't you think I'd need a little practice? You've covered everything else so thoroughly — including *me!*"

The sex-glutton in McLaren's head (or in his balls, perhaps) was thinking hard. "How about this?" he suggested. "I believe a girl's first time with a man should be solo. It's so easy for her to become embarrassed and awkward and burst into tears and so on. So ... if I were to return this evening around six o'clock and gave her a very gentle solo session — just twenty minutes or so to let her feel she's broken the ice — and then came back tomorrow after lunch and spent the entire afternoon in bed with both of you? And you could sort of introduce her to the idea at your leisure tonight — how about that?"

"How *about* that!" Giselle exclaimed happily.

That afternoon Jilly (as she now was to Véronique) lent the girl one of her frocks and took her out shopping — to Peter Davis, and Swan & Edgar, and Swears & Wells, and Lilley & Skinner, and Shoolbred's — for the most wonderful shopping spree imaginable. McLaren had an arrangement at all those places whereby any girl who presented a note with that day's date was allowed to make purchases up to a certain agreed limit with that shop. If they were in any doubt, they telephoned him discreetly and checked her description with him.

They bought armfuls of pretty summer frocks, flowery petticoats, silk lingerie, suggestive knickers, lacy brassières (the first Véronique had ever worn), short gloves, long gloves, gloves of lace and of fine white cotton ... Véronique felt quite giddy by the time they finished at Shoolbred's. Some of these purchases were for Jilly, which she proudly paid for out of her own savings. And it was there at Shoolbred's that something unusual happened.

The assistant who served them was a harassed girl of about Jilly's age — quite pretty, with long wavy red hair and green eyes flecked with brown. She obviously did not get on well with the floor walker, who came over and ticked her off several times for 'crimes' that Jilly and Véronique had not even noticed. Jilly bought two black silk petticoats and a black bra made of the finest gauze. The girl wrapped them up and added them to the pile of their purchases from other shops. "If you like, modom," she murmured, keeping a wary eye on the floor walker, "I can arrange to have all these delivered to you." Then she whispered, "Please say yes!"

"Yes," they said together, intrigued by her manner.

"Ask me to arrange it," she whispered further.

Jilly, rising to the occasion, put on the manner of a grande dame and, tapping the pile of their purchases, said, "Kindly arrange to have these delivered to this address." And she wrote down their Maida Vale address on the sale ticket.

"What now?" the floor walker asked wearily as he came waddling over again. "Is this assistant annoying you young ladies?"

"On the contrary," Jilly replied. "She has very kindly offered to arrange for our purchases to be delivered."

The man smiled ... until he saw the pile they had left. "All of these?" he asked.

Jilly glanced swiftly at the girl, who nodded almost imperceptibly. "Yes, all of them," she replied and started walking away. "If anything has annoyed me, my man, it is your constant interruptions and badgering of this poor young lady. Come along, Rom."

The moment they were out of sight they doubled back behind one of the floor displays and, while pretending to inspect it, strained their ears to catch what the man was saying to the unfortunate girl. He was saying, "We do *not* deliver purchases made at other stores, Miss Keppel. I should have thought that was obvious even to a nincompoop like you. Well, you can jolly well struggle up there with them yourself this evening — and serve you right!"

Véronique explored herself down there and found, to her immense surprise, that she, too, had a little button — a tiny little limp morsel of exquisitely tender flesh, like a lump of sago, or a jelly-baby half sucked away — and just touching it released the most delicious feelings inside her! Had it just grown there in the last few minutes? How had she never found it during all her previous Saturday-night jollifications? Because she'd only been thinking of her *hole,* that's why — which Monica said was all that men were interested in, anyway. She went on fondling it gently, her own little jelly-baby, while she revelled in the variety of pokes McLaren was giving Giselle's quim — some fast, some slow, some deep, some shallow, and each one a delight to Giselle herself.

Next he reached down and, grasping her left thigh, lifted it onto the backrest at the same time as he turned her sideways-on to him. He poked her a couple of times in this strange position but it was obviously not comfortable. Both laughed. Then she lifted her thigh in a high arc between them, like a music-hall dancer's high kick. At the same time she twisted herself round, as if impaled on his prick, using it as a pivot until they were face-to-face.

They smiled at each other and kissed tenderly while he caressed her nipples through the gauze, which she had once again pulled down. She ran her fingers up and down his back and then she lifted her right leg and threw it up around him. In this position Véronique could see again how his prick thrust its way in and out of her hole. She could see Giselle's petals (as she thought of them now) clinging to the pale shaft of his prick, which made them furl and unfurl with each thrust and withdrawal. They were both gleaming wet down there by now and every movement made sticky little noises like people with a hearty appetite smacking their lips.

He started to push it in • 51

just seemed to swallow and swallow and swallow his prick, until the full length of it had slipped inside her. The two of them let out a deep sigh. When he had it all the way in she saw his buttocks tighten as he tried to drive it just that little bit deeper.

That tightening of his buttocks and the powerful thrust it caused stirred something deep inside her. It was the most exciting thing she'd ever seen. She could almost feel his prick filling her own hole the way it must be filling Giselle's. And she could almost feel it, too, when he withdrew and then thrust it all the way in again, much more quickly this time.

The next time was slow again, and his withdrawal was slow, too. And he moved himself a little from side to side. It looked as if he was exploring every little fold and cranny of her hole with the tip of his organ. Not that Giselle complained! She just lay there, bent almost double over the back of the chaise longue, with a seraphic smile on her face and an uninterrupted stream of sighs and whimpers coming out between her slackly open rosebud lips.

McLaren's eyes glazed over. He was moving like an automaton, lost to this world. Véronique just adored the way his buttocks tightened and curled as he thrust and withdrew. She imagined him lying on top of her, doing that, and how her hands would reach down there and hold those thrusting buttocks and feel their hardness and vigour.

After a while he reached for Giselle's shoulders and pulled her upright. She lifted her arms right up and back over her head, back over his, pulling him tight against her. His hands stole round her and fondled her breasts awhile. Then one finger traced a tickly line down her tummy and into her bush, where it obviously found some sort of button that …

Curved like a banana • 47

noticed, was only fondling the shaft. Just occasionally she brushed the red knob part.

He leaned forward and suckled her right nipple — the farther one from Véronique — and gently squeezed the other with his right hand. At the same time he insinuated his left hand into the open gusset of her pantaloons. There he let the backs of his fingers graze softly in and around her bush, making small circular movements over the swelling beneath it. Giselle moaned urgently and lifted her fork toward him. He moved the knuckle of his thumb down into the dark between her thighs, out of Véronique's sight, and started doing things that made her sway and moan in a curious mixture of ecstasy and torment.

Véronique slipped her own hand into her fork and tried to copy his movements but, whatever he was doing to drive Giselle so wild, she couldn't match it. Maybe only a man knew that secret.

He stopped suckling her and just sat there, upright again, caressing both her nipples with his widestretched right hand while he enjoyed her obvious pleasure. She just lay limp, eyes closed, lips parted in a drugged smile. Her hand was still holding his tool but forgetting to fondle it. He gave a jig and she woke to her duties. She gave him a naughty smile and resumed her fondling. He leaned forward and kissed her gently on the mouth. Véronique suddenly longed for such a kiss.

When their mouths parted, Giselle snapped a little love bite on his departing lower lip. He returned hungrily for more and they kissed for a full minute longer.

When they stopped, he eased her farther down the seat until her shoulder-blades were at the base of the backrest and only her head leaned against it. She lifted up her bottom while he grabbed two cushions and slipped them under her.

He pushed her thighs as wide as they'd go and gazed with admiration at her privates for a while.

Véronique moved to another chair to get a better view. She'd never seen another female's quim (her mother's word). Only her own. And only from the angles you could see in a looking glass and a hand mirror. And she'd certainly never seen her own as pink and wet and glowing-looking as Giselle's.

While she gazed in fascination, McLaren put a third cushion as a rest for his chin and went down to ... surely not! But yes! He started licking and kissing and ... well, the only word for it was *feasting*. He was enthusiastically feasting on her quim. Yeurk! And yet, to judge by Giselle's ecstatic reactions, it must be the most scrummy feeling a girl could ever experience.

Her whole body shivered and her breath came in short gasps between moans and whimpers. And when McLaren slipped his arms beneath her thighs and reached up to fondle her breasts, with the same expertise as before ... well, she looked as if she had passed out entirely.

But this position obviously tired him. He withdrew his hands from her breasts and used them instead to press her thighs even wider and flatter. Then he returned to his feast while his hands roamed freely over the insides of her thighs. Giselle started to fondle her own nipples ...

And girls get paid for doing this! Véronique thought. *In fact, Giselle is getting paid for doing it right this minute!* She felt she could not possibly wait for tomorrow or Sunday or whenever it was that McLaren would be initiating her into these delirious mysteries.

After another long feast in that position McLaren rose and went over to the bed. Véronique raced as fast as she dared to get to a chair beside him. When she put her eyes to the window again he was lying on his back on the dark blue sheets with his legs spread flat and wide and his big banana prick waving in the air above him. Once again, Véronique could have reached out and touched him. How she wished the wall would vanish!

Giselle lay on her tummy between his legs and, without any ado, grabbed his prick near the bottom and teased it all over with darts and nips of her teeth and tongue. Little bites. Small, quick licks. Long, luscious, lingering licks that made him squirm and moan as she had done a few moments before.

Véronique realized that, an hour earlier, she might have retched at the very thought of licking a man's prick like that — and at the thought of a man feasting on her quim down there, too. But now it was one of those things — yet another of those things — she could not wait to start doing herself.

The bit McLaren liked best, she noticed, was when Giselle held the knob of it in her wide-open mouth and breathed hot breath all over it, and then closed her mouth all round it and swirled her tongue this way and that — and then, suddenly, opened her lips just a little and drew in a sharp, chilly breath ... and then closed the heat of her mouth all around it once more. By the look on his face, it almost drove him out of his mind — that hot-cold-hot-cold-hot treatment.

Giselle stopped that game just as suddenly as she had started it. And Véronique watched engrossed as, all calm again, the girl now tried to swallow his prick whole — or so it seemed. It reminded her of a python swallowing a rabbit, which she had seen in the cinema once — slow and self-satisfied.

He moaned in greater torment than ever. He rolled his head from side to side and drummed his heels on the bed. And then, in a kind of panic, he jerked sharply out of her, his eyes full of fear. He and Giselle stared at each other and held their breaths as if they'd just heard a policeman's knock at the door. Whatever the crisis was, it passed in due course, and they smiled at each other and breathed easy once again.

Then, swinging his limbs over her head and down onto the floor, he rose, took her by the hand, and led her back to the chaise longue. This time he got her to stand where he had stood before, on the floor behind the backrest.

Véronique raced back to her earlier vantage, eager not to miss a thing. She peeped through the slit and saw McLaren, now naked, standing immediately behind Giselle and bending her forward over the backrest, pushing her down until her long blonde hair spilled over the seat of the chaise longue. His prick was jutting up in the air like the bowsprit of a ship — a rather curved bowsprit, no longer concealed by the spinnaker of his dressing gown. His fingers were easing apart the edges of her harem pants and Véronique could see wisps of pale hair sprouting out between the cheeks of her bottom. With his right foot he pressed alternately against the insides of Giselle's feet, nudging them farther apart, spreading her thighs wider.

Moving to the next chair Véronique could just glimpse the frilly bits of Giselle's quim, pouting like flower petals and looking as if they were just begging him to get in among them. He grabbed his prick again and thrust forward until the knob of it was just buried between those 'petals.' And there he began to move it up and down, quite slowly. He moved it in and out, too, following the curves of her intimate anatomy there. Giselle responded by tightening first one buttock then the other — wagging her tail, so to speak.

Then he paused at one point and started to push it in. Véronique watched in total absorption as the girl's quim

He started guiltily when he saw Jilly and Véronique returning to the counter. "Ah ... er ... is something wrong, modom?"

"Not at all," Jilly said airily. "I simply wish to leave a second address in case there is no reply at the first." When the man continued to hang around she waved an imperious hand at him. "Well — go about your business, my good man! We don't need you here."

Looking daggers he went.

"Now," Jilly said, pretending to write another address, "what's all this about, Miss Keppel?"

"I want to talk to you," was the reply.

"What about?"

"I can't possibly say it out loud here!"

"Let me guess. About leaving your trade and trying ours?" Miss Keppel had a hard time suppressing a smile.

"How do we know you won't simply scarper with our frocks and things?" Jilly asked.

The girl glanced nervously at the floor walker again. "Because I know how much they cost and I'd be very interested in earning that sort of money myself."

This satisfied Jilly. "How will you get to Maida Vale?" was her next question.

"By tube I thought."

"Have you enough for a taxi?"

"Only if I don't eat for the rest of the week."

"Take the taxi. We'll pay him when you come. What time will that be?"

"Soon after six. I have Friday evenings off."

"Six will be the perfect hour. We'll see you then." Jilly passed over the piece of blank paper.

"Gosh, Jilly, you're pretty quick-witted," Véronique said as they returned to the street and flagged down a taxi.

"What are you going to tell her when she comes?" she asked as they climbed in.

"I don't know. But between us — me, Sherry, and his two sons, we'll work out something for her." They climbed into the taxi and she gave the driver their directions. "It's time I told you about Sherry's sons," she said as they settled back into the faded, tobacco-smoky upholstery.

"This taxi reeks of all the people who ever got inside it." Véronique wrinkled her nose.

"So will we if we don't take care of ourselves," Jilly replied grimly. "Sherry's sons are called Terence and Rory. Terence is twenty-seven and is a barrister. Rory is twenty-three and is an army captain. He's in charge of the staff cars for the war office. His unit is somewhere on the edge of Regent's Park. It must be the opposite side from Maida Vale, because he says he works up his appetite while walking across the park and watching the monkeys fucking away on the Mappin Terraces. In the zoo, you know."

"An appetite? For you, you mean?"

Jilly grinned. "You're also pretty quick on the uptake. Yes — for me. And soon enough, no doubt, for you, too."

"Does Sherry know? Will he mind if I call him Sherry?"

"He'll insist on it. But as to whether or not he knows his sons also like to enjoy us ..."

"Both of them?" Véronique swallowed heavily at the thought.

"Both of them — and pretty well every day, too. Believe me, pet, if you've been feeling a bit sex-starved up until now, you're about to meet the cure — in three different forms! Sherry comes to the house every lunchtime. *Every* lunchtime, Monday to Friday, without fail — like today. He takes what he calls his vertical refreshment — that is, a light lunch — for about ten minutes and then you both go upstairs for an hour or so of *horizontal* refreshment, as he calls it. Sometimes he comes on Saturday afternoon, too, but he'll always let you know on Friday. He never calls on Sundays."

Véronique heaved a theatrical sigh of relief. But it was short-lived.

"Sundays," Jilly went on, is when the two boys like to call."

"Together?" Véronique asked in alarm.

"Just listen! They arrange it between themselves. One of them comes about two and stays for a couple of hours. The other calls at eight in the evening and is generally gone by ten."

"Are they married?"

"I don't think so. They never mention a wife. If they are, their wives aren't getting much. I tell you — as practice for life at the Nymphenburg, it's pretty good. Because the sons both call most weekday evenings, too. Though then it's just for a quickie — half an hour with each. An hour at the most. Rory's the unpredictable one. Sometimes, for no reason at all — except that men don't really need a reason for sex, do they! — he gets a letch on him and he'll fuck you six times in a row and he'll be there until midnight. Sherry says he used to be able to do that ..."

"You told him?"

"No! Like I said, or maybe I didn't, anyway, we *think* — Terence, Rory, and me — we *think* Sherry doesn't know. But even if he did, he wouldn't say. So we behave as if he didn't. He once told me that when he used to go to sporting houses a lot, he liked to hang around outside a girl's room while she was being fucked ..."

"Ah ... I meant to ask. Can you say a girl fucks a man?"

Jilly laughed. "What *with*, pet?" Then she looked thoughtful. "Though mind you ..." Then she shook her head. "Never mind. All in due course. I was saying — Sherry, in his younger days, liked to hang around outside a girl's door while she was being fucked and then, when that man left the room, he'd get straight into her and fuck away in the other man's come before she could wash it out."

"What's come?"

"Spunk. Milt. Semen. Roe. Tail juice. Sperm. Sticky — you know — what a man shoots into a girl when he's coming."

Véronique shook her head but the words 'taking all *comers* in her stride' now meant something more to her.

"You don't know about that? Blimey! Well, you saw when Sherry was having those sort of convulsions, right at the end? You couldn't see it but his prick was firing juice up inside me — squirt, squirt, squirt! Not much each time. You'll feel it most on a Monday, after he's laid off for a day or two. It's a couple of teaspoonful in all, I suppose. But you can feel it inside you like a little tickle. And his prick goes ... Hold my arm!" She wrapped Véronique's hand round her forearm and then tensed and relaxed her muscles in spasms, saying, "Squirt!" in time to each spasm. "That's when they get their jollies — all concentrated in one half-minute orgy. Orgasm, it's called — having an orgasm. And then they can't have another orgasm for half-an-hour at the soonest. Some not till next day."

"And what about us?"

"Bless you, pet! You don't know about that, either? We can have orgasms whenever the mood takes us and as often as we like. Once, when Rory got that letch on him, I went on all evening. I lost count at sixty. You'll see."

Véronique's feelings were torn in two at this news. Half of her longed to experience this 'orgasm' for herself but the other half cringed from it in fear. "Does Rory often get these letches?" she asked.

Squirt, squirt, squirt!

"It only happened three times with me but it's quite good when he does because he leaves a little 'bonne bouche,' as he calls it of five sovereigns. Both the sons pay for it, by the way. Not religiously each time but they leave a little envelope of money lying around every now and then. It works out at about ten bob a fuck, which is also good training for Nymphenburg, because that's what a girl earns there." She reached out and gave Véronique's thigh a friendly squeeze. "Feeling a bit nervous, eh, young 'un? Don't worry. The great thing is, even if you *don't* feel like doing it, you can still pretend. It's not like a man who's *got* to keep his prick stiff to have his fun. You can just lie there like dead meat and act your head off — or act your tail off, more likely — and the man will still enjoy himself."

She started to remove her hand but Véronique put her own over it and said, "No — that's nice."

"Really?" For the first time, Jilly seemed at a bit of a loss but she left her hand there on her thigh.

"Were you acting this morning?" Véronique went on.

Jilly grinned wickedly. "Was I hell! That was the best fuck I've had since I started this lark. It is a lark, isn't it! Don't you agree?"

Véronique nodded and leaned back happily in the smelly upholstery. They were passing Lords. Soon be there. She parted her thighs slightly.

Jilly's hand moved a little higher. "Is that nice, too?" she asked. There was a shiver in her voice.

"Even nicer," Véronique said.

"When we go to bed tonight …" Jilly began.

Véronique lifted the hand off her thigh and kissed it. "Shh!" she whispered.

Sheridan McLaren arrived promptly at six, saying he hadn't much time. That was to spare Véronique any disappointment when she learned he wouldn't be staying for several hours of sexual indulgence with her. Long experience with new girls had taught him that a delicate little hors d'oeuvres one evening, followed by the full gourmet feast the following day, was much more rewarding to both parties. However, when he heard the strange tale of their encounter with Miss Keppel, he suddenly discovered he wasn't in such a hurry after all. He made them tell him the story twice, pressing them on every detail. They just finished the second telling as the taxi drew up outside and they saw her getting out.

"She's a good-looker, all right," he said admiringly. His eyes already coveted her and his prick stirred in his fork. Redheads held a special place in his affection, equalled only by blondes and brunettes. He went to stand by the door, listening for her approach.

The girls followed him into the hall.

"I thought you were going to tick us off for taking such a risk," Jilly said. "She could easily have vamoosed with our things."

He shook his head. "In that case she would have given you any other reason under the sun — other, that is, than the one she did, in fact, give. No woman would volunteer such a reason to another woman unless she meant it — and had desperate reason to mean it. Ah, Miss Keppel!" He opened the door to her. "Welcome to my humble home from home. I am Sheridan McLaren and I believe you know these young ladies — Giselle and Véronique."

She shook hands all round. She was trembling like a leaf. "I'm Maxine," she said, accepting the house style.

They went into the sitting room. The taxi driver followed them and made a neat pile of their carrier bags and hatboxes.

Maxine took out her purse but McLaren beat her to it. "A glass of wine?" he suggested. "Or sherry, perhaps? You'd like some sherry, Véronique, I imagine?"

"Sherry can't come soon enough for me," she replied with an absolutely straight face.

He laughed. "Well a *glass* of sherry will help."

While Jilly went over to the drinks cabinet he started quizzing Maxine Keppel — and learned in fairly short order that she was an orphan, the only child of a provincial vicarage. A church benevolent society had obtained for her a place at Shoolbred's and for a time she was happy there.

Jilly passed round the drinks.

When the alcohol had loosened Maxine's tongue a little, she confessed that the change had come when Claude Greene, the floor walker, had got her alone in the stockroom and had put his tongue in her mouth and had tried to pull her drawers down. She had slapped his face and he had made life hell for her ever since. That was two months ago. She'd considered throwing herself in the Thames and then this afternoon, "when these two charming young girls walked in and one of the assistants whispered to me who they were and how they make their living ..." Her voice trailed off and she shrugged as if to say the rest was obvious. She smiled at the girls to show she meant no criticism or disrespect.

"You stop at the most interesting point, Miss Keppel," Sherry said. "Tell us exactly what you felt at that moment."

"I just felt — *yes!*"

"Yes?"

"Like a great big *yes* inside me. You know when you see a hat that's absolutely right for you and something inside you says yes?" She turned to the girls. "Aren't you just dying to open your parcels?"

"Dying!" they agreed in chorus.

"Go on, then!" Sherry told them. "And you, Miss Keppel, you go on, too."

The girls began opening their parcels with half-suppressed cries of delight as at the reappearance of old friends.

Maxine continued: "Something inside me just said yes. It was as if that's what I was made for but I hadn't realized until now. I felt I was born to do ... that. Ooh, those are scrumptious gloves! Where did you get them?"

"Swears and Wells." Véronique had to read the ticket to be sure.

But Sherry persisted. "Let's get this quite clear. You say this other assistant told you what these young ladies do for a living — what exactly did she say to you?"

"She just said they're mistresses. She said Maida Vale is full of mistresses. Is it true?"

"And what is a mistress? What d'you understand by ..."

"A kept woman. A woman who allows a man the use of her body in return for bed and board and a living. I may be a vicar's daughter, Mister McLaren, but I've learned a lot since I had to make my own way in the world. You won't shock me, I think." Her voice faltered a little when she saw the girl he'd called Giselle standing behind him, shaking her head vigorously. Obviously one did not issue such challenges to this man.

"Can't shock you, eh?" Sherry echoed her boast. "What if I ask you to take off your jacket and blouse and show me your bosoms?"

Maxine glanced nervously at the other girls and wet her lips.

"Go on, Giselle," he said without looking round.

Without hesitation Jilly undid her blouse and lifted her chemise clear of her bra. "D'you really want me to go on?" she asked.

A fine pair of naked breasts • 67

"And Véronique?" he added, still keeping his eyes on Maxine, who was fascinated by all this.

Véronique made as little fuss as Jilly had done — and, having no bra, disported a fine pair of naked breasts.

Even then Sherry did not turn round. "Right!" he said and continued to watch Maxine.

"Right!" she echoed and, swallowing hard, unbuttoned her jacket and opened her blouse. She, too, was wearing no bra, so a gorgeous pair of full, ripe breasts shivered beneath the thin art-silk of her chemise, trembling with each beat of her heart.

"Absolutely delightful!" he said admiringly. He especially admired the freckles that peppered her skin.

She blushed and began to rebutton her blouse.

"No, no!" he exclaimed. "Come here and sit on my lap."

Mesmerized, she obeyed, walking like one in a trance.

"This is a kind of test," he explained as he settled her comfortably on his thighs. "You may be best suited for Shoolbred's after all."

It was just the injection of terror she needed to make her steel herself to undergo this test — and Sherry knew it, of course. Giving her no time to resist he slipped his hand under her skirt and moved it rapidly up toward her groin. Soon his knuckles were nuzzling in her bush. She was wearing drawers, with an open gusset in her fork. "Open up," he said gently. "Let's just feel your assets. You could be hiding a fortune down here. A bit wider — come on! This is one area where shyness and modesty don't help."

His middle finger found her groove and ran along it until it reached the soft declivity at the portals of heaven.

"Have you still got a maidenhead?" he asked, slipping it half an inch inside her vagina. "No." He answered his own question. "Where did that go, I wonder?"

She closed her eyes and hung her head in shame. "The choirmaster, when I was sixteen." She shuddered.

He longed to thrust his finger all the way into her, but, in her present mood, he did not dare. He was an artist and girls were his raw material — the rawer, the better, he was fond of saying. And, like all good artists, he treated his material with respect. So he pulled his finger out again, rearranged her skirt, and even helped do up her blouse and jacket. "Another sherry?" he suggested.

"Well?" she asked, flustered now. "Have I passed your test?"

"With flying colours," he assured her. "If you became a man's mistress, you'd have to let him do that to you — and more. You realize that?"

"I told you. I'm not the green little cabbage I used to be."

"And suppose the man who desired to keep you in a little love nest somewhere near here was the living image of Mister Claude Greene? D'you think you could manage it — being nice to him? Dropping your knickers at the drop of his hat?"

Maxine laughed and nodded and shuddered and shook her head all in the same movement.

"You're being rather hard on her, Sherry," Véronique said.

But Jilly tapped her on the arm and wagged a finger in warning not to interfere.

"Come here, little face," he told her without looking round.

Her heart pounding, Véronique obeyed. When he patted his lap she sat where Maxine had sat moments earlier. She knew what was coming — her test.

His hand slipped under her skirts and went snaking up over her stockings to her fork. She didn't need him to tell her to open her thighs. Her quim was there, all ready and pouting to let him in. And in he went — all the way. "Oh dear," he said. "No blushing little membrane of skin there, either! Who took that, I wonder? Another choirmaster?"

"It was the Earl of Almond, actually," Véronique said, proudly holding up the middle finger of her right hand and giving it the name from a childhood nursery riddle. "Only aristocrats for me!"

They all laughed, even Maxine. But Sherry's finger was doing such delightful things to her that she shivered and caught her breath. Then, unable to stop herself, she flung her arms around him and kissed him with passion.

He responded briefly and then broke away. "Upstairs you go," he murmured. "But have another sherry first."

"That's not the Sherry I need," she replied.

"Knock one back just for the hell of it. It'll do no harm." He lifted one thigh to tip her off his lap. "And while you're sipping it you can hear what I'm going to propose to Miss Keppel." He turned to the girl. "You see the difference, Miss Keppel?" he asked. "I needn't labour the point, I trust? Véronique, too, has never been with a man — though we are about to make good that deficiency in her life." He pointed at the ceiling.

Maxine pulled a wry face and nodded. "I *could* behave like that, though," she said.

"I'm sure you could. Up here." He tapped his forehead. "But it would be a life of deceit and misery. If you can't also feel it here …" He tapped his breastbone and left the idea hanging. "However, that is far from being the end of the affair. You may yet have it in you to be a good mistress to some lucky man. I don't think you can possibly go back to Shoolbred's, do you?"

She shook her head.

"Would you consider a temporary place as lady's maid in a gentleman's household?"

Her face lit up at the words, for a lady's maid stood several rungs higher on the social ladder than a lowly shop assistant.

"In *this* gentleman's household?" he asked. "As a maid to *that* young lady?" He pointed at Véronique, who almost dropped her glass.

"You object?" he asked Véronique.

"No," she stammered. "I hadn't even thought about it."

"Well, think about it now." He turned back to Maxine. "You will be able to observe the life of a mistress at close quarters and you will have time to accustom yourself to it and to decide whether it's for you, after all."

Véronique saw the pleading in Maxine's eyes and went to her at once. "Of course I say yes," she murmured. "It was only surprise, not distaste. I took a liking to you the moment I saw you at Shoolbred's. Do say yes! I'm sure we'll have such jolly times here."

Maxine looked from one to the other, tears brimming in her eyes. "Yes," she whispered at last.

"Capital!" Sherry said, standing up and rubbing his hands. "Will it suit you to start on Monday? Why don't you stay here now and dine with us? I suspect you've not eaten yet?"

"Not much since breakfast," the girl admitted.

"Good. We dine in about half an hour. We'll all go out to a restaurant. Giselle will lend you a frock. Now you, Véronique," he said, "I want you to go upstairs to the bedroom, the one where you took a little rest at lunchtime, draw the curtains, light one candle on the far side of the bed, take off all your clothes — every last stitch — get into bed, and wait for me." He took out his watch. "I shall be no more than five minutes."

'Take off your clothes and wait for me' • 71

Véronique tossed back the last of her sherry and floated across the room. Jilly put an arm around her shoulder and kissed her cheek. "Have fun, sweet child," she whispered. "And let who will be careful!"

This is it! a voice inside her said. Now she would be able to do all those wonderful things she saw Jilly doing with him at lunchtime. Except that she knew she'd never manage it. Jilly's actions had been so smooth and easy. She knew exactly what she was doing, what the effect would be, what Sherry liked ... how to mould her body to his ... all those things. Jilly was like a trained dancer whose body did exactly what she intended it to do. But she, by contrast, would be like the merest beginner, shuffling round uncertainly and stumbling over herself at every other step.

And Sherry would be bound to notice the difference, especially after that wonderful session with Jilly at lunchtime. He'd try the same lovely things with her and she'd just fume and sweat and shiver and get everything wrong and end up feeling a complete idiot ...

Perhaps if she went and hid in the bathroom ...?

No! Not now she'd bought all those lovely clothes with his money. She'd have to pay him back, of course — that was part of the bargain. She was to repay him bit by bit out of the money he gave her to be his mistress. So now she was completely trapped. She *had to* perform. That was his cunning.

She hesitated — bedroom or bathroom?

In her terror she almost chose the bathroom but then, in the nick of time, she remembered his finger inside her just now and the melting moments it had given her ... and she chose the bedroom.

It wouldn't be so awful, she now started telling herself. If all he wanted her to do was lie naked in the bed in the dark, with just one candle burning ... and if he meant it when he said they'd dine in half an hour ... well, then — he couldn't be intending to do much to her. With her.

And at that — such is the paradoxical nature of Woman — she felt a bit peeved. She fumed as she took off her clothes. Did he think she wasn't *good* enough to give him the sort of sybaritic pleasure Jilly had given him earlier? She was good for nothing more than a quick poke, eh? Was that it? Well, she'd show him!

Her angry thoughts delayed her so long that she'd only just put her head to the pillow when she heard him enter the room behind her. She flipped round between the sheets — how lovely and soft and silky and warm they felt on her bare skin! — and tried to make him out in the one-candle gloom.

He was wearing a dressing gown of pale blue silk, tied so loosely that his ramrod-prick jutted out like a barber's pole in front of him. It waggled excitedly as he crossed the room to her and again she was reminded of the tail wagging the dog. While she was wondering whether she dared reach up and stroke it, he said, gently but firmly, "Turn around please, Véronique. We're just going to do something very simple this first time together."

"Why?" she asked plaintively. She almost blurted out that she had watched them at lunchtime and felt fully capable of doing the same — and more if he wished. In fact ... whatever he wanted.

He replied, "Because, petal, I think you are going to be one of the truly great mistresses of my life. Yours will be the name I remember when all the others have faded into obscurity. And I want to open you up to the possibilities of the erotic life — the life of sexual indulgence — slowly and carefully ... as one would unpack a rare and delicate orchid from its case."

Well, after that, of course, she was putty in his hands. She'd have crawled around the carpet licking the soles of his feet if he'd asked her.

But he didn't. All he asked her to do was lie on her right side, facing away from him. She obeyed and lay quite still, with her heart beating like a power hammer and a delightful tingle of anticipation down there between her legs.

He slipped between the sheets behind her and grasped her lightly by the hips. It was the first time since her infancy that someone else's hands had held her there, flesh on naked flesh. The tingle in her groin felt like something solid and warm ...

It *was* something solid and warm! And it was sliding ever so slowly along her furrow. By instinct she slipped the fingers of her right hand into her cleft from the front and waited to guide him into her hole when the tip of his prick reached the mouth of it. She was shivering uncontrollably by now and fighting for every other breath. But, apparently, he did not wish her to guide him into her hole. He grasped her hand in his and held it against her tummy, where he caressed and patted it, as if to say it had been a nice thought but a little premature.

With maddening slowness, relishing every little hesitation and tremble, he continued to slide his prick forward along her crevice until he was tucked into her tail as tight as a man could get and still be outside her. And now, at last, he moved her hand back into her fork. There his deft, practised fingers moulded and arranged it around his prick, the knob of which was sticking out in front of her like a short, fat, one-inch prick of her own!

"Made to measure," he whispered. And indeed it was true, for the curve of his prick exactly fitted into the shape of the groove between her petals.

"Mmmh!" She groped her left hand over his body, behind her, and strained to press his left buttock with it.

"What's this?" he asked, amused.

"Make your bottom hard," she said. "Harden the muscles there."

Intrigued, he did as she asked — which, of course, thrust his knob even farther out into her other hand. The movement, and the feel of his buttock hardening in time with it, thrilled her. But the desire to feel his prick inside her was overwhelming and she clutched it even tighter into her cleft. This had the effect of pressing his knob against that little button of joy she had discovered for the first time earlier that day. She gasped at the dart of pleasure it sent through her.

"Yes," he whispered in her ear as his hands left her hips and stole up to caress her breasts. A moment later she felt the tip of his tongue nuzzle in behind the lobe of her left ear. Excitedly she swept her hair aside and offered him the whole of it to pleasure in that way and soon a fresh ecstasy from a new source was radiating all through her.

Meanwhile he was starting to move his buttocks backward and forward, making the hard gristle of his erection slide up and down in her crevice, adding to her joys from that quarter. At first she moved her hand with it but, when it started to pick up the juices of her increasing excitement, she just clamped her thighs tighter together and kept her fingers where they would pick up his knob when it emerged on each new thrust. She had her left hand back on his buttocks by now and so she could time it perfectly — and, of course, as the hot red tip of it emerged she arched her back and held it tight against her so as to increase its pressure on that tiny button of joy.

By now, too, his fingers were doing the most exquisite things to her breasts and nipples. She was in such a turmoil, with so many thrills filling her from so many different directions, that she could not tell one of his actions from another. She was shivering and sweating as if she had a fever — which, in a way, she did: a fever of sexual tumult. The tiny remnant of her consciousness wandered in the whirlwind of erotic frenzy that now consumed her body. Her breasts were on fire. Her nipples blazed. Her stomach was tumbling through infinite space. And as for her sex itself, it seethed and churned with longings and raptures whose very existence she could never have suspected. Nothing she had done to herself during those lonely Saturday nights in her bed at home — her former home — had prepared her to find *these* pleasures hidden within her, just waiting for the touch of a man like Sherry to bring them out.

He started moving faster. Her hand on his buttock urged him to move faster still. The fires in her ear, her breasts, her crevice — all swelled and merged, coalescing into one mighty conflagration that consumed every part of her body. From her toes to her crown she was one vast ocean of burning enchantment. And then, when she felt that nothing could overtop her joy, it was as if his prick put ten thousand volts through her. And then again. And again. And on and on and on …

His tongue could no longer pleasure her ear, his fingers could hardly pleasure her breasts as she twitched and jerked like a mad thing in the throes of her first true orgasm. But he was skilled enough to keep her up there on that plateau until she could gasp no more, cry out no more, think no more — until she went limp in his arms, still riding his erection like a witch on her broomstick. And then he took her back for one last ecstasy while he enjoyed his own.

Now he used both his hands to hold both of hers tight around his leaping, twitching knob. His ecstatic cries of 'Oh!

Oh!' and 'Yes!' raised a response in her mind: 'My body works!' a voice cried out within her. 'I didn't disappoint!'

And then she felt the hot, sticky lumps oozing around between her fingers and his knob.

"Careful!" he warned as she lifted them free. "Try not to get it on the sheets."

He threw them aside and then, wrapping a handkerchief around his by now limp organ, sat up behind her and guided her hands into the light of the single candle. She held his seed between her fingers like a sacred offering.

"That's what it's all about," he murmured. "The human male's need to squirt that stuff into the belly of the human female. And what a desperate, overwhelming, all-powerful need it is, let me tell you, petal. For that ineffable privilege men have parted with all their wealth and more than half their sanity."

The hair tingled at the back of her neck and the tingle ran all the way down her spine. It looked so simple in the candlelight, like lumps of badly dissolved starch. Unthinkingly she raised it to her lips and tasted it with the tip of her tongue. Behind her he stopped breathing. It tasted like ... something sweet and something a bit mushroomy — not unpleasant. Like the rich aroma in a wood when rain falls after a long dry spell in summer. She licked it again, and again found nothing to repel her. She grinned at him over her shoulder and sucked the lot off her fingers.

He let out the breath he had been holding all this while. "You *are* going to be one of the greatest!" he said softly. "A true and worthy heir to your Aunt Connie."

"Why d'you say that, Sherry?"

"Because ..." He lay back and pulled her half on top of him, with her legs parted over his right thigh and her breasts hanging against his chest. "Men and women think quite differently about sex. Quite a lot of women don't think about it at all. Most think about it for about five minutes a day, all put together. Some men never think about it, either, I suppose. But very few. Most men think about it at least hourly. And a few think about it almost all the time — whenever they're not drawing up wills and conveying property and ..." He grinned ruefully.

"I think about it all the time," she confessed. "So does Giselle, I think. Except when buying gloves and frocks and things — but even then, it's adorning one's body, so it's not a million miles away."

"Yes, well, I love talking about sex as well as doing it — in fact, I sometimes love talking about it *while* doing it. So no doubt we'll discover before long exactly why you're so absolutely sensational."

He fondled one of her breasts gently. She shivered. "Is that it for now? When are you going to ... you know — fuck me properly?"

"Daily," he replied. "For most of this summer at least, I should think."

"No, but the next time? Tonight, when we come back?"

"I'm afraid not. I'll return after lunch tomorrow, about two-thirty, and we'll spend the whole afternoon here 'in flagrant delight,' as one of my clerks puts it. I don't know what you think about this, but Giselle wants to make it a threesome. You needn't decide now. Think it over. I'm in your hands — or will be — two hands or four. Oh, what bliss!"

After dinner at a restaurant in Swiss Cottage, Sherry dropped his two mistresses off in Maida Vale and went on in the taxi to drop Maxine, who, he hoped, would be his next mistress, back at her lodgings in Paddington.

Left alone with Jilly again, a sudden shyness overcame Véronique and, like any bashful bridegroom, she lingered about downstairs while Jilly went up to the bedroom. Those intimate caresses in the taxi had laid down a kind of promise for later — for this moment now, in fact. But that moment had arrived at last, and she was unsure about honouring her own side of the unspoken bargain or holding Jilly to hers. When she finally ascended the stairs and went into the bedroom she found her friend at the window, staring through a pair of binoculars. She was still fully dressed.

"Battleship making smoke on the port bow?" she asked jovially.

"No." Jilly laughed. "Sometimes you can see a couple going at it like dog and bitch in the house on the corner. But not tonight. However, I've just realized you can actually see Nymphenburg from here. You could see all the brothels if it wasn't for that tree." She stood aside and handed the glasses to Véronique. "Just between those two houses diagonally opposite. You can't see anything happening, of course. It's too far. But you can just make out the men going in and out. See?"

"Oh yes! There's one coming out now. Like a little ant."

"How long was I up here? Five minutes. I saw three men come out and two more go in during that time. Multiply that up and it's twenty-four an hour. But it can't be. I must just have picked an unusually busy five minutes, that's all."

"You'll know for sure by this time next Monday."

"Thanks for the reminder!"

"Getting cold feet?"

Jilly went to sit on the edge of the bed. She slumped with her hand loosely clasped in her lap. "It's a big leap, isn't it — from this to that. Actually, something Sherry said to Maxine Keppel pulled me up with a jerk — when he asked her if she could drop her knickers for someone like whatsizname Greene, the floor walker at Shoolbred's. I mean, here I've only had Sherry and Rory and Terence, who are all pretty acceptable to a girl. But down there it'll be absolutely *anybody.*" She shuddered. "Fat old goats, pimply adolescents, rough foreigners smelling of garlic ..." She sighed. "When it was just an *idea,* I couldn't wait! But now ..."

"D'you know what I think?" Véronique said. "I think there are — how many? — several dozen girls down there in those houses in Little Venice and they're all managing to work with pimply old goats and fat adolescents — without making too much fuss. They're 'taking all comers in their strides'! So are you saying you're afraid you're not as good as the least of them?"

A smile broke out on Jilly's face as these encouraging words sank in. "You're right," she said, shrugging off her depression. "It's just the thought of changing ... and thinking of Sherry and his boys and all the fine times. Anyway" — she rose again — "I'm for a bath."

"Me too," Véronique said, meaning she'd pop in after.

Jilly smiled naughtily at her and said, "You're quick. Be an angel, go and start the water running."

She was in her dressing gown by the time Véronique returned. "I'll go and shake in some perfume and make it foam," she said.

When Véronique returned to the bathroom, now in her dressing gown, too, Jilly was already in the bath, which was almost long enough for them to lie end-to-end. "Come on in," she cried out gaily. "The water's lovely."

Véronique stepped gingerly in at the other end from her. The water was just hot enough to bear. It felt like a thousand little tingling fingers as she lowered herself through the cap of foam.

"Isn't it lovely being a woman," Jilly said, stretching out until only her face was above the water. She blew foam aside and continued, "To pamper oneself like this. And to *be* pampered the way we are — just because we've got these ... these bits of our bodies that men can't get enough of!"

At that moment Véronique, who had been sneaking her foot up between where she guessed Jilly's thighs were, made contact with her quim.

"Ooh!" Jilly said softly.

Véronique wiggled her foot gently from side to side.

"O-o-o-h!" Jilly responded more urgently and found Véronique's bush with her own toes, too.

They both giggled then; but the ice was broken now and there was no turning back for either.

"Can I come and lie beside you?" Véronique asked.

"And?"

"And this." She lay beside Jilly and started running the sponge all over her body, making random sweeps and circles. "You have lovely lips," she said after a while. "I should so adore to kiss them."

Jilly closed her eyes and offered her mouth. Véronique brushed them with hers and felt the first faint stirrings of those thrills she had discovered with Sherry, earlier that evening. She gave her one long and passionate kiss and followed it with little stabs on her top lip, her bottom lip, the corner of her mouth. At the same moment her hand went to Jilly's breasts and started squeezing and rubbing her nipples. She felt the girl's heart going pitapat under the softness. She kissed her again and then remembered what Maxine said about that man putting his tongue in her mouth. She tried it now with Jilly, who, at first, opened her eyes wide in surprise but then, obviously finding it thrilling, too, responded eagerly. It finished in a fit of giggles.

Rubbing their bodies together

"Wait, wait, wait!" Jilly said excitedly. "Try this. Don't you move, now." And she put her lips back to Véronique's and thrust her tongue in and out of her mouth — in, out, in, out. "Remind you of something?" she asked.

"It makes me want to *do* something like that," Véronique replied. "It's the answer to that question I asked you this afternoon, remember? Can a woman fuck? I saw you hesitate at the time. Is that what you were thinking of?"

"No." Jilly was still a little hesitant. "It's hard to describe, but I'll show you when we've finished our bath."

The rest of their time in the water was more foreplay than horseplay. Now that they knew they were going to do something very exciting together — not here but once they got between the sheets — the urgency went out of it. The evening — indeed, the whole night — stretched ahead of them. They had no very precise idea of what they were going to do, since neither had done anything like it before, nor even dreamed of such a thing, but they had no doubt that it would be anything other than an exciting voyage of discovery. They stood up and soaped each other lovingly, putting their arms around each other and rubbing their entire bodies together, entwining their legs, and kissing again and again.

They took particular care (and delight) in washing each other's crotches, with many a naughty smile and giggle.

"What's it called down there?" Véronique asked. "My mother called it *quim* always."

Jilly raked the ceiling with her eyes. "I should think there's more names for it than there's stars in the sky. *Cunt* is the good old English word. They also call it *oyster* — can you see why?" She spread her legs for Véronique to see.

"Oh yes!" Véronique laughed. "That's why Sherry laughed at the restaurant tonight when I asked for oysters."

"And you said you'd never had them before, and he said he'd had thousands! It's also called the holy-of-holies, or maybe its spelled h-o-l-e-y: holey-of-holeys, home-sweet-home, love lane, the love canal, paradise, the centre of bliss, pussy — because it's furry and likes being stroked — the vertical smile …"

Véronique clapped her hands. "I like that — vertical smile. It is a happy, smiling place, isn't it. Any more?"

"Lord! I'll show you the *Book of Rules*. The rules for the girls here when this was a sporting house. It's got lists and lists of names like that, for pricks and fucking and everything. The girls were encouraged to use some and forbidden to use others. There are a lot of joking names like holloway — hollow way, see? And hairyfordshire — like Herefordshire? And Hornington Crescent … Lapland … the temple of Hymen and low men. Oh, and one Sherry's fond of: the open sea."

"Because it smells of fish?"

Jilly chuckled. "No, because it's 'c' for cunt, not sea like in seaside. When you see it written it's 'c' and three of those star things." She wrote it in the steam on the miror: c***.

Véronique stared at it thoughtfully.

"Penny for 'em?" Jilly asked after a while.

"It looks like those stars they give to hotels, you know — where the number of stars tells you the quality. D'you think men have books where they award stars to sporting girls like that? I'm going to make sure my 'c' will have *five* stars behind it if they do."

Jilly wrapped a towel around her and gave her a little hug. "You really are dedicated, aren't you," she murmured.

"So are you." She kissed her briefly.

Jilly nodded, accepting the accusation. "But I thought I was, you know, a bit odd. Thinking so much about sex." She stretched the towel taut to dry her back. The vigorous movement made her breasts jiggle.

"Wait!" Véronique stood close to her and dried her back in the same way, so that their nipples rubbed against each other's. They kept it up long after their backs were dry and only stopped because it made them even more eager to get into bed together.

"I started talking about that with Sherry this evening, when we were alone upstairs. He said a lot of women never think about it. And some ..."

"The way I see it," Jilly interrupted, "is this. Some women are good at baking. Or needlework. Or nursing. They're made for it, you could say. Born to it. Or something early on in life makes them take to it. And we can all talk about that because, well, everybody knows it and everybody *does* talk about it. 'She's a born nurse,' they say. But when did you ever hear anyone say 'She's a born horizontale' — except as an insult? But some girls *are* born to it. Your Aunt Connie was, according to what you say. And so am I — I *know* it." She tapped her breastbone.

"Me, too," Véronique put in. "Remember what Maxine Keppel said about a voice inside her saying *yes?* That's what I heard inside me when I read my Aunt Connie's letter. I've thought about nothing else ever since."

They left the bathroom and sauntered along the landing, arms loosely entwined around each other's waists.

"And what did you think about before?"

Véronique lowered her voice and, blushing, said, "I used to mastrupate a lot, until I ..."

"You used to *what?*"

"Mastrupate. Isn't that the word for when you diddle yourself?"

"Oh!" Jilly laughed.

"A girl at school said that. She got it wrong, didn't she!"

"Ever so slightly. But I think it's a nicer-sounding word for what girls do. I shall use it from now on. The proper word is *masturbate,* but that sounds so masculine — like as if it was named after a young man called Bates — Master Bates, see? So what stopped you *mastrupating* a lot?"

"I got scared. This same girl, Monica her name was, she told me I'd go blind and end up in the asylum. So I used to ration myself to Saturday nights only — and Wednesdays if I couldn't hold out. But I used to think of it every night and play with my titties ..." She giggled. "I suppose there are names for them, too?"

"Don't start me on names, pet, or I'll be all night — and I think we've got better ways of spending the time, eh?" She hugged her tighter.

"How did you start, Jilly?" Véronique asked as they entered the bedroom.

"I'll tell you later, darling." Jilly took her hand and led her, not to the bed but to a large chest against the wall between the windows. "There's something I want to show you. In here."

When Jilly called her darling, she felt a little thrill run through her.

Jilly lifted the lid to reveal a miniature Aladdin's cave of erotic playthings. There were whips that didn't hurt, manacles that looked fierce but which were lined with velvet, masks, and piles and piles of underwear that no respectable girl could possibly wear. "Sherry claims he's been through all these phases," Jilly said. "He now likes his girls either absolutely naked or in simple things like I wore for him today. And even that was really for your benefit. If we'd been alone, I'd just have been naked. But Rory and Terence love to dress girls up in this gear."

"Did they buy it?" Véronique lifted one erotic wonder after another from the chest.

"No, it was left behind when the brothel closed down. Some of it's been mended since and given modern fastenings. I don't think they had pop-studs back in the Naughty Nineties, did they? Anyway" — she plunged her hand deep into the chest and rummaged among the lower levels — "this is what I wanted to show you." Her hands emerged clutching what looked like an old-fashioned lady's sewing case, all burr walnut with inlaid ivory and fancy brass corners.

She carried it over to the bed and laid it in the middle. She sat to one side and patted the mattress on the other side, indicating that Véronique should seat herself there. She waited while the girl made herself comfortable.

"It's like Christmas!" Véronique wriggled with pleasure.

"What's in here is like every Christmas and every birthday and all the treats you've ever been given — all rolled in one." Jilly raised the lid at last to reveal yet another, and, of course, much smaller, Aladdin's cave. This one was filled with dildoes of every kind — dildoes of ivory, ebony, bone, and rubber ... fat ones, thin ones, long ones, short ones ... dildoes with little reservoirs to fill with starch or gum tragacanth and plungers to make the sticky stuff come flying out at the appropriate moment ... double-skinned rubber dildoes you could fill with warm water and then twist a screw to make them stiffer or softer ... There was one made of gutta-percha thongs braided around part of a dried bull's pizzle from the slaughterhouse; the thongs gave it an exciting texture and the pizzle allowed it to be bent or curved to any desired degree and to hold the new shape during even the most vigorous use of it.

"They call it a dildo," Jilly said, holding up one. "But I call it a 'diddle-o' because we use it to diddle something shaped very like a letter 'o'." She drew them out one by one while they laughed at the gruesome naturalism of this one or admired the elegant abstraction of another — and got themselves increasingly roused by all.

"Have you used all these?" Véronique asked in awe as one exciting plaything followed another onto the bed between them.

"Every single one," Jilly claimed proudly. "Part of my training for being able to deal with pricks of all shapes and sizes, don't you know!"

"Oh yes!" Véronique laughed sarcastically. "Serious professional training, of course. Nothing to do with pleasure! Very high-minded of you! Which is your favourite?"

"This," she replied without hesitation as she drew out a stylized representation of the male organ in its sit-up-and-beg mode — half naturalistic, half formal. "See!" She pointed to a little hole in the base, which Véronique did not recognize as a winding-up mechanism until Jilly fished a key out of the box and wound it up. Then she pressed a button, also in the base, and it produced a low-pitched humming sound. "Feel," she said, lifting it to Véronique's lips. "Kiss it."

The girl obeyed and then leaped back in surprise. "It tingles!" she exclaimed. "What is it?"

"It vibrates. Look. Hold it to your lips again and slowly-slowly turn this ring at the bottom at the same time as you press the button."

Véronique held it in her hands, away from her lips, and did as Jilly bade. The note changed gradually from a hum to a sort of rat-a-tat hammering and the smooth vibrations turned to a tremble and finally to a continuous spasm of twitches.

Greatly daring, she lowered it to her fork ... and then lost her courage.

"Go on!" Jilly urged. "Turn the ring back until it hums smoothly and touch it to your centre of bliss ... your holey-of-holeys ... and all those other words for it."

Véronique pushed half the length of it flat into her crevice and touched the button. It whirred and hummed ...

"Yike!" She dropped it again as if it had burned her.

"Yes!" Jilly said. "The first time I tried it I honestly thought the pleasure was going to kill me. I'm sure I did pass out with it for a time. I don't think a girl can actually die of pleasure, though a lot of them do in the books Sherry has in his library downstairs."

"Library?"

"You just wait! In fact, you will — wait, that is. Girls in our profession spend a lot of time waiting and Sherry's library offers a wonderful way of passing the time. However, to get back to this clockwork prick ..."

"Oh yes, *do!* Can I go first — please?"

Jilly smiled like a magician about to pull the rabbit out of his hat. "Look what I've got!" she said in a singsong and drew forth a second 'clockwork prick' from the bottom of the box.

Or not quite the bottom, for, while Véronique gleefully wound up the second device, she scrabbled within again and came up with the most curious contraption of all. At first sight it was a large, lopsided letter W carved in ivory. "What d'you think that could be?" she asked, handing it over.

Véronique momentarily laid the other toys aside and turned her attention to this baffling new curiosity. Looking at it more closely, she saw that it was more like a 'triple-U' than a 'double-U' — a UUU, with four upright projections. The largest was quite obviously a lifelike male organ in rampant mode, aggressively so. The second one was flattened at the top, like one of those paddles you use for rolling butter into balls; so was the fourth one. Both had slots cut down each side. The remaining upright was a smaller version of the first — a young adolescent's erection rather than a full-grown man's.

"You use the small one to start with and then move on to the bigger one?" Véronique guessed. "Didn't you ask Sherry or his sons?"

"No, it looked sort of threatening, like a chastity belt or something, so I didn't want to encourage them in case it was. But I think I've worked it out since I first saw it. I'll show you."

She rose to her feet, slipped out of her dressing gown and stood facing Véronique with her legs apart. The girl watched in fascination as her friend swung the thing between her thighs, grasped it by the two 'paddles' — one in front of her, one behind — and used them to pull the smaller of the two ivory pricks up, up, up into her hole. And suddenly all was clear. One of the paddles was flat against her tummy, the other against her buttocks, and there, rearing up in front of her, was an erection of which even Sherry would be proud.

"What d'you think?" Jilly asked. "I think some kind of belt or ribbon went through these slots so that one girl could tie it round her and turn herself into a man so as to pleasure another woman. Or even fuck a man in the arse if he wanted it that way."

Véronique's heart was now beating so fast she had difficulty breathing or speaking. "Where's some ribbon?" she asked.

Jilly grinned. "In the top drawer of the dressing table. You'll find scissors there, too."

While Véronique ran to get them she went on, "I don't know if you could tolerate it, young 'un, but I think it would greatly assist my professional education if I could *see* what it's like to poke a girl — to see the whole thing from the man's point of view, don't you know. D'you think you could possibly grit your teeth and bear it for my sake."

"Shut up!" Véronique said with mock severity. "Take it off so I can thread this."

"*Scarlet* ribbon — how appropriate!"

In no time Véronique threaded it so that a single tug would tighten it and two half-hitches secure it. But when she went to fit it back again on Jilly, the girl said, "Let's work up to it, eh? Have a bit of fun with those clockwork pricks first."

Véronique lit the two four-candle candelabra, one on each bedside table, before she switched off the electric lights. Jilly meanwhile swept up all the dildoes but the two clockwork models. The last one was a particularly naturalistic carving in some pale, almost skin-coloured wood with a red-stained knob on the end. She hesitated. "Actually," she said, "before we get carried away, this reminds me to tell you something about Terence, the elder son, the barrister. On Monday evenings he likes a girl to masturbate him — all the way to a sticky end. 'Hand-finishing' he calls it. And it's not as easy as it sounds. There's an art to it, because when you see a man's prick sitting up and begging for relief, you'd think every bit of it was as sensitive as every other. But it's not. Sherry says that Darwin was right and that we have ascended from the apes. And the way apes do it is always from behind, which means that the underneath of the prick here" — she ran a lazy finger up and down it — "gets much more rubbing, much more contact, with the female's hole than the top bit. And if you feel inside your own hole there, on the side nearest your tummy, you'll find it's … you can't exactly call it rougher, but more sort of corrugated. Whereas the bit nearest your back passage is more — in fact, is *very* smooth. So all the sexy nerves are on the underside of the man's prick here. And the top part is nothing special."

She spent a few moments showing a fascinated Véronique how Terence liked a girl to 'hand-finish' him each Monday evening.

"Won't he fuck me at all?" she asked.

"No. Nor on Tuesdays, either. On Tuesdays he likes what he calls *fellatio* — him being a barrister, I suppose that's what lawyers call it." She pronounced it affectedly: "Fell-aah-tieouw! It's what you or I would call 'sucking it off' or 'licking the lollipop'."

"Like you did to Sherry this lunchtime?"

Jilly nodded and gave a self-satisfied smile. "It's very good practice for working as a proper sporting girl, you know. Did you see where I did most of the licking and nibbling and sucking?"

"Here." Véronique ran her finger up and down the underside of the dildo.

"And especially here. Where it looks like a fish's gills seen from underneath, see?" Jilly pointed to the upside-down vee of the glans on the underside of the carving. "God, this is so realistic, isn't it! This loose bit of skin is called the *frenulum*. They love it when you just tweak it gently like this and wiggle the tip of your tongue in the little pockets at the top — well, Terence does, anyway. He likes you to start licking and sucking the top side, where it's less sensitive, and then work your way round to the sexier side. And when he comes... here — see if you can put your middle finger down my throat."

"Won't it make you retch? It would me."

"Not if you keep swallowing. Try it."

Gingerly Véronique did as she was asked. She could only get the very tip of her finger there but she could feel Jilly's throat clamping down all round like soft teeth — or like toothless gums, perhaps.

"You don't retch if you keep swallowing," Jilly said when she'd finished. "And it drives poor Terence out of his mind. He says it makes him come so hard it hurts. But that wouldn't stop him from asking for it — that's every Tuesday."

"And Wednesdays?"

Jilly sat on the bed and picked up one of the clockwork dildoes. "Are you sure you want to hear about Wednesdays?" she asked.

Véronique grinned, picked up the other one, and said, "No." She made a dive for Jilly's fork.

"Steady the Buffs!" Jilly cried. "We've got all night and we can sleep in a bit tomorrow morning, so let's not rush things. Let's seduce each other slowly, starting with a kiss and then a cuddle and then a fondle and, you know, like that. Just one rule when we get round to using these dildoes …"

"What?" Véronique lay down on her friend's left and drew the sheets and eiderdown up over them. She snuggled down on the pillow. "You seduce me. You be the man because I'm the ingénue and I don't know anything — yet. What's this rule?"

"When we're using the dildoes, if one of us has to stop to rewind the clockwork, the other must stop, too — because I don't think I could do even a simple thing like that if you were doing magical things to me down there with yours. Okay?"

"Okay, darling. Call me darling, too. It makes me feel all shivery and nice."

"You are a darling, Rom," Jilly murmured as she closed in with her lips. "You're like the sister I always wanted. You're like me in another skin."

Véronique felt her whole body melting when Jilly's lips settled on hers. She opened her mouth and allowed the other's tongue to explore and ravish her. A moment later she felt her hand on her breast. She gave a little moan and thrust it higher, toward her, feeling at the same time for Jilly's breasts and nipples. All those feelings it had taken long minutes for Sherry to kindle in her that evening Jilly now reignited in seconds. As the incandescence flooded into all her nooks and crannies she relaxed in every muscle. This had the effect of parting her thighs, so that her right knee nudged Jilly's left. Taking it as a hint, she lifted her thigh over Véronique's and snuggled into a new intimacy, mound-on-thigh, thigh-on-mound. And the thighs twitched and fidgeted and stirred in ways that only two girls would know how to twitch and fidget and stir.

Soon, however, that was not stimulus enough and young Véronique wriggled herself completely beneath Jilly, pushing her friend's ankles together with her heels and clamping Jilly's thighs tight by pressing inward upon them with her knees. Now it was mound-on-mound, and lips-on-lips, and body-on-body ... and fingers-on-nipples ... caressing them, squeezing them, rubbing them, folding them in upon themselves with a gentleness only one girl could grant to another.

Both girls were coming freely by now — not with the grand, ten-thousand-volt orgasm Véronique had experienced earlier but with a deep and steady intensity that filled them, possessed them, *became* them.

Jilly broke off her latest kiss and gasped for breath. She raised the upper half of her body on her elbows and scratched her fingernails through her hair as if her scalp, too, were on fire. "I never knew anything like this was possible," she whispered breathlessly. "Did you?" Her breasts hung down, brushing Véronique's lightly.

Véronique could no more speak than fly — indeed, she felt much closer to flying than to anything so intellectually demanding as words. Her response was to put her hands on Jilly's shoulders and gently bear down on them.

Jilly took the hint at once and her head vanished beneath the sheets as her lips and tongue sought Véronique's nipples. Her own breasts hung over Véronique's tummy and, moments later, the darling girl's hands found them there — having first thrown the sheet and eiderdown half off their now burning bodies. Her fingers soon started wreaking a familiar havoc with the myriad nerves that told her brain what thrills her nipples were experiencing.

"Your nipples are like little breasts swelling out of big breasts," Jilly said when she paused for breath.

Véronique now felt such a hunger in her pussy that all she could do was repeat her earlier gesture, nudging Jilly yet farther down. At the same time her thighs spread themselves wider and she jiggled her buttocks in excited anticipation.

Jilly bit and kissed and licked her gentle way down over Véronique's tummy until her lips reached the top edge of her bush — at which point the desperate girl was feeling around for a spare pillow or cushion to slip beneath her bottom and raise her pussy for an even greedier feast. But when she found it, and thrust it in beneath herself, Jilly went down way past the centre of bliss, down to just inside her knees, where she started kissing the insides of her thighs. Then, with exasperating slowness, she kissed and licked her way up again, getting closer and ever closer to a pussy that was now wet and wide open, like a mouth screaming for comfort.

But Jilly had not finished her tormenting yet. When she said they had all night, she meant it! Just when her questing tongue had found its way at last into the hollows of her fork, just between the outsides of Véronique's labia and the tops of her thighs, she pulled back, gripped the girl by the hips and flipped her over on her tummy with a force she could not resist. And in any case she was too surprised to protest. And when she drew breath to plead, instead, the words died in her throat as Jilly's lips started to graze and caress her quivering bottom.

Round and round she went, down into the tucks between buttocks and thighs, up into the small of her back, and down again along the central cleft. A moment later she knew why Jilly, in soaping her body, had lathered and washed her bumhole so delightfully carefully, for now her tongue was in that cleft, pressing tight against the stiff, astonished 'o' of her sphincter and wiggling like a hot glow-worm there.

Another wave of orgasms shook her, subtly different from the earlier ones — and very different from the ones she had experienced with Sherry. And so she learned that women are not just doubly lucky in their ability to come again and again but also that, with a skilled partner to help them, they can come in an endless variety of shades and textures, too. This was like a warm, soft pleasure diffused throughout the region of her bottom and hips but with a sharp, bittersweet, wriggly sort of pleasure at the very heart of it.

When Jilly felt it had run its course she moved on down, keeping her tongue in Véronique's crevice while, with the same smooth firmness as before, she turned the girl on her side. Véronique raised her thigh and bent her knee as she turned. In fact, she clasped her arm behind the knee and hugged it to her shoulder, which simultaneously stretched her pussy and removed all possible barrier to Jilly's rousing exploration of it.

Her oyster! A picture of the oysters she had devoured that night was conjured up in her mind's eye and suddenly she wanted to feast on Jilly's oyster more than anything in the world. She wanted to but could not. Jilly's tongue was doing such sensational things among the folds of *her* oyster that all she could do was lie there paralysed and let the thrills and pleasures go washing all through her.

When she reached the entrance to her holey-of-holeys she pressed her face tight in between Véronique's labia and stabbed her tongue out as far as it would go. More than that, she twisted it round to the left, to the right ... flattened it ... curled the tip ... pulled it back ... stabbed it in again ...

Véronique, meanwhile, thought the last trump had sounded and the gates of paradise had opened to let her in. This new orgasm was no mere warm glow, it was a raging fire that consumed every particle of her, transmuting it to something finer — a transformation that was more spiritual than physical, indeed.

But Jilly did not push her to more and yet more, though she might easily have done, with Véronique so powerless to resist her. Instead, she withdrew her tongue and continued its forward exploration of her cleft ... all the way up to that magic button at its tip, the pot of pure gold at the rainbow's end, the veiled lady in her canoe, pleasure's rosebud. At the same time she turned Véronique on her back again and lifted her thighs to spread them as wide as they'd go.

At first Véronique could not tell what Jilly's tongue was doing there. In the absence of any obvious movement, she assumed it was taking a well-deserved rest after its vibrant exercises in her hole. Soon, however, she realized it was not so and that this was a most subtle form of pleasure, more elusive than any that had gone before.

In fact, Jilly owed the discovery of it to Sherry. He had once made her stand before her mirror with an open mouth and command her tongue to lie absolutely still. She had been astonished to discover she could not manage it. No matter how hard she tried to freeze that tongue in one position, it heaved and writhed and billowed in her mouth. She thought he was going to make some joke about a woman's tongue being never still but he opened his own mouth then and showed her it was the same with a man's. And then, when he laid her on her back and spread her thighs wide and applied his ever-heaving tongue to *her* rosebud of pleasure, she knew why he had first shown her the phenomenon in the mirror.

And so she knew now what delightful and delighted confusion the dainty movements of her own tongue were causing young Véronique to experience.

The girl still did not know quite what was happening down there but she knew that *something* was happening — and an adorable, delicate, heavenly something it was too. So she just lay there and let new orgasmic waves of yet another subtly different ecstasy ripple through her. And the crowning came when Jilly slipped her arms beneath the wide spread of Véronique's thighs and sent her fingers wandering in search of her breasts. She just lay there, panting and fighting for breath, caressing Jilly's hands as they pleasured her up there, too.

After a while Jilly left off and, rising on hands and knees, kissed her way back up Véronique's body until they were mouth-on-mouth and swinging-breasts-on-heaving-breasts again. Then she flopped down beside her and let out a great sigh of happiness.

"Me now!" Véronique said eagerly as she got up on all fours and straddled her friend's exhausted form.

"That's another nice thing about being a woman," Jilly murmured as she snuggled her body down and laid herself open for Véronique's assault of pleasure. "An orgasm exhausts a man, but it stimulates a woman to more and more and more ..." Her voice trailed off into a shiver as

Véronique's lips and teeth and tongue discovered her nipples.

And so Véronique went on to repay all those favours Jilly had just done for her. During that time she made the interesting discovery that, although her erotic desire was still quite ardent, it had nonetheless cooled enough to let her conscious mind act as an observer of all that they did. It was something to do with the difference between being the giver and the receiver of pleasure on such an overwhelming scale. And the cooler observer within her went on to make interesting findings, too.

For instance, when she thrust her tongue as deep inside Jilly's hole as she could get it and performed all those marvels that had just been performed on her, she discovered that, indeed, the back wall of it was much smoother than the front — and that Jilly seemed a little more thrilled by movements against the textured part than against the smooth. She wondered if it had been the same with her but realized she had been too far gone in her ecstasy to notice.

She also saw that Jilly's outer labia — or petals, as she still thought of them — which had been larger than the inner ones in the bath, were now quite small, whereas the inner ones seemed hot and swollen. She licked them with long, slow strokes, waggling the tip of her tongue playfully between them as she moved the flat of it steadily along. That, too, seemed to send Jilly into a frenzy of arousal.

It fascinated Véronique that she could be two persons in this way — the ardent young sexpot *and* the slightly distanced onlooker. Véronique the voluptuary; Rom the onlooker? Rom the ice-cool maiden, the femme fatale; Véronique the insatiable wanton with the ever-open honeypot, eager to take all comers in her stride? The very thought of it thrilled her. She also realized how handy it would be if cool, observant Rom were always *there* to some small degree. Okay, perhaps not in the deep throes of some extravagant orgasm, but if she could be there at all other times, even while Véronique was abandoning herself to the wildest and most lascivious games, Rom could learn and Véronique could enjoy, all at the same time.

Rom must have been standing in the wings of her mind somewhere, waiting for just such a thought to occur. For, even as Véronique abandoned herself to the sweet torturing of Jilly's twitching, ecstatic body, Rom was calmly devising the next level of their pleasure. So that when, some time later, the two girls lay side by side again, panting from their lusty exertions, gazing into each other's eyes, and smiling in wonder that so much pleasure could lie hidden within such fine and delicate flesh, Rom was ready.

Jilly reached for her clockwork diddle-o, preparing to diddle Véronique's 'o,' but her young friend took it from her and laid it beside the pillow again. "One more thing I'd like to try first," she said. "Shift down the bed a bit so as to make room for me in the top half. And lie on your back."

Intrigued by this initiative, Jilly complied. "With my feet over the end?" she asked, kicking the sheet and eiderdown aside, for they were both now hot in every sense of the word.

"Yes!" Véronique said eagerly. "And thighs tight together. Make me work on you to open them. Resist me as long as you can."

While Jilly did as she was told, Véronique knelt in the space above her, reached forward to grab her arms, and pulled them up to where she could kneel on them.

"They'll go to sleep in no time there," Jilly warned. "And then they'll get pins and needles."

"Okay." Véronique freed them again. "But you're to promise not to move them until I say you may. No matter what I do — all right?"

"Promise." Jilly was now more intrigued than ever. "What's got into you, darling?"

"Nothing — yet!" She laughed. "Except your tongue. Wasn't that marvellous?"

"Heavenly. Did you ever do that before?"

"No!" shrieked a shocked Véronique. "You?"

"I've had Sherry and his sons do it to me ..." Her voice caught as Véronique, impatient to begin, started caressing the exposed undersides of her arms with her fingernails. Too light a touch would have been mere tickling; too great a force would have caused painful scratches; but Véronique, with her instinct for the perfect erotic mean, used a pressure — or variations of a pressure — that sent new tingles and thrills dancing in her partner's flesh and silenced all words but the *ohs* and *ahs* of primitive delight.

Up and down her fingers went, beginning at Jilly's elbows and moving a little farther each time. Three inches ... four inches ... five ... half way to her armpits ... three-quartersway ... all the way. And there they lingered awhile, teasing Jilly with the thought that they were uncertain where to go next ... or, perhaps, that they were too shy to go to the obvious place. Meanwhile, the obvious place — her breasts and nipples — were silently screaming for that sensual touch and the loving play that would follow.

Instead, the teasing fingernails went down, down, down over the sides of her ribs, then up again, down again. Just once, seemingly by accident, two thumbs stretched out and caressed two proud nipples, swollen in their longing desperation. Jilly let out a cry as if she had been stung and twisted her body this way and that, seeking that touch again.

Véronique leaned down and put her lips near Jilly's ear. "You promised not to move," she whispered.

"Not to move my arms," Jilly gasped. "Have pity!"

Véronique relented. "Okay," she said. "You can move your arms but only if you find somewhere nice to put them." At the same moment she pressed her lips to Jilly's mouth, and closed her fingers around Jilly's breasts, and cuddled them as gently and skillfully as any girl could possibly desire. A moment later her own feelings dissolved in a new confusion as Jilly's hands touched *her* breasts and lifted them and did all those things which men must learn but that women just know. She spread her fingers wide and cupped her hands around those two hanging fruits, bringing her fingernails in from the outside toward the aching, hungry heart of her nipples. When she touched them at last, and squeezed them and furled them and stroked them round and round, fine strands of fiery heat and icy cold seemed to thread themselves through every nerve and vein in her body.

There was a desperate sense of emptiness between her legs as her pussy mutely craved to be touched, caressed, adored.

For a while they played thus, tongue teasing tongue, fingers persecuting breasts, each braving the other to yield first. And each knew what 'yield' would mean in this loving battle of their bodies — an aching lunge of mouth and tongue and lips for the other's centre of bliss and a feast that would suggest they had endured not mere minutes but long years of abstinence.

Jilly was the first to crack. Not entirely, but she took the first faltering step down the slope that would lead to heedless abandon. She pulled her mouth away from Véronique's and wriggled quickly up to where she could kiss and suckle those full, ripe breasts, hanging into her hands like the most tantalizing of fruits. As the hot sweetness of her mouth closed around one of her nipples Véronique yielded, too, to the temptation of Jilly's two full breasts, shivering beneath her like large jellies on the pale, slender, fine-skinned drum of her chest.

By now they both felt so randy that play of this kind was more of a torment with each new delicious sensation. And this time it was Véronique who surrendered first. Glancing down Jilly's body, so pallid, so defenceless, so appealing in the candlelight, she saw the fine blonde wisps of her bush against the dark of the room beyond and simply could not help reaching out a hand to fondle her there.

"Yes!" Jilly sighed, as if she had waited all her life for such deliverance. She did not, however, open her thighs; instead she reached out her own hand and curled it into her lover's fork, pulling at her eagerly, reaching for her sex already with an eager mouth and tongue.

And now the amorous battle was uneven, for, whereas Véronique had to part her thighs (or crush Jilly's head beneath her knees), Jilly could keep hers clamped firmly together, challenging Véronique to do something so deliriously exciting to her that she would be forced to let her in. Meanwhile she reached up a hand to Véronique's pussy, just ten inches or so above her face, slipped her long middle finger into her vagina and made the tip of it flutter over the most sensitive parts of her hole.

Poor Véronique could not withstand the temptation for long but was forced to lower herself so that Jilly's lips and tongue could do their lascivious best. And oh, how she tried to make Jilly's thighs part and offer her the same favour! She darted her tongue like a snake's, in and out of that tight-pressed slit. She raked her fingernails up and down the insides of Jilly's thighs, or as much of them as their tight-clamped pose laid bare. She moaned and whimpered through her nose, pleading for the flower to open. And all the while her own sex was screaming at her to give up, to lie still, to surrender to the exquisitely tender and loving things Jilly was doing with her mouth and tongue ...

She was on the point of reaching for one of the clockwork toys, which would have been a different kind of surrender, like admitting that a mere machine was, at last, superior to the best of her female intuitions and talents, when her fingers and tongue between them turned the trick. She thrust her tongue as deep into Jilly's crevice as it would go and then curled it backwards, up the groove, until it rested on her button of pleasure, which felt as large as half a bean in its fleshy little nest there; at the same time she was worming her hand in under Jilly's bottom and wriggling her fingers up into her furrow from down there. They picked up a fair helping of Jilly's excited juices, of course, and so, when the tip of her little finger accidentally touched the tight button of her bumhole, it slipped inside a fraction of an inch. Jilly twitched beneath her like a mouse between cat's claws. Her thighs started to open and only a determined act of will enabled her to clamp them tight together again.

Véronique pounced. She changed the angle of her hand and — simultaneously — slid her little finger deep into the hole it had already breached, the next two into the next hole, which was easily large enough (and certainly excited enough) to let them in, and her forefinger went up to assist her tongue in its delectable work. And now it was poor Jilly! She could no more keep her thighs together than the flower can close its petals to the marauding bee. And when she yielded she yielded in trumps, drawing her knees right up until her heels were mere inches from her bottom and then letting her thighs fall slack and wide. And now every delicate membrane of her unprotected oyster lay wide open to whatever lascivious tease Véronique chose to employ — every passionate tissue, every throbbing nerve.

And Véronique lost no time in feasting on every part of it, revelling in Jilly's whimpers and moans, her writhings and sudden jerks, as flesh now stimulated beyond forbearance erupted in one new orgasm after another. She, too, began to come again, though not so turbulently as the other. But it was enough to dull her consciousness to the point where she did not quite realize what was happening when Jilly stealthily tipped her on her side, putting them into the position called (as she would soon learn) *soixante-neuf*.

After a few delirious moments she became aware that Jilly was scrabbling for something and a moment later one of the clockwork dildoes was thrust into her hand. Now she lay, relaxed and contented, with her head on Jilly's left thigh, her face snugly tucked into her fork; Jilly's right thigh was bent right up and lay gently over her, Véronique's, left shoulder. And Véronique lay in a precisely symmetrical position vis-à-vis Jilly. For both girls, then, every inch of their pussies, from clitoris to bumhole, was open to whatever game the other sought to play.

And what games they did play!

There was no position and no point of application in which the gentle purring or the furious trembling of those toys did not provoke squeals of joy and laughter. Laying it in the full length of her crevice, with the tip just touching her clitoris, and setting it to a subtle hum was only the first of innumerable sweet tortures that each inflicted on her lover. Pushing it all the way into her holey-of-holeys and setting it to its most frenzied vibration was the last and finest of all, especially when the questing tongue wrapped itself around pleasure's little button there and brought the torment to its final, stupendous climax. And in between they played every variation the inflamed passions and erotic yearnings of two sexy young girls could devise.

The careful rule Jilly had promulgated earlier, decreeing a truce in their mutual torment while they rewound their toys, was forgotten entirely in their heedless wallow in the hot springs of sensual abandon. They rewound in a frenzy, diddling by hand as they tried to imitate the tremors that the clockwork supplied so immaculately when the magic button was pressed again.

At last, exhausted beyond the reaches of even the most voluptuous provocation, they fell in a kind of waking swoon, panting, sweating, aching ... and glowing all over. Somehow they crawled up to where their heads could rest side by side on the pillow and somehow, too, they drew the sheet and eiderdown up over them again ... and promptly fell into one of the profoundest slumbers either had ever known.

It lasted about an hour, when Jilly surfaced into a kind of drugged wakefulness in which she slowly became aware that Véronique was using the chamber pot, over near the wash basin. The candles had burned to half their length. Downstairs the hall clock struck midnight. She rose from the bed as Véronique lifted herself enough to wipe a tissue through her crotch. The thought of those darling fingers on that darling flesh down there caused a new stirring of lust in Jilly as she crossed to add her contribution to the pot. They kissed in passing but did not otherwise touch. Even the steam off what Véronique had left behind was powerfully stimulating to her — so different from a man's; she wondered if she would ever respond to the touch of a man again.

She had to look down to seat herself accurately. When she raised her eyes again it was to see Véronique holding up the one toy they had not used — the double-dildo that would enable them to take turns in playing the man with each other. She was examining it closely, holding it near the candle.

A little squeal of girlish delight

"Something wrong?" Jilly asked.

"It's just this bit here. It's going to scratch us in a very sensitive place. What's this part called?" She put her finger at the front end of her cleft.

"Terence calls it my clitoris. I call it my clittie. It fits better with pussy, somehow."

"It's going to scratch whoever's-wearing-it's clittie, see?" She held it out to Jilly, who was now returning to their bed.

Jilly saw the part at once. It looked as if the maker of this toy had carved a shallow circular recess in the ivory, about the size of a half-crown. Its sharp edge and the quarter-inch hole drilled through its middle would certainly do nothing to enhance the wearer's pleasure.

Véronique meanwhile had carried one of the candelabra across to the chest full of goodies. She placed it on a nearby occasional table and rooted about at the bottom of the chest. Then, with a cry of triumph, she held up what looked, from Jilly's distance, like a little powder puff. Close-to it proved to be an ivory disc with a little sponge glued to one side — and, sure enough, it snapped into place in the carved recess.

"Now that's what I call a different kettle of fish!" Véronique crowed. "To coin a phrase."

"Shall I go first?" Jilly suggested.

"Of course," Véronique replied solemnly. "Remember now — this isn't for pleasure. It's so you'll know all about fucking a woman from the man's point of view. So I don't wish to hear any little squeals of girlish delight." She slipped the cage between her friend's thighs and squatted down to lift it precisely, so that the smaller, 'adolescent' prick fitted smoothly into Jilly's hole.

Jilly gave a little squeal of girlish delight as it penetrated her and slipped all the way in.

Véronique slapped her legs. "I warned you — that's quite enough of that, miss!" she said severely. "This is serious work. So don't let me hear any more frivolity." She pulled the ribbon as tight as she dared and asked, in a more tender voice, if that was okay.

Jilly licked her lips lasciviously. "That little sponge knows its place, all right," she replied.

"How d'you want to have me first?" Véronique asked, wondering, even as she spoke, how many times she was going to utter those same words in the years to come — to men of every age and size and colour of skin.

"I'll show you all the ways Sherry likes to do it, and Terence, and Rory, okay? Start with you bending over the edge of the bed — they all like that."

Véronique remembered how Jilly had done it that morning — or yesterday morning as it now was — and went over to the chaise longue. "Like this?" she asked, lying forward across its backrest and spreading her legs and wagging her tail in invitation.

Jilly stood back a bit and looked at her, then down at 'her prick' rearing out in front of her. "God, it's strange. I have to try and imagine that all the feelings I get in my clittie are concentrated instead in the knob of this thing. Just bear with me a mo."

She closed her eyes and put her fingers to her temples, as if they were electrodes of some kind, feeding this strange new notion into her brain. "Got it, I think," she said at length, opening her eyes again. She laughed as she gripped the shaft of the thing.

"Are you ever going to start?" Véronique asked impetuously. "I could die of night starvation."

"Just be patient, will you, darling? You'll understand when it's your turn. It's such a *different* feeling." She took a step forward and put her hands to Véronique's hips — but drawing the prick back so that it did not touch her yet.

"Different — how?"

"Power! It's a definite feeling of power. *I've* made you bend over there. *I've* got this great hunk of excited gristle throbbing away in front of me. *I'm* going to push it into you when *I* decide to. *I'm* going to thrust it in and out at a rate and depth of *my* choosing. And *I'm* going to come when the mood takes *me!* Hey — I can understand why men want to do this as often as they do. And why they'd like to do it *more* often, if only they could!"

"How do I look?" Véronique asked plaintively.

"Edible!" Jilly slipped the knob in among the fold and frills of her oyster. "Don't break the spell, pet. Don't get me back to thinking like a girl. This is just fantastic!"

She pushed it in an inch or so and asked how it felt.

"More!" Véronique cried. "I want to feel more. I want to feel it all inside me."

"Yes — I know that longing only too well. But this is what Sherry likes to do often." She jiggled just that first inch or so in and out of Véronique's hole, often withdrawing it altogether to grasp the shaft of it and run it up and down her cleft. Curiously enough the sensations this ought to have aroused in her own vagina — from the complementary motion of the little prick buried there — were quite absent. She was so absorbed in the male aspects of the situation that it produced no more feeling than did the press of the two flat parts against her back and tummy. The stimulation of the sponge against her clittie, however, was as powerful as she might have expected — except that the force of her self-deception transferred it in some strange way to the ivory knob itself. It almost surprised her to find she had such large breasts jiggling there on her chest.

"This is what Terence likes to do," she said, pushing it all the way in. "I don't know if this works because it's not as flexible from side to side as a real prick. But he likes to wiggle his body from side to side once he's right into you so that — hey! It *does* wiggle the opposite way — d'you feel it?"

"Yes!" Véronique gasped. "More!"

Jilly obliged, saying, "I don't know how they do that — it must be some kind of swivel or hinge in it."

"Don't stop!" Véronique cried excitedly. "Does it do it if you wiggle up and down, too?"

Jilly stood on tiptoe, then rocked back on her heels. "Yes!" she cried.

Véronique's response was even more formless and ecstatic. "More!" was the most intelligible word she managed among all her gurgling and disordered sighing.

Jilly wiggled it from side to side and up and down and then all combinations of ways at once while Véronique rose on billows of a now familiar ecstasy. "What does Rory like to do?" she asked breathlessly at length.

"Oh, he likes this!" Jilly grabbed her hips, thrust the prick all the way in, and then poked her with all the vigour her lithe young muscles could muster. "And this," she added, stopping as suddenly as she had started and, pulling young Véronique upright by her hair, hugged her hard and began to fondle her breasts from behind. "Rory likes everything and anything."

Véronique sighed with pleasure and lifted her arms behind her head, and behind Jilly's, too, to pull her forward into a passionate kiss.

But Jilly was too fascinated by the novelty of her adornment to surrender herself in the way Véronique obviously desired. "I'm so glad we did this," she said. "It gives one a totally different view of what fucking's all about."

"How?" Véronique was intrigued despite herself — or perhaps Rom was intrigued while Véronique pouted and put up with it.

"You put it on and you'll see." She withdrew then and started to loosen the ribbon.

"Oh, but we've only just *started!*" Véronique complained.

"I've done all I want. I've learned just what I wanted to discover. If I go on now, I might lose it. I might get all excited — as a girl — and start using this thing like a girl using a toy. Just now I really do feel it's a prick. *My* prick. And I don't want to lose that."

She had withdrawn it from her hole by now, so there was no more point in arguing. Instead, Véronique set about putting it on. And her eagerness to begin grew apace, even as her disappointment about stopping faded.

Jilly, meanwhile, had made a pile of pillows at the edge of the bed. She leaned forward across them and spread her legs. "Sometimes Rory likes you to do this," she said, slipping her hands into her fork and pressing her fingers into her labia so as to spread them wide and allow an unimpeded view of (and access to) her holey-of-holeys.

Véronique did not wait to hoodwink herself into believing the thing wagging its pink head out in front of her was actually her prick. She had an intuition that the very act of gripping Jilly by the hips, and steadying the movement of the knob, and pressing it against the dark, puckered entrance to love's canal, and pushing it inside — that all this would foster the illusion just as well ... even if she didn't feel the clinging, musky heat of Jilly's vagina close around it.

And so, indeed, it proved. Jilly's little gasps of pleasure as Véronique poked away, and the sight of her petals clinging to the shaft as if loath to part company with it, and furling in and out with each thrust — all this merely added to the illusion that she was *every inch* the male, giving pleasure and taking it at his will.

"You were right," she said excitedly. "It *is* quite different when you've got a bit of gristle like this to play with."

Now it was Jilly's turn to cry, "Don't stop!"

Véronique obliged after a perfunctory fashion, poking her with slow, lethargic strokes. Like Jilly, she was much more interested in the discoveries she was making. "We girls don't actually *give* pleasure at all, do we! Except in hand-finishing and sucking-off, perhaps — things like that. But in straight fucking we don't actually *give* men pleasure at all. All we do is we don't prevent them from *taking* it. They give us pleasure — if we're in the mood to let them. D'you know what I mean? What I'm trying to say is that they both give it *to* us and take it *from* us. But we only take it from them — or not, as the case may be. It's so obvious, really — the difference between active and passive. But you don't appreciate it until you put on something like this, do you?"

"M-m-h" Jilly sighed ecstatically. "Talk away all you like, but just don't stop!"

When they woke on the morrow — rather earlier and feeling a great deal more lively than they might have expected — the double-dildo was there, hanging on the hook that usually held back the curtain of the four-poster bed, as if accusing them. Jilly stared at it uncertainly. Véronique spun round, following the direction of her eyes, and turned back again with a grin. "Somehow," she said, "I don't think we'll be using *that* thing again."

Jilly nodded sadly and lay on her back.

Véronique snuggled into her arms. "We're both going to be getting quite enough poking of that kind," she said, "without adding to it artificially. Besides, we proved that, even without artificial aids, girls can give each other a pleasure that's greater than any ..."

"No, don't say that," Jilly interrupted.

"Say what? You don't know what I was going to ..."

"Don't say 'greater than any man could give.' It's not. Men can give you pleasure that's just as great. It's different — I'll agree there. And I could also believe that sex with another girl would be more *consistently* enjoyable — even though last night was the first time I've ever had it. But that's only because we can go on and on — and we know what the other is feeling. But don't think men can't give you the most fantastic thrills, because they can."

"How? Tell me?" Véronique kissed her quickly and snuggled in tighter, like a child asking to be told a bedtime story.

"You'll see soon enough. This afternoon with Sherry, in fact."

"No, but tell me, anyway. I want to know."

"Oh, what an impatient little girl it is!" She raked her fingers gently through Véronique's hair and said, "Okay, here goes. The difference is that men *don't* really know what it's like to be us — at the receiving end. That toy hanging there allowed us to get some vague idea of what it's like to be them, but there's no sort of equivalent for them."

"Well," Véronique pointed out shyly, "they do have *one* hole quite near where ours is!"

"Yes, but even if they got another man to poke them there, they'd still have that solid stick of gristle rearing up in front of them, with all those sexy feelings in the tip of it. So it would never work for them. But I was going to say — *because* they don't really understand our needs, they can do the most surprising things that take your breath away. It's like dancing. Do you go dancing much?"

"I never did." Véronique shook her head sadly.

"Well, get Rory to teach you. He's fantastic. And you'll see how the man leads in dancing and the woman follows. And that's part of the excitement of it because you're waiting and watching on tenterhooks all the time to be sure to follow him. And if he's a real dancing master like Rory, he makes it all seem so ... he makes it flow, one step into another, and before you know it, you're flying round him with your feet doing things you never knew was in them — and which you'd never have discovered on your own. Nor in dancing with another woman. And it's like that when you're being fucked by a man. That's what I'm saying. He can do sudden, surprising things that get you in such a spin — things that no other woman would think of. I can't explain it because when it happens you're in such a dizzy whirl and you've got little fires raging in every part of you, so you don't even know what's happening. You just know it's the most scrummy thing ever and you want it never to stop."

"Which it does, of course," Véronique said glumly. "Stop, I mean. Men being men."

"Yes," Jilly said gaily. "But where we're both going, men are like buses — there'll always be another one along in a minute!"

Véronique bent her knee hesitantly and slid her thigh between Jilly's until it was pressing against her pussy. Jilly responded in a lazy sort of way and murmured, "Save it for this afternoon, eh?" After a pause she added, "Talking of which, how d'you want it to go?"

"How d'you mean?"

"Well, Sherry obviously wants a twosome, but also it'll be your first time with a man, won't it — the first time he gets right inside you, I mean? Wouldn't you rather be alone with him for that?"

Véronique shrugged. She was tugged by arguments in both directions. "Isn't it rather for *him* to decide?" she asked.

Jilly chuckled. "I think I could talk him into — or out of — anything by now."

"Appeal to his reason?"

"No, to his prick. That's the only sort of *reason* men have when they get into bed with us. I'll tell you what I could suggest to him — since you don't seem to have any strong inclination either way — I could suggest to him that we both cooperate, him and me, to make your first fuck as memorable as possible. How about that?"

Véronique had a mental image of Sherry fucking her from behind, like yesterday, only right up inside her this time, and Jilly with her mouth clamped to her oyster, feasting as only she knew how ... or Jilly fondling her breasts and diddling her clittie with one gentle finger ...

"Yes, please!" she sighed.

"So!" Jilly was brisk again. "What shall we do this morning?"

Without hesitation Véronique said, "I think I'd like to go to church."

Jilly sat up in astonishment. "To *church?*"

"Yes."

"What ever for? Are you a Catholic? D'you want to confess?"

Véronique chortled. "No — nothing like that. Quite the opposite, in fact. I'll go there to boast, if anything. I'm not sure I even believe in a supernatural God. But I am sure all those glorious feelings down between our legs weren't simply put there to be denied, or ignored, or suppressed, or *re*pressed, or any of that nonsense. What Sherry and I did yesterday evening was just so *absolutely* right. And what you and I did last night, all those delicious, delightful things — that was absolutely right, too. And so, too, is what you're going to be doing in Nymphenburg next week — and what I'll be doing when I follow you there. We were made for it, you and I. And if what made us was a God of some sort, I just want to give thanks for it, that's all." After a pause she added, "Why are you looking at me like that?"

Jilly gave a baffled laugh. "Here am I, three months ahead of you," she said, "and yet I wonder if I'll ever catch up!"

They enjoyed a light, summery lunch and then had nothing to do but sit and wait for Sherry to turn up.

"This is going to be your life from now on," Véronique pointed out. "Sitting around, waiting for men to come and fuck you."

"Unknown men, too!" A little knot of fear tightened in Jilly's stomach. "The nearer the time comes, the more I wonder if I'll be able to do it after all — and yet I thought it all out before I even started."

"Yes, how *did* you start? Was Sherry the first man who ever fucked you, too? How did you meet him?"

Jilly rose and started to pace about the room. "It's a bit like your aunt's letter from beyond the grave," she said. "There was a home for what they called 'fallen women' near us. And, of course, my mum always rushed me past the place and told me never to stop and talk to the women. Though why she bothered I don't know. They were all really old and broken down. In their forties, you know. So anyway we girls got talking about it at school, prostitution and so on. And as soon as I realized what it was I got really interested and I started reading up in the encyclopedia and so on. Did you know that prostitutes once upon a time were considered *sacred* women? Honest! That's what I thought about when you started speaking this morning about going to church and that. Those Ancient Greeks, they knew a thing or two, I can tell you. So anyway, I waited till I turned twenty-one — key of the door and all that — and I came down to London to look for work. I *said* I was going for typing but inside me I knew what I was going to try. And so there I was one day, knocking on the Hegels' door with my heart going like thunder and me nearly …"

"How did you know about them?"

She bit her lip and smiled guiltily. "I asked one of those girls who stand about on the pavements all over Mayfair. Did you ever go down there?"

Véronique shook her head.

"There's about one every five yards there, all down Curzon Street … South Audley Street … Shepherd's Market. I just took a deep breath and asked one of them, because I always fancied working in a house with other girls and not having to click your heels on the pavements in all weathers. Anyway, she told me — so there I was. And, of course, Madame Hegel saw at once I wasn't ready for it but she gave Sherry a ring and" — she shrugged again — "here I am. The rest you can guess."

"And you were a virgin?"

She nodded. "Same as you — no maidenhead, though. Too much *mastrupation* with the candle!"

They both laughed but Jilly still paced nervously about. After a while she said, "It's not the same, though, is it — working in a sporting house. It's going to be nothing like what I've learned up here with just Sherry and his two sons. I mean … sitting around in the salon and waiting for anybody, just *any*body, to come breezng in and buy the right to take you upstairs and undress you and fuck you — any way he wants it. You can *think* about it all you like, and you can pretend when Sherry's fucking you, or one of his sons, you can pretend it's just *any*body. But it's not the same as when it really is just anybody. And *half a dozen* anybodies, too — every day of the week for three solid weeks ... Jesus! Anything up to a hundred and fifty anybodies in three weeks." She swallowed heavily and shivered. "I wonder if I'll be able to do it."

"Of course you will!" Véronique said encouragingly. "After your first day you'll wonder what all the fuss was about, you'll see."

"Oh, you're a darling!" Jilly exclaimed. She stopped her pacing about and came to sit on Véronique's lap, where she started to kiss her, casually at first, but when Véronique felt how shivery and nervous she was, she responded passionately. And soon they were so lost to the world that they failed to hear Sherry letting himself in.

He stood there rubbing his hands and grinning until Véronique noticed him. "Making friends, I see," he said.

The two girls ran to him and vied with each other to kiss him first.

"So what else have you been getting up to?" he asked.

They vied with each other to tell him that, too, gabbling excitedly all the way upstairs. "I should count it a privilege to watch that," he said. "One of my mistresses in the war, a girl called Debbie, tried to put that double-dildo on but it scratched her in a most awkward place."

Giselle, as she now was again, explained about Véronique's clever discovery. He stopped and took Véronique by the shoulders; staring into her eyes he said, "I told you, didn't I — you have an instinct. When it comes to the business of sex, you have an instinct that is second to none."

She grinned with embarrassment. "Not just the *business* of sex, I hope," she said.

May business and pleasure unite!

"Long may the business and the pleasure of it unite in you!" he exclaimed.

Giselle went on to tell him about going to church that morning and Véronique's reasons for it. Again he looked at her in respect, but this time he was at a loss for words. He merely wiped a lock of her dark brown hair off her forehead. "Amazing," he murmured.

Véronique, thinking this all much too solemn, slipped a cheeky hand inside his trouser belt and plunged down, feeling for his prick. She expected to find a big, throbbing erection just waiting to burst out and get at her; but there was nothing.

"Wait!" he commanded, laughing as he pulled away. "I've got a surprise for you in there."

"I hope so," she replied.

"He can control it," murmured Giselle, who knew what was about to happen. "Just wait till you see."

He overheard her. "For a limited time only," he warned. "So let's be quick."

He kicked off his shoes and raced out of his trousers and underpants. Then he lay on the bed wih his legs slightly parted. His prick was limp and tiny.

Giselle pushed Véronique into a lying position between his knees. "Just watch," she said.

And there it lay, just inches from her face — the magic wand ... the staff of life, though there was nothing magical or lively about it just at that moment. It curled away and down to his left as if trying to tuck itself behind his ball-bag. It looked like an accident of the flesh, a misplaced finger from which all bone had been extracted. She had expected such a veteran, the ever-eager explorer of over five hundred cunts, to be wizened and gnarled, but it looked so smooth, so baby-pink, so modestly asleep ...

"Touch it," he said.

Hesitantly she took it about halfway down (and it was down rather than up) between a thumb and two fingers. It *was* like a boneless finger! She could feel no structures, no hidden parts, inside the slack, soft skin. But that first tentative squeeze did produce some small stirring within. It did not exactly grow firm and yet it nudged her fingers and thumb a little farther apart — and the pale pink head of it gave its first shy peep from the cowl of his foreskin as, simultaneously, it reared from behind the slack folds of his scrotum.

She held it a little tighter, feeling for a pulse or something that would explain its little leap into life. But there was none. She did, however, sense that its two sides were now firmer than its underneath part — there were the beginnings of a structure of some kind inside it.

"Put your whole hand around it," he said as soon as it had swelled enough to lift its head a fraction of an inch into the air. "Not too loose, not too tight. That's it — just hold it at that. Don't let your grip slacken away as it grows." He was up on his elbows watching her face in fascination; he had played this delicious game with more girls than he could remember but few had shown such rapt concentration as this amazing Véronique.

In the grip of her hand it swelled and hardened with every new heartbeat. She could not feel any pulse in the thing itself but it waggled in her hand to the beat of his heart. Its original three-inch length had doubled — and it was still growing. Mainly at the business end. Like a gun emerging from its turret, its fierce, cherry-red knob was nosing out of the slack of his foreskin. The bit she could see, underneath, looked so cute — less like a fish's gills and more like the tiny buttocks of a bright red doll. She longed to lick them but was, as yet, too shy to suggest it.

An invincible lust

And now, although she had tried her best to hold her fingers in the ring they had first formed around it, the massive outward pressure, suggesting an invincible lust, defeated her. When she relaxed her grip at last, the blood rushed in and soon she could not get fingers and thumb to meet at all, so mighty was its girth and so curved its form. And once again a squirt of fear sent a chill through her guts as — all comforting arguments aside — she could not believe that her own tiny hole, which closed so neatly around something as slim as just *one* of her fingers, would ever be able to expand to accommodate *that* leviathan!

And then there was the length of it. Where did it end? Or, rather, where did it begin? For she could see the angry, scarlet knob of it only too well! She scratched her fingernails gently down it, pretending to fondle it but really trying to find where that stiffness just sort of merged with his body in general. She traced it down into his ball-bag but lost it there. It raised a little question in her mind.

"How is it fixed to the rest of you?" she asked.

Giselle began to laugh.

"What?" Véronique was stung.

"Well, darling, most girls are simply mesmerized by what you've just seen. Me included. Only you could ask something as down-to-earth as that."

"But I want to know," Véronique insisted.

Sherry reached down and lifted his ball-bag out of the way. "Feel down under there," he said.

Her fingertips rummaged around between his thighs. "Oh yes!" she exclaimed. "It goes on down there, too."

"I never knew that," Giselle said. "Let's have a feel ... oh, yes. I see what you mean." She giggled. "My goodness! It's lucky that half of it *is* buried back there or it would come out through our mouths!"

Sherry let his balls fall back again. "Make friends with him," he said. "He's going to be a good friend to you."

Véronique needed no second invitation. She wriggled up the bed a little and took her 'good friend' between all ten fingers and thumbs. She put her lips to the very base of it, where the stiff shaft vanished into his ball-bag, and kissed it. And licked there with little darts of her tongue. And bit it with gentle nips of her teeth.

He lay back with a long sigh of satisfaction and nodded at Giselle when she offered to complete his undressing.

Véronique explored with her tongue and lips all the way to the knob. She could now clearly feel the two stiff sausages under the skin, on each side of the soft, squashy tube that ran up the middle. She remembered what Jilly had told her about all the pleasure nerves being concentrated in that bit where shaft turns into knob. So she teased him by ignoring it and going back to the bottom again, this time to give it one big, luscious lick, the way she would lick a sorbet on a stick. She repeated this several times and was rewarded on each occasion by a little gasp of frustration from him.

Then, to tease him further, she skipped her tongue over that sensitive bit and, pulling his erection down until it was pointing straight at her, stuck the very tip of her tongue into the spermspouting hole at the end and jiggled it gently around. How like a gun it was! Not so much in its form as in its air of menace. When you saw men in ordinary life, elegantly dressed and doing civilized things, you never thought of this big, stiff, fleshy howitzer hanging down there between their legs. You never thought of it cranking itself up, just like a howitzer, until it was almost vertical. And you certainly never thought of it firing salvo after salvo!

It was as if each civilized man were like a Jekyll and Hyde. All those suave Jekylls who made pompous speeches at

She explored it with her tongue • 121

school prize days, or put on a dog collar and led a church service, or thundered at criminals from the bar and the bench ... they all had this primitive ape-man bit, this primeval Hyde, seething away down here, ever ready to mock their pretensions.

"What are you thinking now, little face?" Sherry asked when her tongue fell still and her eyes went vacant.

"Sorry!" She came back to the present with a jolt and made up for her absent-mindedness by popping the whole of his knob inside her mouth.

But he lifted her away again. "Go on," he said. "Tell us."

She sighed. "I was thinking that sporting girls must have a very different picture of men from the rest of the world. The world may see a respectable man in a top hat cutting a ribbon or taking a salute or singing hymns with his family in church ... but she sees a naked ape with this rod of gristle dancing a jig out in front of him."

He laughed and pulled her head back over his knob. "At least I've never pretended that the naked ape is not the real me," he said.

Véronique tried the trick Jilly had told her about — trying to swallow the whole thing, and to keep on swallowing so that it did not have the usual consequences that follow when you put your finger down your throat. When she found it worked she varied it by pulling an inch or two back, so that it just filled her mouth, and exploring the surface of it with her tongue, which made more discoveries of detail than fingers or even eyes could achieve.

Giselle had meanwhile undressed and put on a pair of powder-blue silk stockings, held up by a slender, lacy girdle of the same tint. But when she straddled Sherry's head and offered to lower her pussy to his face, he pushed both girls away and sat up, blowing urgently on his prick to cool its dangerous ardour. "Let's decide whose benefit party this is," he said. "Mine? Or Véronique's? Or Giselle's?"

"Yours," Véronique said.

"I vote it's Véronique's," he said. "For her first real fuck."

Giselle grinned. "Me, too — and don't you think the old harem ritual would be appropriate, Sherry? The initiation ceremony?"

Their grinning eyes said yes!

Véronique, thinking of coopers' apprentices being rolled in barrels and Tom Brown standing on a table and singing while the other boys threw bread at him, was full of misgivings — especially when Giselle went over to the chest and pulled out one of those whips which, she promised, 'did not hurt.' She wondered what 'not hurting' meant in this case. "Initiation?" she asked.

"Yes!" Sherry rose to his feet, folded his arms, and assumed a stern mask — so stern that, even with his erection wobbling in front of him, Véronique did not feel inclined to laugh.

And for Giselle, of course, the sight of a man in that usually secret condition was now so familiar that even the possibility of laughing did not occur to her. She simply handed the whip to him and went down on her knees, eyes modestly downcast.

"Slave!" he said to Giselle. "Take this new plaything to the initiation room and prepare her to receive the Marks of Submission."

"What is all this?" Véronique asked as Jilly led her out of the room and up one more flight of stairs.

"A joke," Jilly said. "But it works best if you pretend to take it seriously. It's based on something Sherry found. Remember I said this used to be a brothel? Well, the man who inherited it after it closed never lived here, so when Sherry bought it *everything* was still here. And I mean

A new virgin in the harem • 123

everything, all covered with dust. The *Book of Rules* for the girls, for instance. It's not just a list of dos and don'ts. There's one section that's full of suggested fantasies — for customers with no imagination. You can read them all. Rory's quite keen on them. Anyway, among them was this Oriental Harem fantasy. There are lots of Oriental ones, in fact, but this particular one is for the initiation of a new virgin into the harem."

She pulled aside a curtain on the landing to reveal a rather ornate door, carved into the onion-shape of Oriental doors and richly inlaid with 'gold' and 'jewels' — otherwise known as gilt and coloured glass. She opened it and said, "Fanfare of trumpets! Or shawms or whatever they use out there. A new plaything for the sultan!" She prodded Véronique inside. The room was dimly lit because the windows were almost entirely obscured behind richly carved and heavily pierced screens of ivory and black-lacquered wood. The walls in between were painted with Persian-style hunting scenes and pictures of courtly life. On closer examination the 'hunting' scenes consisted of hunstmen watching animals copulating and the courtly scenes all involved one sultan *in flagrante* with several slave-girls or courtesans. The bed was decorated with carved odalisques whose arms were entwined behind their heads and whose bare breasts were coyly peeping out behind garlands of flowers stretched between their nipples. The floor was of linoleum patterned to imitate marble; several animal-skin rugs softened its coolness beneath the bare feet.

But the centre of the room was dominated by what looked at first like a gymnastic horse, though of a highly ornamental kind, carved and decorated in the same Oriental style as the rest of this fabulous room. Jilly went forward and patted it. "The virgin's defloweriing bed!" she said. "Come on — take off all your clothes. We'll play the game seriously now. I forget what I'm called. The Mistress of Novices? No, that's in the Convent Room next door, of course. Matron of the Slave-Girls, let's say. Hurry up, child! I can hear the Sultan coming up the stairs."

Véronique unhoooked her bra while Jilly almost ripped her drawers off her. The moment she was naked, Jilly bent her forward along the length of the 'vaulting horse' and, taking what Véronique had thought were two ornamental tassels hanging beneath it, brought them up and knotted them tightly around her waist.

"I can't move," she complained, trying to wriggle a bit of slack for herself.

"You just wait, child!" Jilly replied grimly. "I've only just started binding you down. Remember now — not a sound when you are whipped, nor when …"

"Whipped?" Véronique struggled in earnest now — which was made still more difficult by the fact that Jilly had buckled and tightened two straps, one round the top of each thigh, binding her even more tightly to the horse.

"Shush, little one. Submit! Submit! These laws are decreed by our lord and master, whom we *must* obey on pain of death! Think only of that. Pain of *death!*" Slipping out of character she stooped and kissed Véronique's generous bottom, murmuring, "God, I could strap on that prick and enjoy you myself!"

She went to the other end of the horse and started strapping Véronique's arms to two buckles in the leather there. Véronique herself now decided to take the game seriously. "What a privilege it is," she murmured as she closed her eyes and sighed ecstatically, "to enter the service of so wise and potent a sultan and to dedicate my body to his exclusive pleasure!"

The cat-o'-nine-tails in his hand • 125

"That's the ticket!" Jilly gave her bottom a playful slap. "Can you move?"

Véronique squirmed as much — or rather as little — as she could. "Delightful!" Jilly said just as the Sultan entered the harem. He was wearing nothing but a large gold-lamé turban. The cat-o'-nine-tails was curled up in his hand and he slapped his legs with it ominously.

"Is the slave-girl ready to submit?" he asked solemnly.

"Yes master," Véronique whispered.

"And will you accept these six stripes as the marks of love?"

"Yes master."

"One!" He raised the cat and brought it down with considerable force across her naked back. The effect was something between a sting and a tickle. Véronique, who had been expecting quite a painful lash, had a job not to giggle with relief. The Sultan's prick, she noticed, had grown stiffer than she'd ever seen it. It was so stiff, in fact, that its fiery red knob struck his belly with every movement — and he was not at all a portly man; indeed, his belly was as flat as any young athlete's.

"Two," he said as he raised the cat again and brought it down, this time across the generous moons of her derrière. They, being more tender than her back, stung more than they tingled but it was still nothing you could call painful. In fact, a moment later, a delicious warm sensation spread throughout that part of her body, and her pussy began to long for the touch of him. Maybe there was something in this whipping business after all.

"Three!" This time he stood well back and swung it horizontally toward her naked posterior, so that just the tips of the nine tails flicked in between her parted thighs, as near to the top as possible without touching her pussy itself.

Again it stung more than it tickled but again she bore it without a murmur — and was rewarded, as before, by the most thrilling glow that spread throughout her thighs and belly.

He skipped to the other side of her and transferred the lash to his other hand. "Four!" he cried as he struck again, this time near the top of her other thigh, again on its inside. And now the sting was a sting no longer but a sweet, sharp stimulus to frank erotic pleasure. It was all she could do to stop herself from begging him out loud to end her misery. Her virgin misery. For, despite the many things, living and artificial, that had invaded her holey-of-holeys down there, no man's gristle had yet stretched its walls nor shared their ardent heat. She could just about stop herself from crying out but nothing could prevent her derrière from wriggling. And she was filled with a silent triumph when she heard how the sight of her girlish, sixteen-year-old's tail, pinioned for his delight and squirming in her bondage, made him gasp.

As he drew near, Giselle moved toward her head, where she began to fiddle with something in the two sides of the horse. A moment later that portion of it which had until now supported her breasts fell away, leaving them dangling freely. Three things then happened at once, not by accident but by well coordinated nods and winks between the Sultan and his Matron of Slave-Girls. Giselle's hands began to fondle her breasts, doing unbearably rich things to her nipples; the Sultan's hands gripped her round the hips and held her wriggling body still; and the tip of the Sultan's prick nuzzled its way in between the thick, and by now very juicy lips of her pussy.

The physical pleasure of these contacts, combined with the physical torment of her anticipation, almost robbed her of her senses. She fought for breath. She strained against

His slow, easy thrusts 127

the cords and straps that held her, and against the masterful grip of his hands, to reach her pussy out toward him and suck him inside her if only she could.

But then she realized he was not just letting the tip of it rest there. He was very slowly moving it in and out, feeling for every subtle change of texture inside her, exploring and enjoying each fresh millimetre — knowing that no man's prick had ever been there before his. From the changing grip of his hands alone she could tell how much it excited him, both the thought and the physical act. But she had no need to seek the signs of her own increasing excitement. They filled her entire body by now — the tocsin of pleasure, the gathering of muscle and sinew before the chaotic release of orgasm. It was not far off now.

She willed every fibre of her body to relax, to yield, to submit, to open up, to receive. And on and on he went in his pioneering exploration of her vagina. She could not tell that any one of his slow, easy thrusts was any deeper than the one before but over any half-dozen taken together she could feel that higher and higher reaches of her hole were being progressively stretched by that magnificent organ, which could truly be called a magic wand now, a staff of life.

In, out, in, out ... she heard the sticky little noises it made as it stirred among the juices of her excitement and broke their feeble hold on his flesh. They coincided with the delicious stretching and contraction of her vagina as he filled her and then withdrew again. And again. And again. Giselle could hear it, too, and could see each thrust that caused it; she timed her caresses of Véronique's breasts to synchronize with them so that the whole of the girl's body seemed stretched on a rack of impossibly sweet pleasure. When at last he gave the thrust that crammed the whole of his splendid organ inside her it brimmed over her cup of joy and she dissolved in the most body-shattering orgasm she could ever have imagined. It possessed her every fibre, flooded every vessel, tightened every sinew.

But when he became aware of it he stopped, as if her present ecstasy were only some way-station on the route to something grander yet. He undid the straps that held her thighs while Giselle took care of her wrists and the cord around her waist. Then between them they carried the half-swooning Véronique to the bed where they laid her out upon her back and parted her legs at a modest angle.

"Five!" the Sultan cried out before she was even aware he had picked up the lash again. And this one fell with all the force of the earlier ones across her breasts. But now she was so stupefied with lust and a longing for more that it was like being lashed with silk ribbons — more tickle than sting.

And it was the same when, with a cry of "Six!" he brought it down across the lower part of her tummy, with her Venus mound as the bullseye of his target. All she did was let her thighs fall slackly apart in mute invitation and watch him through half-closed eyes, drugged with pleasure, as he climbed on top of her. Giselle, reaching under his balls, helped him pocket the red in a single stroke.

Something within her knew she had been waiting all her life for this, for the weight of a man upon her, for his knees between hers, for his fingers in her hair and his kisses on her lips, for her hands on his firm, masculine buttocks, feeling them harden like steel as they pushed his gristle in and out of her with such devastating effect upon her sanity. Once again she felt her body dissolve into the chaos of orgasm. She felt as if she were expanding to fill the whole universe ... or as if the universe were shrinking, casting off all its inessential parts and preserving only its all-important heart, of which her vibrant, pulsating flesh was the sacred beat.

Her thighs fell slackly apart

Faster and faster he thrust, more and more frenzied was his breathing, wilder and wilder the amazement in his eyes. And when at last he came, in one almighty spermspouting gusher, and his prick recoiled from each effort like a siege-gun on wheels ... and she felt the kick-kick-kick of it deep in her belly, it was an arrival at the end of a long, confusing journey. It was the knowledge that confusion is no more. He had come but she had arrived.

A cup of tea and a slice of cake in the drawing-room below — which had once been the salon of the sporting house — seemed laughably incongruous after that. They all felt it and, for a while, they sat, decently clad in silk dressing gowns again, and stared into nowhere, smiling as at the happiest of memories.

"Well?" Sherry asked after a while.

They were both looking at Véronique.

"I remember an opera singer came to give away prizes at school once," she said dreamily. "She described the moment when she first made that sound from her throat, the sound that carries over a chorus of eighty and an orchestra of a hundred and twenty. She said she couldn't believe it was *her* throat making it — though, of course, she knew it was. And that was the first time she knew with absolute certainty, without the slightest twinge of doubt or hesitation — she just knew that she was born to make that noise. And today *I* know, too. I know what *I* was born to do."

She pulled aside the seams of her dressing gown and let her thighs fall slackly apart. The little hump of Sherry's prick gave a visible twitch underneath the silk.

Véronique saw it and said, *"That's* what I was born to do. Now it's Giselle's and my turn, Sherry, to make *you* the centre of attraction."

They sauntered upstairs again to the principal bedroom, where the two girls had had such fun the previous night. There Sherry, looking exhausted all over − except for his half-alert prick − lay flat on the bed while Giselle took off her stockings and girdle. Then the two girls climbed on top of him, sharing him as best they could, to give him a slow, sensual, all-body massage. After innumerable contortions in which they rolled over and over and turned end to end many times, he finished up on his back once more but now with his face drowing in Véronique's pussy and his prick deep in Giselle's throat. Their session finished, however, with his prick deep in Giselle's other gullet − and her on top of him doing all the work (and loving it) − while the ever-inventive Véronique, having stuck her little finger in a pot of cream, now had the tip of it firmly lodged in his bumhole while she shook her hand as if it were palsied. It fetched him off again in no time at all.

They rested side by side for a further half hour and then Giselle said, "Now me!"

Sherry groaned and did not move.

Véronique, who by now felt she could *never* get enough, climbed over him and settled on top of Giselle. She kissed her and fondled her breasts and pumped her buttocks up and down as if she were wearing that double-dildo again. After a while she whispered, "Shall I go and get it?" and Giselle, knowing full well what she meant, just kissed her for an answer.

Sherry opened half an eye, then two halves, then two big, round, whole eyes as an excited Giselle helped an even more excited Véronique strap the toy on again. He slipped his hand between the sponge pad and her clittie and said, "I see!"

"You can do that any time you like," she told him.

He came alive again and crawled around them on all fours, watching now from one side, now from the other, as Véronique, lying on top of Giselle, pleasured her slowly, with long, shivery, voluptuous strokes. Eventually the stimulation became too much for him and his prick grew as stiff as it ever had been. He pushed the girls on their sides and, taking the pot of cream Véronique had used, smeared it over the tip of his prick and Giselle's bumhole. Then, without preliminary, he thrust it into her there, timing it with one of Véronique's withdrawals.

Giselle squealed with joy and wriggled her bottom backward and forward between her two lovers — backward for his thrusts, forward for Véronique's. And he continued to make sure that his thrusts coincided with her withdrawals. "Oh God, oh God!" she moaned, "I can't belie-e-e-ve it!"

Her cries became incoherent when Sherry slipped his hands round between their two pairs of naked breasts and set his fingers wriggling like little worms between their nipples. A moment later he started rising to his third climax of the afternoon. Véronique sensed it and withdrew completely, scurrying down the bed to stick a slim, wriggling finger in Giselle's hole and feast on her clittie at the same time. When Sherry stayed rammed inside, to the very hilt of him, while his gristle went twitch-twitch-twitch! as it pumped his emptiness into her, Giselle began to jerk and twitch like one in a palsy.

His hands were still on her breasts and Véronique was caressing her hips while she continued to feast on pussy down there. Sensations were filling her tormented young body from every possible quarter, filling her until she felt as if she had exploded among the stars.

"Rules of Comportment within the House: [Véronique read]

"The word 'naked' in these Rules does not mean completely bare. The only time a *fille-de-joie* is permitted to be completely bare in this house is when a customer requests it. At all other times she will wear a minimum of black silk stockings and a fancy corselette with stocking suspenders attached. When we open our doors at noon, *filles-de-joie* will be dressed as any lady would dress for an At Home or a visit to an art gallery. From 6:00 p.m. *filles-de-joie* will change into evening *déshabille* — namely a loose silk cloak, house-coat, or dressing gown such that, while it will cover her charms modestly, it will not deny a gentleman access to her body in order to evaluate her charms and so determine his choice. From 9:30 on a *fille-de-joie* may parade naked in the salon, as above defined.

"Even then a *fille-de-joie* will not parade provocatively, making wanton signs and flirtatious gestures to try to captivate gentlemen who might otherwise choose another. She will walk and sit and converse as if she were fully dressed and among exclusively female friends. This rule is to prevent *filles-de-joie* from entering into ruinous, fatiguing, and ultimately self-defeating competition among each other at a time when all are tired after (we may hope) a strenuous day's work on their backs. For if one girl begins to ogle the men and to 'strut her mutton,' as the vulgar say, all must join in or lose trade. Therefore any *fille-de-joie* who indulges in such behaviour will be fined three shillings for each and every occurrence.

"Nor will any *fille-de-joie* seek to poach a regular customer of another *fille-de-joie*. Naturally, if a gentleman known to be a regular customer of Girl A should arrive a few minutes after Girl A has gone upstairs with another customer, and if that gentleman should then select Girl B, then Girl B should not refuse. But nor should she set out to canvass such a choice by saying, for instance, 'Oh, last time *he* took her upstairs they were at it a full hour!' Or, 'The girls have told me so much about *your* prowess as a lover, sir!' and similar inducements. Any *fille-de-joie* who indulges in such behaviour will, similarly, be fined three shillings for each and every occurrence.

"I like the name *fille-de-joie,* don't you?" Véronique said. "Girl-of-happiness ... daughter-of-joy ... filly-of-gaiety. It's so much nicer than moll or buttock or squirrel. Why squirrel, anyway? Because we squirrel money away?"

"No," Jilly replied. "Because, like the careful squirrel, we cover our backs with our tails. *Some* of the old names are nice, though. I like merrylegs and wagtail and horizontale. There's a list of them at the back of those Rules — names the girls are permitted or forbidden to call themselves. D'you know that clergymen used to call us Athanasian wenches? Because the Athanasian creed begins *'Quicunque vult ...'* which is Latin for Whosoever desires ...' Honestly! The lengths we humans will go to, all to avoid saying the obvious!"

Véronique found the page and her eye skipped down the list at random: bangtail, Bankside lady, bat, bed presser, bit of muslin, buttock ... yes, buttock was there along with more than a hundred others. "So many!" she murmured.

"There are more names for us than for any other profession, Sherry says," Jilly replied. "More than for coppers, vicars, and lawyers combined. That must mean something. Also the way I'm really Gillian or Jilly but for business I'm Giselle. Funny!"

"I'm always going to be Véronique, on duty and off — business or pleasure. So far I see no difference, anyway." Her eyes were straying down the page. "Look at all these other words! This is where you got all those names for our holey-of-holeys, I suppose. Just look at them all! Civet. Chink. Moey. Muff. I like muff — something nice and warm and welcoming and covered with fur! Periwinkle. Commodity. Placket — what's a placket?"

"It's a slit or pocket in a woman's skirt. Haven't you ever heard the word."

"Oh, I see. Then there's teazle. Dumb glutton — hey, that's good, too. Dumb glutton! I've got a dumb glutton between my legs. She can't get enough red meat but she can't open her lips and call out for more!" She giggled.

"She can weep for it, though!" Jilly came to sit beside her, reaching across to turn the page. "And what about those?" she asked. "Names for the male priap."

Véronique read, again at random, wherever her eye settled in the three close-printed columns: Belly ruffian. Lollipop. Ladies' delight. Eye-opener. Beard-splitter. Plaything. Girlometer …

"Girlometer?" she queried.

"A measuring rod for girls," Jilly explained. "For measuring one special part of us."

Véronique laughed and continued: Crack-stopper. Nightstick. Cranny-haunter. Cannon. Piledriver. Ramrod. Baton. Truncheon. Weapon …

"It's all very warlike, some of it," she said.

"I expect it is a bit of a battle at times," Jilly commented. "Which d'you think is the best name?"

"Gristle," Véronique said without hesitation. "Isn't that exactly what it feels like — says she after her long experience of just one of the things!"

"Well, I've only felt three so far, but I agree with you. Gristle is exactly what it feels like." She turned the page again. "And all these words for fucking. The ones in sloping letters were permitted to be used by the *filles-de-joie,* the others were forbidden."

"Fuck — they couldn't say fuck!" Véronique laughed and read on: *Horizontal refreshment. A bit of snug. Dip his wick. Do a knee-trembler.* Shafting. Frigging. Grinding. Screwing. *Give him soft for hard. Jigajig. Have some nooky.* Rogering. Give the old man his meat. Stuff a girl. Pocket the red ...

"It's enough to make your head spin," she said. "Look there's a note here at the bottom of the page which says that gentlemen are to be discouraged from using the coarser of these expressions."

"You should see what it says about the use of a girl's bumhole!" Jilly told her. "Talk about Victorian hypocrisy and how to be coarse while trying to be coy!"

"Where?" Véronique began to turn the pages excitedly.

"Later," Jilly said, taking the *Book of Rules* firmly from her. "We've got to get ready for Terence. He'll be here in an hour."

"How d'you know? Was that him on the phone?"

"I told you."

"Sorry. I was lost in that book. Anyway ..."

"Yes, anyway — he wants us to be dressed like a *grande horizontales* of the *Belle Époque.* And that's going to take an hour, believe me!"

"Shouldn't we have a bath first?"

"No!" Jilly almost shrieked. "Never wash or bath before any of Terence's visits. He went on a walking holiday in France just after the war and met two farm girls who'd been harvesting all week and saw no point in taking a bath when they'd only get dirty again next day. They reeked like goats, he says, and they gave him the best crinkum-crankum he ever enjoyed. There's another word for it."

Despite the no-bathing edict she led Véronique to the bathroom, saying, "The only place you wash for Terence is your bumhole, which we do on this thing. It's called a bidet. You know the joke about bidets? There's this innocent English rose who sees one for the first time on her honeymoon in Paris and says to the hotel porter, 'Oh, is that for washing babies in?' And he replies, *'Mais non, madame* — it's for washing babies *out!'* Anyway" — she hitched up her skirt, kicked off her knickers, and sat on the thing — "you keep your pussy covered like this, because he prefers the taste of girl, he says, to the taste of coal-tar soap. And you turn on the tap ... eek! And you wash your bumhole, inside as well."

"Inside?" Véronique queried.

"As far as your finger will reach. I tell you — he's got some queer habits, Master Terence has. He's a nice enough fellow but he's got some decidedly strange ways. He says it's good practice for any girl who's going on to work at Nymphenburg, because there are lots of men who go there to do things with the girls that they couldn't possibly do with their wives. Licking our pussies is only the start. And getting us to suck them off."

When Véronique took her turn on the bidet she remembered wryly how hesitant she had been, last Thursday night, about putting her finger in her vagina — and now here she was, only four days later, sticking her finger inside her bumhole with gay abandon! "Why not, I wonder?" she mused. "Why wouldn't a wife do that? It's very nice to have one's pussy licked. And, when you hear how the man moans with pleasure, it's quite a good feeling to know you're the cause of it. Why wouldn't a woman want to do all that with a man she loves?"

"Search me!" Jilly took care not to wipe her oyster as she dried her bumhole. "I don't suppose a man could even ask his wife to let him *undress* her the way Terence is going to undress us in ... crikey! In forty-five minutes. Come on!"

Their 'working clothes' for the afternoon were in an ornate wardrobe in the *Belle Époque* salon at the other end of the landing from the bathroom. They were:

- A black satin corselette that started below the breasts and finished above the belly-button. It had a frilly gauze fringe at the top, which made some half-hearted gesture toward supporting a girl's breasts. Fortunately both *these* girls were superbly endowed in that department and needed no such support.

- A black gauze bustière to be tied around a girl's neck with a black velvet bow and furnished with two drawstrings at its lower end, one at the front, beneath her breasts, and the other at the back, at the level of her shoulder-blades, both being tied beneath her armpits; this flimsy garment was furnished with holes to permit her nipples to protrude, each nipple being then covered by a detachable butterfly of silver-steel wire and crimson velvet.

- Glossy black silk stockings with a dozen little bows in scarlet velvet all up the back seams.

- A narrow suspender belt in scarlet lace, elasticated to hug a girl tightly around the waist and with long ribbon suspenders, festooned with white silk flowers and bows.

- A heart in white silk and crimson satin designed to hang in a flap from the back of the suspender belt, half covering the girl's buttocks; easily detachable.

- Two little lace frills to cover her hips, ditto.

- Another heart, to hang at the front over the girl's Venus mound and round into her fork, where two thongs of something furry and elastic ran back outside the girl's labia and hooked into the heart over her buttocks; this second heart was in black lace trimmed with red sequins; in her fork it had two flaps designed to open like window shutters — 'for gentlemen [the original sales catalogue said] who desire to throw wide the casements and rise at the crack of Dawn ... or of any other filly!'

- A pair of drawers in crimson silk, with an open gusset right through the girl's fork; composed of two separate pieces of material held by a knot on each hip and two pink bows on the inside of each thigh; 'the gentleman [the catalogue, again] may thus relieve his paramour of this provocative garment without disturbing the lascivious posture of her figure.'

- Five lace flounces to encase each leg, namely: at the ankle, the calf, the knee, the thigh, and as close to the centre-of-bliss as possible, each long enough to overlap the one below and each held by hooks and eyes at the front; 'to be worn over silk stockings and to facilitate the step-by-step disclosure of female allurements whose abrupt revelation to the lusty male eye might precipitate an equally abrupt and hapless detumescence.'

- High-heeled shoes of scarlet silk; fingerless arm-length gloves of black lace; four cotton and two silk petticoats; a small wickerwork bustle; tortoiseshell hair combs; a feather boa and large ostrich-feather fan; and a silver-filigree diadem holding a glass jewel on the forehead.

Over these alluring undergarments Jilly put on a skirt of pale blue silk shot with fine vertical stripes in primrose yellow; her bodice was of blue muslin embroidered with primroses and violets. She smoothed it down and gazed wistfully at the effect in the looking glass. "We were born into the wrong age, Rom," she said with a sigh. "A girl was a girl in our mother's day. God, a man would have to pay a female to take all *this* off her body, eh! Flounce by provocative flounce."

Véronique chose a dress of mulberry-red velvet with a separate bodice and leg-o'mutton sleeves. She chuckled at the effect. "I remember my aunt coming to tea in a dress exactly like this — before the war, of course. I must have been about eight or nine. Hey!" The hair suddenly prickled on the back of her neck. "What if it was this exact one! It could be. She and Sherry being such old friends. Maybe she passed it on to him in her will." She took Jilly's hand and squeezed it. "Sometimes I think she's directing me from beyond the grave, you know."

"How creepy!" She closed the wardrobe doors.

"Not really," Véronique said. "It gives me a feeling of strength."

"Ask Sherry if it is your aunt's."

"No. I'd rather not know for sure. I'd rather just imagine it is. Well!" She smoothed her dress and turned away from the wardrobe. "What do we do now?"

Jilly seated herself on an elegant sofa upholstered in black-and-yellow striped silk. "Once again we wait. Like good little fillies-of-joy, we wait for a man to come and fuck us. To 'cure our night-starvation' — did you see that advertisement?" As Véronique sat beside her she went on, "It wouldn't work if men dressed up in silky-lacy-frilly stuff like this, would it! I shouldn't feel at all amorous in peeling it off."

Véronique stared at the bed, equally elegant in its matching coverings and carved corner-posts.

"Would you?" Jilly prompted.

"I think … you know how you pipe whipped cream all over cakes? I'd like to have a man with certain bits of him covered in whipped cream. And I'd lick it off him. I think *that* would make me feel amorous, all right."

Jilly laughed with delight. "Don't suggest that to Terence," she warned. "He doesn't like a girl to take any initiative at all — which is quite easy in one way because he's very straightforward. He says what he wants — no embarrassment, no shyness. Then he expects you to do it. And not to make up tricks of your own. Whereas Rory is never happier than when you do something to surprise him — even though he's always got some new idea of his own as well. Terence thinks women's bodies were made entirely for men's pleasure. He doesn't mind if you enjoy it, too, as long as it doesn't interfere. But Rory says it's like digging for gold in an inexhaustible mine — there's always something more to be got out of it. And if we all cooperate, we'll get more of it quicker."

"I like the sound of Rory better," Véronique said.

"He is more fun in bed," Jilly agreed. "But Terence is probably better training for the Noblest Profession."

"Don't you mean Oldest Profession?"

"You call it what you want. I'll call it Noblest. It'd be a lot easier on the nerves to gratify half-a-dozen Terences per day than half-a-dozen Rorys. Of course, we need a bit of both. Variety is the spice of life." She giggled. "Talking of spice — did you notice in those heart-shaped things in front of our pussies ... they're stuffed with lavender?"

"No!" Véronique was intrigued. Then, suddenly distrustful, she said, "Go on!"

Jilly put her heels apart and reached forward to pull up her skirt and all six petticoats. "Take a sniff," she offered.

Intrigued, Véronique arranged her skirts carefully as she knelt between Jilly's legs and intruded her head under seven hems. "Seven hems guard the seventh heaven!" she laughed. Her excitement mounted as she moved her head up between Jilly's thighs. Her cheeks were caressed by all those lace flounces and her imagination aroused by dimly lit glimpses

Glimpses of silk drawers • 141

of silk drawers and hearts and satin and gauze. She could just imagine how it would excite a man to frolic and carouse among all these adornments long before broaching the delightful things they adorned.

"Well?" she heard her friend's voice from far away.

The chief aroma in those dark, silky confines was the musky perfume of civet that Jilly had so carefully *not* washed away in the bidet earlier. Four days ago that, too, would have repelled her but now it just set the blood racing. And there, sure enough, almost overpowered by it but still faintly perceptible, was the sweet, clean fragrance of lavender. The smell of old ladies in church. It was delightfully incongruous and Véronique stayed to enjoy it until Jilly said enough was enough.

But Jilly never spoke. It was Terence who said those words instead as he grasped her by the waist and hauled her back to her feet, leaving Jilly's — now Giselle's — skirts in disarray on her lap.

"That's how I'd like to see *you* sitting, too, young lady," he said with a smile. "Véronique, I presume? I'm Terence."

Véronique, now sitting, blushing, at her friend's side, shook his hand and then lifted her skirts upon her lap, too.

He went down on his knees in front of Véronique and started lifting her petticoats even higher, inch by inch. He was casually dressed, as if for golfing, as gentlemen of his class often are on Sunday afternoons. He was tall, dark, and decidedly handsome, with his slender, clean-shaven face, firm chin, chiselled lips, and dark, deep-set eyes. But his manner, as Véronique watched him carefully rolling back her petticoats, was notably solemn, as if this were some kind of religious ritual.

He did not speak until he had everything rolled up as far as it would go. Then, after pausing to feast his eyes on the complex but delightful impediments that still lay between him and heaven's gates, he slipped a finger between the 'crack of Dawn' flaps, got the tip of it into her hole, and said, "This is my temple, Véronique. Here is where I worship whenever I can. And these" — he laid gentle hands upon her thighs — "are the pillars of the temple wherein I worship. I wonder if you can guess where Samson is hiding? I wonder if you can give him the strength to push these admirable pillars apart?"

So it *was* a kind of religious ritual for him!

"I think I can, Terence — both guess his hiding place and give him the strength." She would have jumped up to begin the game at once, but she recalled Giselle's warning never to take the initiative with Terence.

"Well," he said, "we shall see. And now, girls, I should like you to walk up and down in front of me here."

He sat while they rose, and he pulled his feet in under the sofa so that they could walk near. And so it was "walk up and down ... lift your skirts before you ... and now behind ... stand before me ... part your legs ... turn round ... bend forward ... curtsey ... kneel ... unbutton your bodices ..." At last he stretched himself full length on the carpet while they lifted their skirts a foot or so off the ground and walked a careful path over him, 'giving him an eyeful' each time they passed.

All this he took as calmly as a vicar celebrating a service for the thousandth time.

He made them kneel beside him on the floor and remove their unbuttoned bodices. He gently peeled away the silk butterflies that hid their nipples and played with them awhile. He unhooked their dresses so that when they stood up — Véronique first, followed by Giselle — the material fell upon his face and torso. He repeated the fun with each of their petticoats except the last, which were of silk, embroidered with little Cupids and floral cartouches all around. He sat them back on the sofa and dived beneath their petticoats — first Giselle's, then Véronique's — and 'sniffed the civet,' as he called it.

He stretched out on the bed and got Giselle to lean over him and brush his face lightly with her nipples, exposed as they were through her gauze bustière; meanwhile Véronique carried out the first of her boasts — to find where Samson was hiding. She had noted the bulge in his trousers many times already, and so, when she took off his boots, his plus-fours, and his nether underclothes, she was not particularly surprised at the 'Samson' who now reared his big bare head and one weeping eye toward her. Unlike Sherry's it was circumcised, therefore pink and dry rather than radish-red and wet. It was also much knobblier, with several changes of direction and a distinct curve to the left. Nonetheless, it looked well up to the task of pushing aside the 'pillars' of her particular 'temple.' She did not intend offering any resistance to his worshipping there.

He crossed the room to the washstand and got Véronique to take off her gloves and wash it while Giselle removed his shirt and tie. "This is my penis," he said and went on to give the other parts the names he wished her to use: glans, frenulum, testicles, scrotum, pubis. She repeated them after him; the same words on her lips seemed to excite him.

Now he was naked and his *penis* squeaky-clean. And they were stripped to their last twenty-two garments, all of them underwear of various fancy kinds. He led them to the bed, laid Véronique on her back, lay on top of her himself, and got Giselle to lie on him; and Véronique fought uncomplainingly for breath while he and Giselle writhed and wriggled above her awhile.

He placed them side by side and grazed over their bodies with his lips and hands. He undid the lace flounces at their ankles and kissed the gleaming black silk of their stockings. He sniffed again at the civet and lavender. He undid the flounces around their calves and kised their stockings again. And again he buried his face in their forks and sniffed his fill there. He undid the flounces at their knees and turned them on their stomachs while he buried his nose in their forks from that side and snuffled deep draughts of their natural perfume. He laid them on their backs again, undid the flounces halfway up their thighs, and kissed the black silk until you'd think his lips must ache. And he sniffed in their forks again, and turned them again, and sniffed in their crevices and licked at their bumholes between the two furry thongs. His tongue felt like some hot, excited little animal, quivering with lust.

He lay on his back between them and got Giselle to straddle him and hang her breasts in his face. He suckled and fondled her nipples awhile before asking Véronique to slip the two knots beneath Giselle's arms and take the bustière away. He cavorted with her naked breasts for a time and then made the girls change places so that he could do the same with Véronique.

Putting them on their backs again, he returned to their *pudenda,* where he unhooked the last of the lace flounces, the ones at the very tops of their thighs. Now he had the silk stockings and the bare thigh-flesh and the hearts over their *pudenda* to delight his lips and the little crannies and crevices between them to seduce his tongue. He kissed and licked. He drew apart the flaps and kissed and licked again. He turned them on their stomachs and, with the tip of his tongue, unhooked the thongs that held the two hearts, front and back, together.

He mounted them by turns • 145

He slipped pillows beneath them and kissed their bottoms all over. He buried his nose between their buttocks, where they had washed so meticulously, and licked his way down to their bumholes, where he sank his tongue as deep inside them as it would go. He removed both hearts and laid them on their backs again and indulged in a riot of licking and tongue-poking in and around their *pudenda*.

He lay on his back and made both girls try to kiss each other with his *penis* in between their lips. He made them nip it gently with their teeth from bottom to top, then down, then up again.

He made Véronique squat and rub her *pudenda* all over his face while Giselle gave him *fellatio*.

He got them kneeling on all fours with their pale, girlish bottoms swaying slightly in the air and he mounted them by turns, doggy fashion. Véronique, whose erotic ardour had been raised to fever pitch by these games, cried out in her ecstasy the moment his *penis* slipped inside her. He transferred his exertions at once to Giselle, and so Véronique understood that she must do nothing to disturb him on his relentless march to orgasm.

He did her right, though, about ten minutes later when, with both girls on their backs for the final time, he first brought Giselle to the point where she brimmed over and then, transferring to Véronique, lifted her effortlessly back to the plateau of orgasm and kept her there until — as he would no doubt have said — his *penis oscillated in the convulsions of seminiferous ejaculation.*

Certainly the *ejaculate* ran thick and starchy from her *vagina* when she ran back to the bidet some ten minutes later, after he had dressed, thanked them, shaken hands, and gone.

"A common prostitute sells but a single commodity, namely her body." Véronique was reading aloud to Jilly from the *Book of Rules,* cutting and embellishing as she went, while they waited for Rory to arrive. "A *fille-de-joie,* by contrast, sells two — her body and her spirit. Her body will always be clean, wholesome, and alluring; her spirit friendly, cooperative, tactful, and willing. A *fille-de-joie* is not alone in this. The same could be said, to varying degrees, of all who meet and deal with strangers — of nurses, waitresses, hotel staff, and assistants in shops. Hey, Maxine Keppel should read this bit."

"Go on," Jilly said. "The part where it says about how many men a *fille-de-joie* should pleasure each day — top of the next page."

"D'you know it by heart?" Véronique asked in amazement.

"By every organ in my body, I should think. Go on. The rest of that page just talks about how everyone who works with their body — dancers, acrobats, coal miners, et cetera — have to balance effort and income over their expected working life. And it says we're no different."

"Here it is," Véronique said, flattening the page. "The street walker, who gives little or nothing of her spirit to each customer, can easily service (we shall not say 'pleasure') two dozen and more men a day; indeed, she must do so if she is to keep body and soul together, for the pay is niggardly. The very highest class of Parisian *courtisane,* on the other hand, will seldom pleasure (and here the word may be too feeble) more than one gentleman a day, exceptions being made for Bastille Day, New Year's Day, and so on. The *fille-de-joie,* as one might expect, lies somewhere in between."

She sniffed. "They could have made a joke there. She *comes* in between. Anyway ... One cannot lay down absolute rules but one may take as a starting point that four lovers a day is the ideal number and six the maximum. Wow! How many is it at Nymphenburg?"

"Six is average, my friend Fleur says. But whoever wrote that book reckoned the girl should give the man at least a full hour. It was a more leisured age, obviously. Whereas Madame Hegel says forty minutes is adequate. And six forties is the same as four sixties, so they're both saying the same, really — that four hours of men thrusting their gristle up and down your love canal is enough for any girl! Go on."

"Now it must be allowed that some girls enter the Profession — they always spell it with a capital-P — quite right, too — some girls enter the Profession for a brief period only, one or two years, say, while they earn enough for a small haberdashery shop or a dowry, or to finance some costly operation for a member of the family. Setting one or two years against the expected ten to fifteen (or indeed more) of the true Professional, one can admit that such Passing Professionals, as one may call them, may easily pleasure up to a dozen gentlemen a day — Jesus! That would be *twelve hours* of gristle thrusting away inside you! — without harm over so short a span as one or two years."

Véronique fanned the pages, stopping to read here and there at random, and to herself. "The French have much nicer names for things, don't they," she said after a while. *"Concon* is much more delicate than cunt or cunny or pussy — though pussy's not bad, I suppose. Pussy and muff are the nicest in English but *concon's* still best. Your sweet little *concon!"* She reached across into Jilly's groin and petted her there. "She's going to have to traffic for four hours every day from tomorrow on."

"Wednesday on," Jilly corrected her.

Véronique's eyes gleamed. "Are you staying till Wednesday now? You can help me seduce Maxine. I'm sure she's got the makings of ..."

"No!" Jilly laughed. "I'm going down there on Monday — tomorrow. But Madame never starts a girl in the salon on her first day. Nor the second day, either — usually. The first day she goes in shopping for appropriate lingerie and corsets and things. And she reads the books on how to recognize disease and female hygiene and stuff like that. And the second day — if she's still got the stomach for it after those repulsive pictures, they've got a room where people can watch. Like the one you hid in Friday lunchtime. And she just watches how the other girls do it. And then only on the third day — which will be Wednesday for me — does she go into the salon herself. All sweet and clean and ready for service, as they say."

"Gosh!" Véronique was awed. "They really take trouble over us, don't they!"

"We must be worth it. If you think about it — ten girls bring them in at least thirty pounds a day ... almost two hundred and fifty quid a week or between twelve and thirteen thousand a year."

"Two people could sail first class around the world six times for that!" Véronique said. She suddenly became very thoughtful. If ever there was a precise moment when her ambitions in her chosen profession were defined, that was it. However, if some fairy godmother had stepped in and offered her the chance to take Madame Hegel's place, then and there, she would have refused; she was far too curious about the Game — from the viewpoint of the players rather than of the managers.

"When is Rory coming?" she asked.

"In twenty minutes. But it's no good planning anything. He might want us all in the bath together, pretending it's asses milk and we're degenerate Romans. Or he could ask us to make up one of the servants' beds in the attic and get in it and pretend to go to sleep so that he can burst in and ravish us. Or ... you know ... anything. Also you can never tell when he's being serious."

Véronique flung herself on the bed and closed her eyes, trying to imagine she was a *fille-de-joie* already, down at Nymphenburg, waiting for the doors to open and business to start. All over London unknown men were checking their purses ... eighteen, nineteen, twenty shillings! Got it! And a two-bob tip. And a shilling for the taxi. And two bob for dinner ...

"Penny for 'em, darling?" Jilly said.

"I was just thinking. It really is an extraordinary business. There's Mister Smith who woke up in Finchley this morning with a letch on him that just won't go away. And he thinks, 'I must go to Little Venice and pay a girl to get rid of this.' And all during the day — several times an hour — his prick goes all stiff at the thought. And he gets more and more excited until in the end he can't think of anything else. And his hands are sweating and trembling. And why? All because of a warm, wet, hairy hole about halfway up this girl called Giselle who he hasn't even met yet!"

Jilly laughed. "And what's this Giselle doing meanwhile?"

"She's having a bath and putting on clean undies and powdering her face. And she's not thinking about Mister Smith at all, but she can be absolutely sure that he — and half a dozen like him — are all being drawn toward her as if they had rings through their noses. Or through their pricks, more likely, connected to her by invisible but unbreakable threads. And she doesn't even need to tweak them. Just the fact that they know she's *there* with her hole all clean and sweet and ready — her and dozens like her — and that she'll spread her thighs and let them inside her to put out that raging fire. D'you think our *concons* have got something like a wireless transmitter inside them, sending out waves north, south, east, and west? And men's pricks are like receiving antennæ, sticking up in the air like that? Antennæ specially designed to receive the signals our *concons* send out? And once they pick up the signal their pricks will give them no rest until they've obeyed it? D'you think that's it?"

Jilly laughed and said, "You are a funny one. Don't you ever think about anything but sex?"

"No," Véronique replied. "Do you?"

"No."

Rory was shorter, rounder, and much jollier than his brother. And Jilly was right — you never could tell when he was being serious. When she introduced him to Véronique a message flashed between her eyes and his, each assuring the other that they liked what they saw and were certain to have a lot of fun together in the weeks ahead. Then he turned to Jilly and said, "There's one more thing I meant to tell you, pet. Remember when we were discussing the *other* things a girl can do — to earn extra money — down the road there at Nymphenburg?"

"Yes," she said. "Your father's been helping me and ..."

His jaw dropped. "You didn't tell him *I* said ..."

"No! Of course not. I said one of the girls down there told me. My friend Fleur ..."

Rory turned to Véronique. "'My father must never, *never* know that Terence and I come visiting here, too."

"I promise he'll not learn it from me," she assured him earnestly.

A little vigorous spanking

He chucked her under the chin. "That's the kiddo! I like you already more than I can say."

Giselle (as she was to him, too) broke in. "I'm sure my bumhole is now well able to ..."

"No, there's something else," he said. "Very important. Can't think how it slipped my mind."

"What?"

"Spanking."

"Spanking?"

He nodded. "Nymphenburg is not one of your Marquis de Sade houses where men pay small fortunes to skin a girl alive with the lash. But the Hegels do permit a little vigorous spanking with the bare hand — provided the girl agrees, of course. D'you want to try that?"

Giselle took an uncertain step away from him and then laughed. "You! I never know when you're serious."

"Oh, I'm serious now. Honestly. You can earn two bob for each spank. Half a crown each if it's more than six spanks. D'you want to try just one?"

"I will." Véronique stepped forward. "What do I do?"

"Oh." He was taken aback. "I hadn't thought of ... I mean I don't really know you yet. Besides, you're not starting at Nymphenburg tomorrow."

She grinned at him. "You've never spanked a girl, have you!"

He tried to look offended. "How d'you know?"

"Because if you enjoyed doing it, you *would* have done it before and you wouldn't particularly care which of us you did it to. Therefore your offer to spank Giselle — and the reasons you gave — are quite genuine." She smiled again and added sweetly. "And so, by the way, is my offer."

"Pwhoo!" He looked deflated. "How old are you — if I may be so bold — Véronique?"

"Seventeen — soon."

"Two thousand and seventeen," Giselle said. "She's a reincarnation of every *grande horizontale* since Ancient Greece. I promise you, Rory, when she's finished with you, you'll be resigning your commission and signing on at the nearest monastery." She winked at Véronique.

"I say!" He giggled and loosened his collar.

"Come on, then!" Giselle stepped forward. "What do I have to do? And if you've never actually spanked a girl, how d'you know?"

"I've watched it, that's all. I thought I paid to watch one of the pater's past girlies *in flagrante* with a customer and the bugger went and spanked her! So I had a chat with her after and she said it just stings a bit and doesn't leave a bruise. Money for jam, she said."

"Do I bend over a chair or what?"

"No. I get undressed and wear just a schoolmaster's gown and you wear a schoolgirl's gymslip and those thick black stockings and flannel knickers. And I bend you over my knee and pull them down and caress your botty a bit as if I hate what I'm going to do. And then I spank you. And then you blub — boo hoo and all that — and then I roger you while you're still tingling and you tell me it was the most wonderful rogering you ever had and you want me to come back another day and spank you all over again. I mean this bugger had a whole rigmarole where the girl made a mess in her exercise book and had to kneel and beg for mercy. But I couldn't do that without laughing …"

"Let's try," Véronique said.

They both turned to her.

"Let's do it properly. Otherwise Giselle might burst out laughing down there at Nymphenburg, which would ruin everything. Besides, I think it sounds exciting."

'I think it sounds exciting' • 153

"I say — do you?" Rory grinned. "I must admit the sight of it got me pretty horny. But I wouldn't dare go down *there* and …"

"We're wasting time," Véronique said. "There are schoolgirl outfits in the chest in the main bedroom. I saw them there. And a teacher's gown and mortarboard. I wondered what they were for."

They raced to the main bedroom and opened the Aladdin's cave of a chest. This time they ignored the toys and rummaged among the dressing-ups, where they soon found two schoolgirl outfits. Rory, meanwhile found one of the dildoes, which he held up with a cheeky grin for Véronique. She took it from him, kissed it, and put it firmly back. "Days and days of bliss," she murmured to him. "Now, where are we going to do this spanking?"

"The Ecclesiastical Room?" Giselle suggested.

"Capital," Rory said. "Just the ticket."

"We'll go there and get ready," Véronique said. "And we'll push the door slightly ajar when you can come in."

He licked his lips and nodded. His breathing was fast and shallow.

The Ecclesiastical Room was like a chapel-of-all-faiths-and-none, a piece of scene painting apparently built in monastery stone. By suitable use of drapes and props it could become a cell in a monastery or convent, the apse of a church, a pagan temple, a mortuary, or, as now, something not too far removed from the fusty old study of a reverend schoolmaster in a Victorian public school for girls.

The two girls in question were already scantily dressed so they were naked in no time. And oh, what excited giggles there were as they put on their navy blue flanelette knickers and their black lisle stockings!

"Such memories!" Giselle said.

"Except for these skirts. Our gymslips were never this short — look, you can see half my thighs!"

"That's because these are gymslips for twenty-two-year-old schoolgirls in the chorus line, not your typical spotty thing with puppy fat and pigtails."

"Pigtails!" Véronique said. "We've got to do it properly."

But they decided there really was no time for pigtails, so they gathered Giselle's long, fine blonde hair into a ponytail and Véronique made two bunches of hers, sticking out, one at each side.

"I've got it," Véronique said as they tied each other's bows. "We both cherish an undeclared pash on this cruel, masterful teacher and secretly we want him to roger us. So we won't wear any bras or bustières and …"

"Did you wear bras at your school?"

"No! We practically had to bandage them flat. Swaddlings was more like it. Anyway, we won't wear anything at all over our breasts and we'll leave buttons undone on our blouses so that when we kneel in penitence before him, we can give him little glimpses of our charms and drive him wild with desire. D'you think he'll catch on?"

"Rory is no first-class-honours candidate but where sex is concerned, believe me, no one catches on quicker! You and he are going to click."

"Why?"

"Because you catch on pretty smartly, too. Are you ready? How do I look?"

"Naughty-naughty-naughty." Véronique giggled.

Giselle reached her hand under her own skirt and eased her knickers in her groin. "God, I thought I'd had all my jollies for today — with Terence. But I'm as wet as a duckpond down here. Why am I so excited? D'you think it's really going to hurt?"

"I'm going to open the door. You kneel. I think he should find us kneeling, don't you?"

"With hands praying?"

"No. With hands behind our backs, protecting our poor little botties, although we know it's useless. Also that'll make our breasts look bigger." Véronique opened the door and raced back to kneel beside her friend. And there, with heaving bosoms and downcast eyes, they waited. And waited. And waited.

Rory was delayed because he had trouble getting into the jackboots he had found in one of the wardrobes. By the time he managed it he was so randy and so eager to get at the two girls that he left the rest of his dressing-ups where they were. And so, clad only in mortarboard and gown — and jackboots — and swishing a wicked-looking riding crop in his right hand, bringing it down with stinging relish on the open palm of his left, he strode along the landing to his rendezvous with the miscreants.

He looked down and grinned at his prick — an iron-hard stub of flesh gazing straight up at him with one happy eye. He was inordinately proud of his proud organ. True, at *almost* five inches, it was not the world's longest; but its seven-inch circumference could stretch a girl's vagina to the point of absolutely-no-complaints-thank-you-sir. And, when the letch was on him, it was utterly tireless. And by Harry the letch was on him tonight! Move over, Casanova! Those girls were going to be begging for mercy before midnight and Giselle would be going to Nymphenburg tomorrow in search of blessed relief!

And this new Véronique creature was an absolute scorcher. That naughty glint in her eye owed nothing to artifice. She was one of those rarities — a *young* girl who was as fascinated by sex as any male. He knew quite a few thirty-year-old women of that sort, and they were not without their charms; but to find a sixteen-year-old in that class was ... well, top marks to the old man!

He almost shot himself in the eye at the sight of the two young penitents in their short little gymslips, with their blouses half undone, and their full, firm breasts straining at the shoulder-straps.

"Well!" he spluttered. "Here's a pickle! What have you two wicked little girls been up to this week, eh? Answer!" He towered over them, goggle-eyed as he peeked into their blouses.

"Please, sir ..." Véronique and Giselle spoke at once.

"One at a time!" He slapped the riding crop hard against the leather of his jackboot, managed to contain a cry of pain, and resolved to hit less hard next time. "You — Miss Giselle."

"Please sir, we've been very naughty," she replied.

Véronique thought this much too vague and perfunctory. "Please sir, Matron caught Miss Giselle in my cubicle, sir," she said in a low, penitent voice that was almost a whisper. It amazed her that, although there was part of her that wanted to laugh at this absurdity (perhaps the part she called Rom?), the Véronique part of her personality was utterly caught up in the charade. In fact, for her it was not even a charade. It was a drama. Almost a real-life drama.

Giselle was right — Rory was quick on the uptake. "Caught in your *cubicle*, Miss Véronique?" he asked in tones of horror.

"Yes, Mister Whackford, sir. Matron took down our knickers and gave our poor little botties a good hard tanning with her shoebrush, and it really hurt, sir. But she said it wasn't enough, sir, and she sent us to you for the severest punishment. Oh please, sir — spare us, sir. Don't hurt us

Into strange, uncharted depths • 157

and we'll do anything ... I mean *anything* not to be hurt by you."

He stared at her in amazement. Those were real tears brimming in her eyes! He began to feel uneasy, too. What had started out as a shallow little fantasy — *his* fantasy — about a little harmless smacking followed by a jolly good rogering was starting to take him into strange, uncharted depths in his own psyche. *Pull back!* his wiser self advised.

He was on the point of following that advice when Miss Véronique lowered her head and slumped a little — which had the effect of thrusting out the seams of her unbuttoned blouse ... which, in turn, bared for him the tops of the two most delightful young breasts he'd seen in a long time. Well, for several days, anyway.

He swallowed heavily and said, "I suppose Matron expects me to let Kubla Khan here" — he waggled the riding crop before their terrified noses — "discover the colour of your blood?"

"Yes, sir," they whispered.

"Well then, young ladies, if I'm to spare you — and I only say *if*, mind — then I must know *exactly* what Miss Giselle was doing in your cubicle, Miss Véronique."

The two girls glanced at each other as if uncertain who should speak first. "You!" Giselle whispered. She was as wrapped up in Véronique's imaginary drama as was Rory by now.

"We were playing Lost in the Alps, Mister Whackford, sir."

He frowned, genuinely bewildered. "I beg your pardon?"

"We scrumpled up my sheets and we were pretending they were snow, see? And we were lost. And so we huddled together for warmth, didn't we, Giselle? And all of a sudden we started shivering — genuinely shivering! And we didn't know why? It wasn't with cold, because we both seemed to be on fire. It was with some strange kind of excitement inside us, and we couldn't understand it, but we couldn't stop, either. And that was when Matron caught us. Please sir, what did we do wrong, sir? Was that wrong?"

"Well ..." He could not resist it. He reached out with the riding crop and pulled the loose edges of Véronique's blouse wider apart, leaving her naked breasts pressing against the broad blue serge of her shoulder-straps. "You are growing into a big girl now, Miss Véronique. And so are you, Miss Giselle." He did the same to her and fought to stay in character though his hands itched to be all over those four soft, trembling swellings.

"But what was that strange excitement inside us, sir?" Giselle asked. "Was it bad or was it good?

"I wasn't there," he said, "so how can I say?"

"We could show you, sir," Véronique suggested slyly.

"Very well," he said, seating himself in a large medieval-style chair. He longed to play with his prick but, realizing it would be out of character, had to content himself with draping his gown over it and tweaking the cloth surreptitiously every so often. "Show me."

"Well, sir, Giselle was lying on my bed like this — we'll do it on the mat here, so you'll have to imagine the sheets — and I was keeping her warm like this." She lay fully stretched out on top of Giselle, who whispered in her ear, "You're a bloody marvel!"

"And?" Rory asked, clutching the armrests to keep his hands off his prick.

"Nothing, sir. I just started shivering, like this ..."

"And to give her support I moved my leg like this," Giselle put in, slipping her thigh up into Véronique's fork. "And she did the same to me."

Véronique complied, adding, "And that's when we got those funny feelings in our tummies. Nice feelings. Scrummy feelings. They didn't feel bad at all. *Was* it so very wicked, sir?"

"Come here, my child," he replied in an unexpectedly kindly tone.

Véronique, looking as if she feared the worst, approached him reluctantly.

"Don't be afraid," he said. "Just park yourself on my lap for a moment. That's the ticket!"

Hesitantly she obeyed, sitting as far as possible from that big black tent where his prick was lofting the cloth of his gown.

"Closer," he said. "Now don't be alarmed but I'm just going to slip my hand under your gymslip a mo ... see?" He fondled his way up between her thighs until his knuckles were grazing her knickers in the region of her Venus mound. He pressed gently and massaged her there. "Was it a feeling like that?"

"Oh, no, sir!" she replied in a fluttery, melting voice.

"No?" He was surprised.

"No — that is ten times nicer than the nice feeling I had with Giselle, sir. Come, Giselle — let him do it to you, too, and see if you agree."

"Just a mo!" Rory held her as she made to yield her place to Giselle. "If I touch you here ... and here" — he touched her nipples and squeezed them lightly — "is that the same feeling?"

Véronique gasped and collapsed against him. "It's even nicer still, sir! Oh, what *is* it that can be so nice? Can you explain it, sir?"

"I think I can," he answered solemnly as Giselle took Véronique's place.

Taking her cue from Véronique she responded with similar rushes of ecstasy — not entirely forced — when Rory massaged her sex and fondled her breasts.

"But first," he continued, "we must settle the business of your punishment. Matron expects to hear a good six thwacks, accompanied by piteous screams, coming from my study. And I don't think we should disappoint her, do you?" He gave them a conspiratorial grin.

Intrigued and relieved, they agreed wholeheartedly.

"So, Miss Giselle, since you are the elder, you may go first." He rose and arranged a large pillow over the back of the chair he had just vacated. "If you will kindly drop your knickers to your knees and bend over beside this 'whipping girl,' as we may call it …"

Giselle complied. Her slender, almost boyish buttocks trembled in their defenceless nakedness. There was something about their absolute vulnerability that invited an assault. Véronique was surprised — and slightly ashamed — to realize that it would not take much in the way of lost inhibitions for her to pick up Rory's riding crop and give her a cut in earnest.

Giselle gave out six very convincing screams for 'Matron's' benefit, each one coinciding with a loud thwack of Rory's riding crop upon the defenceless pillow. Watching him, Véronique felt quite sure that, despite all his earlier disclaimers, he would actually love to be letting that cruel leather bite into their soft flesh for real. The gleam in his eye and the way he could not help grasping his prick and squeezing it each time, confirmed it.

"Now you, Miss Véronique," he barked over his shoulder, again for the benefit of the supposedly listening Matron. "You wicked, wicked girl. Let's see how you like the kiss of Kubla Khan!"

As she dropped her knickers, lifted her skirt, and bent over the hard oak of the chair, it was on the tip of her tongue to tell him that he could, if he wished, give her one cut of the crop in earnest — just to see what it felt like. Luckily she suppressed the suggestion in time, and the six-of-the-best fell harmlessly on the pillow while she gave out the most bloodcurdling yells. But the thought and the memory lingered.

"Now!" he said as she rose and pulled up her knickers again.

She was shivering and panting and rubbing her bottom as if the punishment had been real. Belatedly, Giselle did the same. It was a curious situation — a fake drama inside a drama that was also fake. They began to feel reality blurring at the edges.

"Now!" he repeated. "You must have *some* punishment, young ladies. What you did was still very wrong. So I shall chastize you with my hand on your bare posteriors and …"

"But why was it wrong, sir?" Véronique asked plaintively. "It felt so pleasant."

"It was wrong because you did it with each other."

"But then who should we …" Her voice trailed off as understanding dawned.

"Yes!" he said, delighted to see that they understood at last. "You should do it with a *man!*"

"But how, sir? I mean …"

"I shall show you, my children. First I shall chastize you, then I shall show you. You're not in a hurry are you? Have you much prep to do tonight?"

"I've finished all mine." Véronique looked at Giselle, who said, "Me, too."

"The correct English is '*I*, too,' Miss Giselle. For that you shall receive one extra smack of my hand. Come! You are now delaying me deliberately and that will only make me angry again." He sat on the chair, pulled the pillow onto his lap, and patted it. Giselle, slightly mystified, made to sit on it but he manhandled her roughly until she was bent over his knee, face down.

Véronique put a three-legged stool near her head and set a small cushion on its seat before helping the girl to lay her head upon it. She remembered her own position during the slave-girl ceremony yesterday, especially how Giselle had played with her breasts during the 'whipping.' Now it was Giselle's breasts that hung so temptingly in the space between 'Mister Whackford's' lap and the stool. She crouched there, ready to play her part, and looked up into the man's eyes.

He was now completely absorbed in the business of baring Giselle's buttocks for punishment. His lovingly lickerish fingers lifted the brief skirt of her gymslip up over her back. His eyes gloated on the sight revealed as those same wanton fingers peeled her knickers slowly down. He rolled and nudged them all the way to her knees, where gravity did the rest. He seemed mesmerized at the sight of her slim young buttocks, squirming on the pillow on his lap; and, as Véronique saw when she caught sight of the scene in a mirror across the room, there was something appealing in the way her body bent and tapered in from the width of her hips to the narrowness of her tight-together knees.

He could not resist stroking it. Nor could his fingers hold back from toying with the wisps of her bush where they curled out of the 'hot-cross-bun' of the clefts around her buttocks and between her thighs. At length, however, he recollected himself and raised his hand high for the first smack.

When Giselle's buttocks tightened and flinched against the expected assault, he murmured, "No, laddie" — and

Véronique was sure he said 'laddie' not 'lady' — "tightening only makes it worse. Didn't they teach you that?"

But Giselle could not relax and his hand came down an almighty smack on the right cheek of her bottom. She let out a shriek of anguish, genuine this time — which was just as well because Rory, dropping quite out of character, bit his lip in equal anguish and flapped his hand to cool it and blew on his fingers as though they had been burned. Véronique looked away rather than catch his eye, for they would surely have dissolved in laughter.

"Are you sorry now, Miss Giselle?" he asked sternly, snapping back into character just in time. He clamped his smarting hand under an armpit to soothe the pain.

"Yes!" she said fiercely — and was about to add, 'I mean I'm sorry I ever agreed to this!' when he barked, "Yes *who?*"

"Yes, sir," she mumbled reluctantly. Then, to the surprise of both: "Actually, it *glows,* if you want to know." And she wriggled a little, as if adopting a more comfortable position, and her bottom relaxed absolutely, and her thumb went up into her mouth, and she closed her eyes, and smiled and sucked ... sucked and smiled.

Véronique and Rory exchanged anxious glances. A quick decision was needed — to persist with the old fantasy, in which the smacks were controlled and the terror counterfeited, or to follow Giselle off down this new path, which led ... heaven knows where. Véronique's answer was to lift her hands to Giselle breasts and fondle them, paying particular attention to her nipples. Rory was a split-second behind her as he brought down his hand again, less fiercely this time and then, as the sting turned to glow, caressed that same hand gently, round and round over her wriggling bottom and down into the cleft where the moist wisps of her luxuriant bush protruded coyly.

Giselle let out one long, happy sigh and writhed with the whole of her body. Rory pointed silently to the strawberry patches of excitement that flushed the small of Giselle's back. Véronique stretched her left hand wide to torment both Giselle's nipples at once while, with her right hand, she gently reached into the gymslip and raked the fingernails up and down the girl's spine and over those strawberry patches.

Smack followed smack in well-spaced timing, with more and more fondling and fingering in between, until at last she stretched out rigid and, with one huge sigh, half-swooned in the grip of a mighty orgasm — which yet more caressing and fingering prolonged still further.

Then it was, "My turn! My turn!" from Véronique, who kicked off her knickers and hitched up her skirt even before she laid herself across Rory's lap and the little stool. Now that Mr Whackford and his Naughty Girls were dead, Giselle smacked her, too, at the same time as Rory. The first double-thwack was a bit of a breath-taker, she had to admit, but she soon felt the glow that had changed Giselle's mind so swiftly and, moments later, felt the first stirrings of those internal thrills that lead on to the glory of a full orgasm. It was not long in coming ... so to speak.

And then it was "My turn! My turn!" from Rory, too, much to their surprise. "Not with your hands," he said, throwing off his mortarboard and gown. "This!" And he picked up his riding crop and handed it to Giselle. "And like this," he said, kneeling on the pillow on the chair and bending over its backrest with his hands hanging down.

Véronique, seeing his prick poking out beneath the curly X of the struts, had an inspiration. She placed another chair where his head and shoulders could rest on its backrest and then, squatting on the floor, slipped between them to where she could lick and suck his prick.

In happy copulation

"It's loaded," he warned.

"That doesn't bother me," she replied, giving it a welcoming lick just as Giselle gave him the first cut with the crop.

The twitch of his muscles carried it into her mouth and she followed it as he tried to withdraw, keeping it there in the warm. It was too short for her to get it down into her throat — and in any case it was too fat to go that far. It filled her mouth and stretched her lips taut as it was. At the same time her hands caressed his thighs and balls.

Giselle plied the crop rather half-heartedly but the marks it left on his buttocks made her feel she was being hard enough. Véronique was fascinated at the way his prick leaped and seemed to swell even bigger and to harden still further with each fresh stroke. Before long, of course, the inevitable happened and his prick went kick-kick-kick like a howitzer in her mouth and she felt the liquid salvoes of his come going splat-splat-splat against the back and roof of her mouth — which was already so full of prick that the liquid bulged her cheeks and squirted out all round her lips and went up into the back of her nose and drooled out by her nostrils.

He moaned and whimpered in his gratitude and ran his fingers through her hair and kept her head there around him until long after the last little kick had come and gone. But it did not soften his prick by the smallest fraction of an inch. He laughed with delight when he saw it still firm and said, "The letch is on me tonight, lassies. Hold on to your hats!"

And he hurried them back to the huge four-poster bed and laid them on their backs and passed from one to the other in happy copulation for the next hour or two or three ... until neither they nor he could come any more.

They had promised each other no tears but both Jilly and Véronique broke down when the moment for parting came on the following morning. Jilly said she'd come back for a visit at the first opportunity. Véronique said she'd be working at Nymphenburg herself in a couple of months or so — when Sherry wanted fresh blood or when she felt ready. But somehow it only produced more tears, more hugs, and more kisses.

"I have the feeling I'm making the most ghastly mistake," were Jilly's last grim words as she waved farewell and the taxi pulled away.

Within ten minutes Maxine Keppel arrived, on foot and with a battered cardboard suitcase so like her own that it brought a little lump to Véronique's throat. "I have the feeling I'm making the most ghastly mistake," were Maxine's very first words.

"Come on in," Véronique said soothingly, "and I'll write you a fake reference on Mister McLaren's notepaper. I'm sure we could get you in at Selfridge's — or even Harrods!"

Maxine let herself be comforted by that. "You take everything so calmly," she said. "I wish I could be like that. Doesn't anything ever surprise you?"

"Lots of things. Come on — I'll show you your room. This is Gerty, by the way — the housekeeper-cook and maid-of-all-work. She doesn't talk much but she keeps the house immaculate and cooks two wonderful meals a day, and ..."

"Only two?"

"Yes, well, Mister McLaren pays a visit every lunchtime and food isn't exactly the main thing on his mind! We have a quick, light luncheon — and then ... crinkum-crankum!"

"Ah!"

Véronique had never noticed that when redheads blush their freckles get darker.

"I say! What are all these rooms?"

"Oh, you know, just rooms. I haven't studied them at leisure myself yet." She pulled a guilty face. "Been *rather* busy! Anyway, this is the main room — which is my bedroom, too." She opened the door and preened herself while Maxine gasped. "It could all be yours one day soon — remember," she added.

The girl licked her lips and resurveyed the room with fresh eyes. "I don't know," she said with a sigh.

"Next door is called the Ecclesiastical Room. You can make it what you want — nun's cell, abbot's chamber, part of a church, a mortuary ..." She showed the room off briefly, to Maxine's increasing bewilderment, and went on, "Next is a room with a mock railway carriage. Come and see."

"Did Mister McLaren build all this?" Maxine asked. Her bewilderment mounted with every new revelation.

"No, he bought it just as it is ... furnishings, carpets ... drawers and chests full of clothes ... everything. Voilà!" She flung open the door of the railway room. "Did you ever see the like of that?"

Maxine advanced and touched the carriage as if she was not sure it was there at all.

"Go on in," Véronique urged. "Once you're inside you're not aware that it has no wheels. And look ... sit there!"

They were in a replica of a first-class compartment with windows on both sides. Jilly had shown Véronique some of these marvels that same morning, before she left, so she knew exactly what to do. She drew the blinds over the windows on the side by which they had entered and then flicked a switch above her head.

Maxine gave a little cry of surprise, just as Véronique had earlier that morning. The carriage began to rock. Lights came on outside the other windows. A machine made clicketty-clack noises. And a painted landscape began to move past them, giving the most lifelike sensation of a train travelling through the countryside. Maxine grinned, and Véronique had a glimpse of the happy little girl she must once have been.

"Why?" she whispered, still lost in amazement.

"Can't you guess?"

Maxine shook her head.

"How often have you sat in a railway compartment with a man sitting opposite, ogling you? And you know jolly well what he's imagining — what he'd like to be doing to you. Well" — she waved at the arrangements all around them — "here he can. With the right sort of girl sitting there where you're now sitting!"

Maxine jumped up as if stung and looked about her in horror.

Véronique laughed. "Come and look at the next compartment. It's a replica of a suite on the Orient Express."

It was, too — a replica of one of the most opulent, luxurious conveyances ever built ... a riot of burr walnut, tulipwood, birdseye maple, ivory inlay, chased brass, buhl, cut glass ...

Maxine no longer needed to ask why. And her horror was turning to a shocked kind of amazement. "The lengths to which they'll go!" she murmured.

"Come on!" Véronique switched off the current and stepped back into the room. "You'll get accustomed to it sooner or later. See what's next door."

'Next door' was the *Belle Époque* room. Maxine ran her hands over the silks and polished furniture. "The money they'll spend!" she said.

It's not just physical

"Are you complaining?" Véronique asked.

Next door — the slave-girls' quarters in the harem — was the last straw. "I never imagined!" was all she could say. "I never realized." A little fear troubled her brow. "Is this a ... you know. Is it one of *those* houses?"

"It was," Véronique replied. "Not in Mister McLaren's time, mind. As I said — he bought it lock, stock, and barrel."

Maxine put down her suitcase and wandered back to the other rooms. Now she touched everything as she passed, as if afraid that it was *all* fantasy. Eventually she returned to Véronique. "So it's not just ... you know," she said.

"Not just what?" Véronique asked, though she had a good idea what this was leading up to.

"You know! Not just ... physical."

"What isn't just physical?"

Maxine flounced away, toward the bathroom and the rooms on the rest of that landing. "You know jolly well what I'm talking about. What girls *do* in these houses. It's not just physical."

Véronique ran after her. "I know jolly well what you're *not* talking about ... avoiding talking about. It won't do, you know — not in this house."

Maxine turned and leaned against the balustrade. "I know," she replied glumly. "I said it was a mistake."

"You're talking as if you've got to decide here and now. But you don't. All you have to do is look after my clothes, brush my hair ... that sort of thing. And keep your eyes and ears open. And talk about it with me whenever you like. I'm not afraid of talking about it, even if you are."

"Your clothes!" Maxine said scornfully. "Having seen these rooms, I can just imagine what sort of clothes *they* are. And brushing your hair! To make you beautiful for ... all *that* sort of carry-on!"

"You've changed your tune, haven't you? What happened to this great big *yes* you felt inside you when ..."

"I've been thinking about it all weekend and it's turned to no."

Véronique gave a hopeless shrug. "Well, in that case there's nothing more to be said, is there. What else can you do? Typing? Singing and dancing ...?"

To each suggestion she shook her head. "I liked working at Shoolbred's — apart from Claude Greene, of course." She looked to be on the verge of tears.

Anxious to avoid a scene, Véronique asked, "What d'you *really* want to do, Maxine — in life, I mean?"

A smile spread over her face. "Own a little shop — a haberdashery, say — a little shop all my own." The smile faded. "But what's the point!"

"A haberdashery." The word rang a bell with Véronique. "What would such a place cost to buy, I wonder?"

"Five hundred pounds at least," she replied grimly. "One in a good situation would be more like eight."

"Is that all?" Véronique asked lightly.

"Hark at Lady Muck!" Maxine replied. "If I starved for ten years and never bought new clothes and slept in the park, I could just about save five hundred from the pound a week I get at Shoolbred's — or got at Shoolbred's, rather."

"Call me what you like, but I'll be earning a pound in under two *hours* at Nymphenburg. What you earned in three weeks, I'll be earning every *day*. Don't look so shocked — you've just seen what men will spend on fantasies and illusions. What we can offer them between our legs is the grandest fantasy of all. So why the surprise? You need eight hundred for a really good-class haberdashery? I'll earn more than enough to cover that in my first twelve months at Nymphenburg. And so could you!"

Maxine stopped breathing. "You? In ...? You mean, you ... *you* ...?"

"Little me — and little pussy down here. Work it out for yourself if you don't believe me. Three pounds a day for twenty-one days is ...?"

"Sixty-three pounds," Maxine replied impatiently.

"And there are thirteen of those twenty-one-day spells in a year. Thirteen times sixty-three?"

"Eight hundred and nineteen pounds!" she said in amazement.

"And you already have one of the necessary qualities, Maxine."

"What?"

"You're a lightning calculator!"

Sherry had rushed over last Friday because Véronique and Giselle were there. On Monday he rushed over again — to see Maxine and Véronique. His cup of delight was truly running over for, although he did not dare count the Maxine chicken until it hatched, the very fact that she might one day open her thighs and let him in was enough to get his blood racing. Plus, of course, the fact that Véronique most certainly would open her thighs (and any other convenient hole) and let him in.

It amazed Véronique to see the way Maxine flirted with him all during their hasty lunch. It was not the sort of flirtation she or Jilly might have employed, which would have been a prelude to a happy coupling in one of the rooms upstairs, it was the sort that immature girls often indulge in, girls who have no real idea of sexual intercourse but who have picked up certain tricks from vamps in the movies and trashy novels and are delighted to find that they have some encouraging effect on the predatory male.

For Sherry the excitement of having her in the house was also a disadvantage. He was intrigued at the untutored gusto Véronique showed for all things sexual. The girl who last Thursday, by her own admission, had not known that men move their pricks in and out of a girl's pussy but who had imagined they just let it soak there until something vague and wonderful happened, had certainly come a long way in the four days since then. The things Rory had told him on the phone, all about her spontaneous embroidery of the Naughty Schoolgirl fantasy, had him sweating and trembling to see her in a gymslip for himself. And yet to ask her boldly to put on one of those things would be to risk revealing to her sharp little mind the collusion that existed between him and his sons.

"How d'you want me today, Sherry?" she asked as soon as the door closed behind them.

He gave a baffled laugh. "I don't know, petal. It's one of those rare moments in life when I'm at a loss. You suggest something. Surely you've looked through all the dressing-ups?"

"Is it my fault?" she asked. "Something I've said? Or done?"

He threw his arms about her and hugged her. "Something you *are,* my dear. You suggest that the possibilities for enjoyment are infinite with you. You fill me with fear that, in choosing one possibility, I shall forfeit all the others."

Gerty had drawn the outer curtains. Véronique now drew the inner ones, which darkened the room almost completely. "There might be a way to enjoy them all at once," she said mysteriously.

"How?"

"Well — there's only one place where it's possible," she replied, and tapped his brow. "Up there. But let's see how much I can help it along. Take off your clothes and lie on the bed."

Intrigued still further, he obeyed while she sought for something among the chaos of the dressing-ups and mumbled that she must get Maxine to tidy it all up. At last she found what she was looking for — a black velvet blindfold, a mask without eyeslits.

"What now?" He chuckled as she tied it firmly around his eyes.

"Now," she said. "I am as good as your fantasy will let me be."

His erection was as mighty as she had seen it at any time last Saturday. She took a pot of cream, covered her hands with the lubricant, and began to massage it with both hands. She gripped it, pulled the skin taut in one hand, and slid the other up and down. She let the skin go slack and, gripping the shaft halfway, moved her fist up and down, making the skin slide over the underlying gristle. She let go and made her fingers go pittapat all up and down it. She forced the foreskin back up over the knob and lightly scratched the taut skin underneath, from the top right down over his balls and back up again. And to each of these delightful manipulations he responded with a moan of pleasure, a shifting of his body, a thrusting of his sweetly tormented prick toward her sweetly tormenting fingers.

She worked in silence and when he once tried to speak she put a finger to his lips. And then he understood that *she*, Véronique, was not actually there; in her place was some kind of universal fantasy female who, although she took the initiative, was 'really' conjured there by him. And so for the next half hour she offered him visions of all that he and Véronique might enjoy when she came back to him — not a catalogue of all the things they might do together, but windows that offered visions of this bright path or that. She gave his mind's eye enticing glimpses of sexual delights which, though he might have tasted them all many times before, would nonetheless be unique and fresh because *she* would be there to serve them, and would taste them, too — and for the very first time.

"What did you do?" Maxine asked her when Sherry had gone back to his office.

"I learned …" she replied, and then the words failed her because she had learned so much.

"Oh," Maxine said flatly, thinking she was too naïve to be told any more.

"I learned that girls are born with sexual knowledge … sexual cunning. The world may preach it out of us or scare it out of us — or even flatter it out of us by drumming it into our skulls that we are pure angels who would much rather be nuns and only condescend to sleep with men for the sake of the Empire. But it's there in all of us still. And when it comes to flattery, we females are the biggest flatterers of all. The master flatterers."

"The *mistress* flatterers?" Maxine suggested.

Véronique laughed and said, "You've got the makings, darling! Let's go for a walk in the park. It's such a lovely sunny day."

Ten minutes later they set out toward St John's Wood and the park. Maxine, picking up the threads of their conversation, asked what Véronique had meant by flattery.

"Even a dear sweet man like Sherry," Véronique replied, "who knows more about a girl's sexual nature than any man in London, I should think, still believes we absolutely *need* men."

"I don't understand. Are you saying we don't need them at all?"

Do girls need men?

"No — that's leaping to the other extreme. We need them, but not absolutely. I'm sure Sherry thinks that if there weren't men around, we females would just knit and chat and chew and snore — with never a sexual thought in our minds. I'm sure he thinks it takes a man to awaken our desire, to light the fire and keep it burning. But that's the way it is with *them,* not us. They need *us* to light their fire — and put it out, in their case. They need us either in person or in pictures in their minds."

Maxine smiled at this. The suggestion that she, too, was stronger and more powerful than any man pleased her. "But how can you be sure?" she asked.

"We're walking toward Regent's Park, right? Sherry's son Rory hangs out on the far side — he's an army captain stationed over there. And every night and every Sunday afternoon or evening, he drags himself across these two miles to have a nice time with me. So does his elder brother, Terence, who lives even farther away. I have a nice time with them, too, of course, but they're the ones who do the travelling and they're the ones who pay for the pleasure. So who *needs* whom?"

Maxine whistled at the grandeur of the thought.

"You noticed yourself back at the house," Véronique went on. "You marvelled at the amount of money that had gone into creating all those fantasy rooms — what men were willing to pay to put a bit of living flesh on their dreams. *Our* flesh. And they still are. And always will be. So whose *need* is greatest, eh?"

At that point two dogs came up from behind and almost bowled them over. They scurried past and turned at the next corner, tongues slavering, eyes bright.

Véronique chuckled at the coincidence. "Guess what we're going to see in a minute or so!" she said.

And sure enough, when they reached the corner, there was a bitch being covered by a dog, frantically and vigorously, while half a dozen others stood around, panting and drooling, with big red carrots under their bellies and stupid grins on their faces.

"Look into their eyes!" Véronique said. "A batallion of machine-gunners wouldn't drive them away!"

"I'm looking at the bitch," Maxine replied. "Just standing there so patiently. What's *she* thinking?"

"*I'm* the one who's dishing out the orders here — that's what she's thinking," Véronique said confidently.

Maxine shook her head. "She's thinking, 'How happy I could be with any one of you if only the rest would just piss off'!"

Véronique looked at her askance. "Such language from a vicar's daughter!"

Maxine grinned.

The bitch started snapping at the dog who had been covering her — in fact, still was covering her. He obviously wanted to get down and she obviously wanted him to go but it was no use. His prick seemed to be glued inside her. They trod a circle, snapping and snarling, but could not part.

"Dog-notched," Véronique said, dredging the word up from some forgotten incident, when such a sight would have meant nothing to her. "That's what they call it. I wonder why it happens?" She laughed. "It's a good thing it doesn't happen with humans or a girl could never earn her living!"

"Those two dogs who almost knocked us over," Maxine said as they resumed their walk. "How did they *know* this bit of fun was going on here?"

"Scent, I think. Bitches in heat give out a scent like aniseed, I've read. Crooks throw police bloodhounds off the scent by dragging aniseed always." She chuckled. "Jilly and I

What is the bitch thinking?

had this fantasy where we imagined our ... where we imagined that girls have some sort of transmitter between our legs and that when a man's *thing* goes all stiff ..."

"Prick," Maxine interrupted. "I'm not afraid of the *words*, you know. Prick, cunt, arsehole ... I do know them. So when their pricks go stiff ...?"

"They act like receiving ærials, receiving these secret signals from our ... *concons*. I prefer the elegance of French, you know. Did you know that most men wake up every morning with an erection?"

"No!" Maxine's eyes went wide with surprise and her grin almost divided her jaws. "Why?"

"Jilly told me. She said Sherry told her. It stops them pissing the bed, he says. They call it piss-proud. Because a man can't piss when he's stiff, see."

"Oh, good! That was one of the things that had me worried, you know, at the thought of letting one of those things inside you and then ... yeurk — you'd be full up with his piss! You're sure it can't happen?"

Véronique shook her head. "If we keep talking, perhaps we'll take care of *all* the things that have you worried still. Jilly and I had this fantasy where sporting girls have specially powerful transmitters so that all those men, all over London, who wake up piss-proud can feel the waves radiating out and, like those dogs just now, they *have to* obey the call."

"You miss her, don't you," Maxine said. "You miss Jilly."

"Not really. A little." Véronique slipped an arm through hers. "It'd be much worse if you hadn't come along and rescued me, darling. Besides, we'll be seeing her again soon enough."

There was a powerful tension in Maxine's arm. Véronique wished she could find something to say that would calm her a little.

"Did she tell you lots of things?" Maxine asked. "About sleeping with men and so on."

"Told me," Véronique said carefully, "and showed me, too."

The girl swallowed audibly at her side. "Showed you?"

"We slept in the same bed for the last three nights." She held her breath, wondering whether or not to make the offer.

Maxine held her breath, too, as she wondered whether it was a maid's place or not to suggest sleeping with her mistress. "I see," she said at last.

Both girls breathed again, leaving the idea hanging uncomfortably between them.

That evening Terence came promptly at seven for his Monday-night masturbation at her hands — indeed, at, in, on, and all over her slickly greased hands. Being circumcised his knob was much less sensitive than his father's and she was able to do more things to it without risking a premature crisis. He told her, as he lay down, that he wanted it to last about twenty minutes. And for twenty minutes she sat naked beside him, and partly on him at times, as she rubbed, stroked, pulled, pumped, tickled, fondled, fingered, scratched, mauled, palpated, cradled, and otherwise pleasured and delighted that vibrant gristle. She experimented with different grips, different pressures, different rhythms. She held the tip of it between a thumb and two fingers and fluttered her hand as fast as she could. She held it still in her fist and squeeed, squeezed, squeezed. She stretched the skin tight to the base and let her grip slide up and down it, now hard, now barely touching him. And when he neared his climax — which she could tell by the frenzy in which he tightened his buttocks and tried to poke the empty air — she teased him by slowing down. The faster he jigged, the slower she pleasured him and the tighter she gripped.

His climax came at last. At first the hydraulic force of his semen as it came gushing up the tube on the underside of his gristle made her think he had a muscle there, long, thin, and immensely powerful. She let go in shock, and a big white thready gobbet of the stuff came flying out of the end — two circling drops orbiting each other on glutinous threads, captured by her astonished eye before they fell on her bare thigh, very near her fork.

He groaned at the ecstatic pain of so violent an orgasmic squirt with no warm vagina to resist and contain it.

She grabbed his gristle again in time to feel the next mighty surge. This time, more knowingly, she released the pressure just in time for this salvo, too, to go flying through the air and land a little farther down her thigh. And so, too, with the next, and the next, which landed hot but swiftly cooled upon her knee. The next few spurts, trapped by their own gooeyness, welled out of the spermspouter hole and drooled down his bloated knob. She went on squeezing and releasing until long after the flow had ceased, holding him tight there until she felt his prick twitch, when she'd let go, watch the purple of his knob become flushed with crimson, and then squeeze again. And she continued thus until the whole organ turned limp and shrivelled between her fingers. The process was as fascinating to her as his father's demonstration of a swelling erection had been.

Terence just lay there, gathering his scattered wits and faculties. "You are the best fricatrice I ever knew," he murmured at length. "You must surely have been a man in some previous incarnation! You must have tossed yourself off a million times. Else you could not possibly know such things."

These lighthearted words had more effect on Véronique than he intended. At the time she laughed off the thought as no more than an amusing fantasy; but the more she thought about it the more she felt that she did, indeed, have an uncanny fellow-feeling for that poor, greedy, tortured, ravenous organ of the male, whose hunger was never met, whose thirst never slaked, and whose dreams were never fully realized.

"Oh, Terence!" she exclaimed. "There were so many things I did *not* try this evening. If you could only spare me twice as long next time …?"

Rory, who arrived half-an-hour after his brother, had not been able to get the delights of those schoolgirl gymslips out of his mind.

"Back you go to your schooldays, pet," he commanded cheerfully. "Gymslip on, blouse buttoned up to the neck, crucifux between your breasts, no bra, no chemise, no knickers, just …"

"No knickers?" she queried.

He shook his head. "Just a naughty suspender belt and some naughty suspenders. Oh, and shiny black silk stockings, not that awful lisle."

The fantasy this time was that she was a schoolgirl left behind when all the other girls had gone home on exeat and that she was thinking of going on the Game when she left school and had put on that suspender belt and those stockings to see how she looked in them. And then he, a lonely, sex-starved sports master, had come upon her admiring herself and was now going to give her a taste of what she might expect as a sporting girl.

"The exeat lasts all week," he murmured as he took her on his lap. "So we'll start with a few simple skirmishes tonight and work up to the heavy cavalry by the end of the holiday, eh?"

The few simple skirmishes involved groping inside her blouse, groping under her gymslip, fingering inside her pussy, and, eventually, slipping her onto his 'pego,' as his sports-master character called it, and asking her to wriggle around until she felt it jumping and squirting inside her. Meanwhile, what one of his hands did to her nipples and the other to her clitoris had her jumping and spinning well before his crisis.

Last thing that night, just before going to bed, Maxine brushed out Véronique's hair and asked her, in a slightly loaded voice, if there was anything else she required. Her hand shivered and her wrist was weak.

"Yes," Véronique replied at once. "I should like you to read to me aloud from the *Book of Rules,* which you'll find lying in the top of that big chest there."

She knew that Maxine would find, also lying in the top of that same chest, a selection of dildoes, including that intriguing double model in ivory. She watched the girl hesitate as her eye fell on the toys. There was a long pause as she took in their shape and, most probably, worked out their purpose. However, all she did was take up the book and close the lid again. "Which part?" she asked as she came back to sit in the chair beside the bed.

Véronique took the book from her and found the place. "Here," she said, passing it back.

Maxine read: "A *fille-de-joie's* relations with her customers have much in common with the relations between an actress and her audience, especially if she has a part in a drama that is enjoying a long run. In truth, a *fille-de-joie is* an actress, and her particular drama has enjoyed, and will continue to enjoy, the longest run in human history. Not for nothing is hers known as the Oldest Profession."

"Jilly always said the Noblest Profession," Véronique interrupted. "Sorry. Go on."

"Think how you would feel if you paid your hard-earned money for a seat in the stalls only to find that the actress was plainly bored with the play, spoke her lines in a lacklustre voice, moved with all the vivacity of an Egyptian obelisk, and clearly could not wait for the curtain to fall! Suppose you went backstage afterward to remonstrate with her. How much would it mollify you to know that the poor creature had only spoken those identical lines and made those identical movements in matinées and twice-nightly performances for the past four years, amounting in all to not far short of three thousand times?" Maxine raised her eyes from the page. "They do lay it on with a trowel, don't they!"

"Go on! It's a good argument, don't you think?"

"Would you not still feel entitled to ask for your money back, all the same? Yet how would you, as a self-respecting *fille-de-joie*, feel when faced with a similar request — and for similar reasons — from one of your clients? Not too thrilled, we venture to suggest. Gosh, this writer is psychic! Sees right into a poor girl's heart!"

"Get on with it!" Véronique laughed.

"A good *fille-de-joie*, who is neither too greedy nor too lazy, may expect to engage in over sixteen hundred performances of her especial 'drama' in a working year. Sixteen hundred times she will admit a gentleman to her room and permit him the liberty of her body for an agreed span of time — *and* will leave him feeling he touched some special chord in her ... Ha! As long as it wasn't her *spinal* cord, I don't suppose she'd mind."

"Stop putting in bits of your own. Go on."

"For him, as for each new audience at a theatre, the encounter will be the unique experience of the week, or the month, or perhaps even of the whole year. Something he has saved up for, looked forward to, and, he hopes, something he will remember with gratitude for a long time after. For her, by contrast, it will be one of half-a-dozen very similar performances given that day and every day. Of course it is hard to put on the same 'genuine' smile, cooperate with the same 'genuine' enthusiasm, respond to his amorous acts with the same 'genuine' incandescence of passion. Yet it is not impossible. Somehow the good *fille-de-joie* reaches into the rich store-cupboard of her personality and finds just the ingredients she needs to make the feast." Maxine sniffed. "Inspiring stuff!"

"It is," Véronique insisted. "And you're not as indifferent to the argument as you're pretending to be. I can tell."

"You must be psychic, too, then," she mumbled.

"I wish I were," Véronique said. "Then I'd know what's going on inside your pretty little head."

The compliment sent poor Maxine into confusion.

Véronique tightened the screw. She said, "In fact, it's more than a pretty head. It's rather beautiful, I think."

The girl's freckles darkened charmingly. "Is it?" she asked shyly. "How beautiful? I mean in what way?"

"Beautiful like this." Véronique rose to her knees and kissed her as gently as she could on the lips, neither hurrying nor lingering over it. "Go up to bed now," she murmured. "And we'll read a bit more tomorrow."

"And talk?"

"And talk a *lot* more."

Half an hour later, however, just as Véronique was dropping off to sleep, the door clicked open and then closed again and she heard the swish of mercerized cotton as Maxine tripped across the floor and came to rest beside her bed again. "That bed's cold and damp," she said. "I can't possibly sleep there."

Her voice shivered up and down over an octave or more.

"Naughty bed!" Véronique said, lifting her covers by way of invitation. "Tomorrow we'll take it out in the garden and shoot it."

Maxine thought this so funny that she collapsed in hysterical laughter at Véronique's side. Then, of course, the laughter turned to tears and she wept uncontrollably for a time. Véronique did nothing except put a hand to the poor confused girl's head and scratch her lightly behind the ears and round her neck. "Go to sleep now," she whispered at last.

"Don't you want to …?" Maxine could not finish the question.

Véronique kissed her chastely on the forehead. "Of course I do, darling," she replied. "But not in this mood. Don't worry — time will tell."

When she awoke in the morning, Maxine had already risen and gone.

And so the whole week passed for Véronique, in happy noontide and eventide copulation with the three McLarens, followed by chaste, girlish confidences and conversations with Maxine at night. And a few kisses. Sherry kept asking how the girl was coming along. His long distrust of twosomes had been weakened by his happy experience with her and Giselle and he was eager to put another nail or two in its coffin. But all she ever said was, "She's coming along nicely but isn't ready yet."

"What's she waiting for?" he asked petulantly.

"I don't know. And nor, I think, does she. But we'll both know it when it finally comes along."

Véronique had a shrewd suspicion that Maxine's difficulties had to do with Jilly, whom she saw not so much as a rival but as a yardstick beside whom she, Maxine, would measure very small. There was no way of disabusing her of this delusion, not without making her feel small, anyway. She just hoped that when Jilly called on Saturday morning — *if* she called at all — it would change the picture.

Saturday morning came round, and so, at last, did Jilly. In fact, she came at ten, which was rather earlier than Véronique had expected. She and Maxine were still eating breakfast so Jilly, who had already had porridge and kippers down at Nymphenburg, joined them for bacon and egg and whatever was going in the way of toast and marmalade. "I'll tell you one thing this life gives you," she said. "And that's a good strong appetite. If you have any picture of just lying on your back and letting it all happen — forget it! It is hard work, believe me."

"Tell us!" Véronique urged, looking at Maxine, who nodded enthusiastically.

"Let's go out and sit in the garden, eh? We don't see much of the open air down there."

They took their coffee out to sit in a small summer house at the end of the little town garden. It was an octagonal structure of wood resting on a circular rail so that you could sit on the wicker sofa and, by pumping a handle beside one of the armrests, turn it to face into the sun as it moved across the sky. It felt private enough inside there for them to lift their skirts right up to their waists and take off their stockings so as to tan their legs from top to toe.

"So what's it *really* like at Nymphenburg?" Véronique asked when they were all settled comfortably.

"Whoo!" Jilly fanned her face. "Where to begin! D'you want to know the best first — or the worst?"

"The worst," Maxine said.

"The best," Véronique put in at the same time.

They all laughed. "The worst is that no one and nothing can prepare you for those few *ghastly* minutes when you go into the salon for the very first time and sit there and wait for a man to come in and choose you. And the best is that no one and nothing can prepare you for what happens after he has chosen you. There now!"

"Start at the beginning," Véronique urged.

"No, the beginning is awful — the first day, I mean — when you look at pictures of diseased sexual organs, men's and women's. The women's are worse because you can almost *feel* it. They put them in to warn you what you'll get if you ignore the symptoms on the men's. And then there are pamphlets on female hygiene which, if you didn't know it already, you ought to be shot. And then Tuesday was quite interesting — watching other people fucking. Which is something *you've* already seen." She nodded at Véronique and noticed how surprised Maxine seemed. "You didn't tell her?" she asked. "Or show her?"

"What?" Maxine asked.

"All in good time," Véronique replied. *"We've* got a room like that in this house. I'm not supposed to know about it but if you'd be interested in seeing Sherry and me *in flagrante* — or me with either of the boys — just say the word. I could probably talk them round to it." She turned back to Jilly. "Anyway …?"

"Yes, anyway, I spent Tuesday buying what Madame Hegel calls 'snaky' lingerie — bras that just go under your breasts — tit-slings, we call them — and knickers that have big holes where we've got small ones — that sort of thing."

'His was the biggest I've ever seen'

"You wear them in the salon?"

"Not the knickers. I'm coming to that. The doors open at five and close at one in the morning — except that certain privileged customers can call at any time and the night porter will let them in and wake up the girl. And even if she's fast asleep, she's got to please him."

"There's a night porter?" Maxine asked.

"Yes, well, some of the customers who come before we close at one decide to stay the night. There's almost always one or two. It's six quid for the whole night — three quid to the girl and she can sleep on till noon, so it's not unpopular. There's one man who ... no, I'll tell you about him later. Anyway, where was I? Oh yes. Five o'clock Tuesday evening. All the girls troop into the salon where there's three or four men already waiting. There are usually two at least. Jumpers, we call them, because they try to jump the starter's gun. So there I am sitting upstairs, staring into an empty workroom through my little one-way mirror ... which actually isn't so little."

She gestured something measuring about three feet by two. "You feel ever so visible but you aren't at all. It's amazing. And you can see *everything!* Every little pubic hair. So in comes my friend Fleur with her first catch of the evening. Not much of a catch, mind. A short little bloke with a kipper-tail moustache and big, mournful eyes — and a prick sticking out of his flies like Nelson's column! Well, not really, but bigger than Terence's, which was the biggest I'd seen until then."

"And since?" Véronique asked.

Jilly laughed. "Don't ask!"

Véronique held her fingers about seven inches apart and said to Maxine, "Terence's." Maxine's reaction made her wish she hadn't.

"So Fleur takes him over to the basin and washes it. They've got running hot and cold in every room, you know! Then she takes him near the lamp and looks at him carefully. No smiles. Nothing. You'd think she was a nurse or something. But when she's satisfied, it's all smiles and flirting and caresses while she finishes undressing him …"

"Is she naked?" Véronique asked.

"Oh, I should explain that. In the salon all we wear is that tit-sling I told you about. Someone tried to kid me it was invented by a German engineer called Tietzling — and I believed it! Well, you do when you're new and nervous, don't you. But they're lovely girls down there, honestly. I thought they'd all be bitchy but it's not like that. It's like we're all in this fight together, all on the same side. Where was I?"

"The tit-sling?" Véronique prompted her. "And what else?"

"Oh yes! When we go in the salon we wear a tit-sling, which is like the bottom half of a bra with two ribbons going round each side of your bosom to a strap at the top — I mean the whole top half of your bosom is bare, and the nipple, too. Plus you wear a suspender belt and silk stockings."

"No chemise?" Maxine asked. "No camisole?"

"Nothing. No panties. No knickers. No drawers. It's all right there, open to all comers, as they say. Of course you wear a snaky housecoat or dressing gown over it. And fluffy pompom slippers. It's very comfortable. Most men just take off your housecoat, see the rest, like it, and leave it."

"And that's what Fleur was wearing — tit-sling, suspenders, and stockings?" Véronique said.

"Right! Oh, I could sit in this sun all day! So I thought she'd start fucking him right away. You *can* say a girl fucks a man, by the way. Our sort of girl anyway. But she didn't. She spent a lot of time letting him play with her. And just looking at her in different positions. Like she'd lie on the bed with her knees drawn up and legs spread wide while he lay between them and just gazed his fill. That sort of thing in lots of different poses. Then she knelt over him and rubbed her tits in his face and chest."

"Did he kiss her?"

"Not her lips. They can kiss you anywhere but your lips. That's been the Hegels' rule ever since this big flu epidemic started. Madame says she'll keep it on after, too, because girls were always going down with thrush and mouth ulcers. Anyway, she romps and messes about with him for more than half an hour, so the real business, when she finally lets him get inside her, only lasts about six minutes. So I thought, clever girl! That's the way to keep it fresh and young and not to wear it out! But when I asked her after — because the girl who's doing it for the benefit of a newcomer like me, she always has a little confab after where she explains what she was doing and why — so Fleur tells me that she knew from the start, when she washed his prick, that he was what they call a 'hair-trigger man.' He almost came in her hand. Which is a disaster because Madame will fine us double what we earn if we don't give a man a good forty minutes. So if a man comes in the first five minutes, you've got to work your tail off to give him a second go."

"And if a man comes after thirty minutes?" Véronique asked, remembering that even hardened (so to speak) lechers like the McLarens could easily be satisfied within that time.

"You just lie there with him, cuddling him and chatting him up until it's safe to come out. A lot of men come inside half an hour. They're just flattered and pleased when you don't seem to want to kick them out — which is what happens in the cheaper establishments. Madame knows we do it, of course. There's nothing that woman *doesn't* know, I think. Nothing that goes on there anyway. But she says it's why men keep coming back to us and why Nymphenburg's got this reputation. After all, a cunt is a cunt is a cunt!"

"So how many fucks did you watch that night?" Maxine asked.

Véronique stared at her and then remembered not to; the girl had never used that word before. Something was loosening up inside her.

"Well, when a new girl is being trained behind that one-way mirror, they always try to put the next girl there as soon as the place is empty — which it never is, of course, for more than a couple of minutes. So I saw ten couples fucking there that night. Funnily enough, Fleur no sooner went out to the salon than she was back again — this time with a clergyman!"

She glanced nervously at Maxine, who just laughed and said she wasn't surprised.

"This one was about sixty. Poor bugger! He had a fine erection when she washed it but he lost it between there and the bed. So she sucked him back stiff and sat on top of him and fucked him for about twenty minutes. Very gentle and loving, she was. From the way she treated him you'd think he'd been visiting her for years but she said she'd never seen him before. Anyway, he went all limp again and she had to suck him stiff some more. And then she asked him would he like her to suck him all the way. And he said yes. And when she finished him off he still had fifteen minutes. By the way — his prick was limp again by the time he started coming. Just sort of half stiff. She said that can happen with old men. If you use a vibrator on them — hey! They've got *electric* vibrators down there. Mind you, I still think the clockwork ones upstairs here are better. Anyway, if you use a vibrator

Choirmaster took her virginity

on them, they can stay limp all the time and still have an orgasm!"

"More coffee?" Maxine rose to fetch a fresh pot from the kitchen.

"What's she like?" Jilly asked when she'd gone.

"Lovely. Good company. Interesting. But very nervous. I think that choirmaster who took her virginity did more than she's ever hinted at."

"Have you talked about it?"

"No. I'm afraid of doing more harm than good — raking up bad memories."

"Do you and she ... you know? Like we did? Oh, I miss you, darling! Hurry up and join us and we can share a bed again. D'you know — in some houses the girls get whipped for loving each other up — honest! But not at Nymphenburg. Mind you, Madame is a raging lezzy herself. She's got her eye on me, I think. What was I saying before? Oh yes — do you and Maxine ...?"

"No — not yet. We share the same bed, which is a start. And she doesn't mind being kissed. But that's as far as we go. I think she wants to, but something inside her has got to snap first."

"Try a drop of port and cider — the good old leg-opener!"

"Maybe. But it would be better if it was something she couldn't turn round and blame after. She's never said 'fuck' before today, so I think something's happening. Shush now, here she comes again."

They sipped the coffee and made appreciative sounds.

"So that was it, really," Jilly said. "My first evening as trainee-voyeuse. It was very good, in fact. I think I saw every style of fucking there is. One man went at poor Dinah like a demented machine. Another lay down with his prick *just* inside Georgette so you could hardly see him moving. There was another who fucked just about every fuckable part of Raquel — her elbows, the backs of her knees, between her titties, her mouth, her bent neck, her … no, I mustn't say bumhole." She put on a prim expression and said, "Miss Brown. And Miss Laycock." She giggled. "Have you read that bit in the *Book of Rules,* yet? No? It's near the end, before all those lists of naughty words. They recommend, for the very best class of trade that the arsehole be called Miss Brown and the cunt, Miss Laycock! When I told the girls down there, they just hooted. Now it's our new fad. We all pretend to be very prim and proper young ladies and we ask each other at breakfast, 'How is Miss Brown today, my dear? Oh, I'm so pleased to hear it. And pray how does Miss Laycock? Oh, capital!' And so on."

They all laughed till it threatened to get out of control.

"So!" Véronique brought them back to earth — back to the earthy, indeed. "What did eight hours at the one-way mirror teach you?"

Jilly took a sip of coffee as she gathered her thoughts. "How to seem interested, lively, and engaged even when you're feeling apathetic. How different one customer is from another. That's what I mean when I say that the best thing about it is that nothing can really prepare you for the work. No two men are ever exactly the same, not even in looks — and certainly not in what they want of you. I saw Fleur fuck three men in there that night. The third one was some kind of wrestler or strongman. Fortunately he didn't have a prick to match or he'd have killed her. Talk about piledrivers! She moved a foot every time he rammed that thing into her. As I say — she was lucky it was on the small side. But she just smiled and sighed like he was giving her the time of her life. What a girl!"

All three of them sighed but none smiled.

Jilly resumed her tale. "There's one class of man that even Madame doesn't mind us finishing off quick. I haven't met one yet but they've all warned me. We get a couple every week."

"Goodness!" Véronique exclaimed. "Are they dangerous or what?"

"No. She wouldn't let a dangerous man across the threshold. No one plays tricks with Wolf Hegel. He may be getting on a bit now but he knows more ways of fighting dirty than most men know ways of fighting at all. But this kind of man hates himself. Some of them castrate themselves when it gets unbearable. They just can't bear the necessity to fuck. It builds up in them till they *have to* do something about it. I suppose some of them go out and rape a woman. They *all* would if we weren't there because — well, you've seen it with Rory — when the letch is on a man's back like that, *nothing* will satisfy him but to fuck and fuck until it's all quiet on the southern front again. But they don't enjoy it like Rory does. They just hate the necessity. And they hate the fact that we see them at their weakest, giving way to the impulse. So there's no point in being nice to them for forty minutes. You finish them off as quick as you can and let them escape back to their misery. But, like I say, a house like Nymphenburg will only get a couple of men like that a week, so it's not an excuse a girl can reach for too often if she finishes a man off in record time."

Véronique threw her grounds out into the grass and poured herself another cup — cold by now but, as the day was warm, it was all the more refreshing for that. "It *is* interesting, though, isn't it, Jilly? So far, anyway."

"Interesting?" Jilly echoed. "I tell you, it's absolutely fascinating. You are going to *love* it."

"Honest? Tell us how *your* first night went. That's what we really want to hear all about."

"Oh!" Jilly pulled a face and flapped her hands. "Now that was something altogether different. The one bit you aren't going to love — and yet there's no way of avoiding it — is when you troop into the salon for the very first time and sit down and wait for a man to come along and choose you. A dressing gown never felt so flimsy, and you're as good as naked underneath it, and you're the only person there who's never done this before, and you've got two heads and both have headaches, and your stomach's been hollow since you woke up that morning, and you've been sweating and trembling about it all day, and then this fat, sweaty man takes you on his lap and you pray please don't let it be him ... don't let it be him!"

"This is what really happened to you?"

"This really happened to me. He stuck his finger in my pussy and sniffed it and, without a word, just tipped me off again and went to one of the other girls instead. So then, having prayed don't let it be me, I got furious, of course! Why *not* me? What's *wrong* with me? I could have killed him I felt so humiliated. And then it happened again. This middle-aged man, early forties, good looking, slim, nice manners, takes me on his knee and fondles my titties and has a peep at my pussy and says, 'I think we'll go upstairs now, my dear.' And my heart starts singing again, all humiliation forgotten — because I could really enjoy it with someone like him. But then old Hegel comes up to him and says, 'You've got the pick of the house tonight, Mister Lamb!' And Lamb asks why, and Hegel explains, and then Lamb gets cold feet and says he'll maybe wait a week or two until I've gained a bit of experience! And off he goes with Nina, instead. I wished the ground would open!"

"Oh, poor darling!" Véronique put her arms about her and hugged her tenderly. "How terrible for you."

But Jilly grinned. "Just wait!" she replied. "This is what I mean when I say you just can't predict from one minute to the next. These humiliations seemed to last a lifetime but actually it was only five or ten minutes. We opened at five, right? At quarter-past the salon is suddenly full of gorgeous young men in their early twenties, all looking for nookie! Well, I tell you — you never saw girls perk up like the girls of Nymphenburg that night! They'll swear to you they don't care any longer if they fuck Adonis himself or some dry old fart with a prick like my little finger. But the gleam in their eyes said different. And the colour in their cheeks said different. And the swelling of their chests. And their smiles a mile wide. And the strutting of their meat — it all said different."

"But who were all these young Adonises?" Maxine asked.

"Ah, well, this sort of thing happens several times a year. Usually it's boat-race night or some big varsity match, or a cup final — you know? When people come up to London once or twice a year and decide to make a night of it. And one of the things they do, some of them, is visit the best sporting house in town."

"So what was it this last Wednesday?" Véronique asked. "I don't remember any ..."

"It was a party of naval cadets passing out or finishing a course or something down at Greenwich. Twenty of them! Well, of course, Madame explained there were only ten girls, some of them already *occupied* — in every sense of the word! So they laughed and said they were only the advance party. They knew the limitations and were painting the town red in shifts — one lot at the music hall, one lot dancing at the Palais, one lot drinking and eating, 'and us'!

So it seemed that a second wave of twenty would descend on us poor girls about quarter to seven, a third wave about nine-fifteen and the final wave about ten-forty five. Eighty cadets and only ten girls! They had it all planned like a military operation."

"Except for telephoning to arrange it in advance," Maxine remarked.

"Madame would probably have said no. Or arranged to parcel them out among other houses in Little Venice. But they calculated, rightly as it happened, that she wouldn't turn away so much business even if it meant some desperate reorganization. Of course, looking at those gorgeous hunks of virile young manhood, I was just dying for her to say yes. And there was a cheer among all the girls when she did. Because — say what you like — if you're going to be forced to take at least eight comers in your stride in one evening, it does no harm if they're all young, slim, fit, and of the officer class, does it!"

The other two stirred excitedly in their seats and agreed that it did no harm indeed.

"So then it was Madame's turn to get it all laid out like a military operation. She saw they couldn't possibly be allowed forty minutes each."

"Why not?" Maxine asked at once. "Ten girls could give twenty lads forty minutes each in eighty minutes, leaving ten minutes to spare."

Véronique chuckled and said, "Maxine is a human calculating engine."

But Jilly smiled patiently. "And who'd fuck the regular customers? She could turn away casual trade for one night but not regulars. So what she did was she struck a special price with them. Fifteen bob for thirty minutes instead of a quid for forty. And of course they said okay because at that age most men can still come twice inside thirty minutes, which is all they wanted. In fact, it would be better to go back to Greenwich and boast of getting their end away twice inside thirty minutes than inside forty. She's a shrewd woman, Madame Hegel."

"Seven girls could manage that," Maxine said, "leaving three for regular customers. If the three worked almost without a break, they could manage seven regulars in an hour and a half — or twenty-eight over the six hours the cadets would be *occupying* you — in every sense of the word!"

Jilly was impressed. "Did you just work that out in your head?" she asked.

Maxine nodded. "I've always been pretty good at mental arithmetic."

"So the young lads agreed?" Véronique prompted her excitedly.

Jilly nodded, closing her eyes and smiling at the happy memory.

"And?" Véronique almost screamed. "Who did you get first?"

Jilly stretched out full length in the sun and stroked the tops of her thighs with her finger nails. "He was *gorgeous!*" she murmured. "A-lex-an-der ..." She spoke each syllable so lovingly that the other two girls felt pangs of jealousy. "Talk about Adonis! He has the body of a young ballet dancer and thick-thick curly golden hair. And pale greeny-blue eyes that just melt you at a glance. And lips you just want to kiss and kiss and hang on. And not a hair on his body except the one place where you'd want it. And skin as fine as a baby's. I thought I was in paradise as I walked upstairs ... what am I saying? *Ran* upstairs with him. And then what happened? I drop my dressing gown and I'm standing there, just dissolving away in the admiration in his eyes as he stares at my titties and my derrière ... and I'm helping him undress and I'm planning all the marvellous things I'm going to do for the unbelievably beautiful organ that's emerging from his trousers ... when it starts leaping and twitching and flinging great gouts of sticky all over me and him and the door and the wallpaper!"

She buried her face in her hands and pretended to weep. "I could have killed the fucking traitor — except that he's in a worse pickle than me, poor lad! He's laughing and crying and swearing 'shite and onions!' all at the same time. Then he breaks down in tears and begs me not to tell any of the others, and ... oh, it was just awful. So I got him onto the bed and I started playing with it again — and let me tell you, anyone who's learned the care and feeding of the male priap under the tuition of Terence McLaren and Rory McLaren and the great Sheridan McLaren himself knows more than most sporting girls learn in a lifetime. Five minutes later I had that gristle as big and as rock-hard as he'd ever known it. And he just sat there staring at it, laughing with disbelief and telling me I'm a miracle worker. So we had twenty minutes left in which to stop it from going to waste — which we did. Stop it going to waste, I mean." She stretched and sighed again.

"Your first twenty professional minutes," Véronique murmured enviously. "Talk about falling on your feet!"

"I fell all right. It's a sort of code of honour among the girls there that they don't come with customers. I don't know how they stop themselves. And I'm not so sure I want to know, either. All I know is that I came every minute Alex was fucking me — and I'm not ashamed to admit it in present company, though I said nothing down there, of course. And I came with the next young fellow, too. And the next. And after that I don't remember. I came a few times more. But I have to admit that after seven or eight fucks in a row, with just a walk downstairs and then up again in between, it does rather ..."

She broke off and tried to think of some way to explain it. "You know if you say a word — the same word — over and over ... ice-cream, ice-cream, ice-cream, ice-cream, ice-cream, ice-cream, ice-cream ... suddenly the word has no meaning? You may absolutely *adore* ice-cream but suddenly it doesn't mean anything. Well, it was like that. I found myself looking up into the grinning face of this handsome young cadet, who's having a wonderful time with my heels up by his ears and his prick as deep inside me as it can go and his tummy going slap-slap-slap against the backs of my thighs, and all I could think was ... what on *earth* are you doing to me, young man? I wasn't affronted. I wasn't peeved. Not even weary. I mean I felt bright as a button and ready to take on the army, too. Just utterly perplexed. It no longer had any meaning. Maybe that'll become permanent one day, but I hope not. That was *the* most thrilling night of my life so far — no question. Any questions?"

"Yes," Maxine asked at once. "How many men did you fuck that night altogether?"

Jilly gave a dry laugh. "Well — some of them came back for more. The early ones, who got randy all over again. So — I didn't fuck any of the regulars that night, because mostly they already have their favourite girl. So I just fucked cadets. Eek!" She gave a squeal of joy. "So I fucked" — she looked all round and lowered her voice — "fourteen in all that night."

"Was Alex among those who came back for more?"

Jilly grinned and said, "Yes and no. Or, rather, no and yes. No, he didn't return *that* night. But yes, he returned on

Thursday night. And again last night, too. And yes, he's stinking rich and can easily afford it. And yes, he says he's going to come and fuck me *every* night until he's posted out of London. Every weekday night, because he goes down to the country at weekends — to build up his reserves for me, he says."

An appreciative silence followed in which Jilly swung her legs happily. "I tell you," she said at last. "It's *the* life for a healthy young girl with a good body and an abiding interest in the things that can be done with it!"

"What about getting babies?" Maxine asked.

Jilly nodded ruefully. "You're more cautious than I ever was, Maxine. Full marks to you. I never asked that question because I was scared of the answer. I just didn't even want to think about it. But the answer was there in one of those pamphlets they gave me to read. Of course we use chemicals and whirling sprays and stuff like that, but they're probably unnecessary. The funny thing is that you'd think a girl who fucks six men a day would have six times more chance of breaking her leg than a girl who fucks only one. But the truth is exactly the opposite. A girl who fucks six men a day stands almost no chance of 'copping a basket,' as they say. D'you know why?"

Mouths agape they shook their heads.

"Put six boys in a playground and what happens? What can you guarantee will happen before very long?"

"They'll fight," Maxine suggested.

"Right! And so will those little swimmy-tadpole things in their sticky."

"Sperms," Véronique said. "You mean sperms fight each other?"

"To the death. Did you ever see a dog and a bitch get dog-notched tight together?"

Véronique and Maxine exchanged glances and laughed. "Only last Monday, just round the corner," Véronique explained.

"Did you ever wonder why that happens?"

"Only last Monday, just round the corner," Maxine repeated.

"That's the dog's way of stopping the bitch fucking another dog for half an hour or so. It's all explained in that pamphlet. Dog sperm can swim faster than Captain Webb. So, if a dog has shot his load into a bitch, and if he can stop any other dog doing the same for a while, his sperm has a better chance of winning the race. And perpetuating his part of the race, too."

"You mean the dogs do it deliberately? That one last Monday didn't look too happy about it," Véronique said.

"I don't think they can help it. Almost everything to do with males and sperms and sex is in the sorry-I-can't-help-it category — thank heavens or we'd be looking for some other kind of work!"

Maxine screwed up her eyes as if trying to recall something and then said, "Oh yes! You said there was one customer you'd tell us about later."

"Did I?" Jilly frowned.

"Yes. You were talking about the night porter and overnight customers and ..."

"Oh yes. A man called *Roger* — wouldn't you know it! He's especially fond of playing his little trick on new girls at Nymphenburg."

"Like you?"

"Like me — the night before last. It's not a trick, really. It's a kind of fantasy, I suppose. He likes to call about three in the morning and then he either picks a girl he knows or he asks the porter if there's anybody new. And the day before yesterday the porter said, 'Giselle's new!' So Dan, that's the porter, he came and woke me up and told me to piss my bladder empty because I wasn't going to be able to do it for the next hour. And then, after I'd done that, he told me to get into the bed in the working room at the top of the stairs — because we sleep in tiny attic rooms at the top, not in the working bedrooms, see? And I was to pretend to be asleep. And I was to stay alseep when this Roger climbed into bed, *and* when he lifted my nightie, *and* when he fondled and kissed me all over, *and* when he slipped his prick into me, *and* when he fucked me, which would go on, all very sleepy and leisurely, for about an hour. *And* when he shot his sticky up me. And he'd pay four quid for this privilege, of which I'd keep two. And if I could act like a girl having her jollies without waking up, there'd be a tip in it, as well."

She laughed and, fearing that her thighs might be burning, threw her skirt back down over them. "It's the most uncanny feeling — lying there in the pitch dark, pretending to be asleep, almost falling asleep for real, and then some man you've never met, and whom you'll probably never even *see*, slips into bed behind you and starts fondling and caressing you all over. And then he slips his gristle inside you and gives you the slowest, surest poke you ever had. For easily a whole hour. I mean, I truly did fall asleep a couple of times. Not deep sleep. Quite shallow, in fact, and full of dreams."

She closed her eyes and shook her head. "I'd almost forgotten it. I had this dream all about pricks. I simply can't imagine why!" She laughed again. "These pricks were all dressed up like Edwardian swells — you know? Top hats, canes, silk scarves, white tie and tails. Just a six-foot prick and balls dressed like the man who broke the bank at Monte Carlo — monocle and all. Dozens of them, all sauntering up and down …"

All very proud and stiff

"With an independent air," Maxine sang. "You can hear the girls declare …"

"Just so!" They all laughed again and Jilly went on. "Of course, every prick *is* a millionaire — with millions of sperms to spend. So maybe that was why I dreamed it. I believe in symbolic dreams, don't you?"

"Dare we ask what all these swells *did* in your dream?" Véronique said. "There's more symbolism for you — swell, swoll, swollen … swollen pricks … you ought to be ashamed of yourself, having dreams like that!"

Jilly giggled. "That wasn't the worst. I wasn't really *me*, you see. I was a six-foot cunt, dressed in furs and standing at the top of these steps. It was a long flight of marble steps. And all these swell-pricks were climbing up toward me on my left — very proud and stiff …"

"Okay, we can guess what they did," Véronique said.

"Well, they *didn't!* That was the odd thing. They just strutted up and down in front of me, like swells on the promenade at Brighton, and then — I didn't actually see it happen — but there was this equally long line of bent and broken and collapsed pricks going away from me, down the same flight of stairs to my right. But there was no bit where they fucked me in between. And I kept falling back into that same dream, just me standing there, and this parade of swell-pricks climbing on my left and the cortège of broken ones slinking down again on my right. And every time I woke up there was Roger, still with his gristle inside me, still rogering away as slow and dainty as possible! Analyze that, eh?"

"It doesn't take much analysis, surely?" Maxine said.

They turned to her.

"The pricks are all customers. The cunt isn't you but Giselle, the *fille-de-joie* — where's the mystery?"

"But why no fucking?" Jilly asked.

"Because fucking for you, Jilly, is still fun. It represents fun. The dream is telling you — advising you, maybe — maybe even warning you — that fun *isn't* part of the Game. I don't know. I'm just talking rubbish." She pulled a guilty face.

"If you're right," Jilly told her, "then *you*" — she turned to Véronique — "are right, too. I *should* be ashamed of myself for having dreams like that." She turned back to Maxine. "I just hope you're wrong, pet, that's all. Fucking is *still* fun for me, even with men who don't particularly inspire, and even if I don't see all the stars in heaven. And I'm going to hold on to that for as long as I can."

"How many men *have* you fucked, darling?" Véronique asked. "Since you started last Wednesday?"

Now it was Jilly's turn to pull a guilty face as she reached into her handbag and took out a little notebook with a tiny propelling pencil in its spine. "Fourteen on Wednesday," she purred. "Seven on Thursday, plus Roger in the small hours. And six last night."

"Twenty-eight," Maxine said.

Jilly looked skyward. "I suppose you can already tell me what I've earned, too?"

"Five guineas the first night. Two pounds for Roger. And six-pounds-ten for the other thirteen. Thirteen pounds and fifteen shillings — plus whatever you got in tips."

Jilly laughed. "Plus what I earned for smacks on my 'bare posteriors'! I got a quid for eight smacks on Thursday night." She snapped the book shut. "I don't know why I bother with this," she complained. "I could just ring you up every morning, Maxine, and add it to the running total in your head."

Véronique reached a hand out. "Can I see?"

Jilly clutched the book to her chest. "You won't laugh?"

"Of course not."

"Promise?" She handed it over hesitantly.

Maxine came and sat beside Véronique. Together they read:

WEDNESDAY 7th June, 1922

1 Alexander 2/-(!!!!!!).
2 Rodney (short, dark: !!).
3 Philip (medium, muscular: !!!).
4 Michael (tall, blond: !).
5 John 1/6 (tall, medium, l).
6 Charley 1/-(average, fair, l).
7 Mickey (average, dark, s).
8 Frank (short, dark, th).
9 Terry 2/6 (average, medium, av: !!).
10 Steve (tall, medium, s).
11 Philip 2/-(again).
12 Avrion(?) (average, ginger, l: !!).
13 Guy 1/-(short, brown, s+th: !).
14 Rodney 2/6 (again: !!).
Finished 01:25.
FEES: 5gns. TIPS: 12/6. = £5/17/6.

"I had to work almost three hundred hours at Shoolbred's — nearly six weeks — to earn that much!" Maxine said. "What a cockeyed world!"

Véronique laughed. "It's a world ruled by a cock with one eye, all right!"

"The money after their names," Jilly explained, "is the tip they gave me, if any. Madame says we must never show the slightest disappointment if they don't tip us. Some regulars tip only once a month. And anyway we must remember that they have already paid us a big compliment by choosing us in preference to all the other girls who were available to him in the salon at the time."

"And the underlined letters?" Maxine asked.

Véronique laughed. "What d'you think they mean? If th is 'thick' and l is long, what's s and av, eh?"

"Oh!" Her freckles darkened prettily.

"For the next day," Jilly said, turning the page, "I added a few more details."

THURSDAY 8th June, 1922

15 Graham 2/6 (45, moonface, plump, short, balding, av+th — 69, standing, sitting, lying, Miss B: !).
16 Colin 2/-(35, foxyface, tall, slim, dark, l+c — fellatio, doggy).
17 Michael 1/6 (30, monkeyface, slim, average, dark, s+th — cunnilingus, heel-over, wheelrim, levrette: !).
18 George 2/6 (50, Mr Bumble, bald, important, s — 8 smacks for £1, doggy, revenge, Miss B).
19 Martin 2/-(25, Valentino, slim, handsome, l — 69, entwined, climbing ivy, wurlitzer, wheelbarrow dance: !!).
20 ALEXANDER — !!!!!! (tip refused)
21 Gary 1/6 (30, puddinghead, fat, short, dark, av — 69, fellatio, pillar, revenge, capuchin).
Finished 00:45.
Then: 22 Roger £1! (?,?, l+th — one hour from behind: !!).
Finished 03:30.
FEES: £3/10/0. TIPS: £1/11/6. SMACKS: £1. = £6/1/6.

NB: This was really my first true night as a professional. I'd have done any of last night's young men for a lark or for fun. But tonight's definitely only for money!

"Finished?" Véronique asked Maxine.

"Yes," she responded eagerly.

They turned the page and read without further comment.

FRIDAY 9th June, 1922

23 Pete 1/-(40, rabbitface, short, dark, chubby, sh+th — breakers, free-spread, knee ride, gentleman's relish: !).

24 ALEXANDER — !!!!!! (tip refused but perfume accepted)

25 Phil 1/-(20, lemurface, tall, bookworm type, long dark, sallow, av+th — 69, pillar, capuchin, half free-spread).

26 Felix 2/-(35, Sancho Panza, florid, foreign, gold teeth, l — 69, cunnilingus, heel-over, morning pride, Miss B: !!).

27 William 2/6 (55, Bignose, thin, tall, grey, l+th — handiwork, fellatio, titfuck, armpit, Miss B).

28 Neil 1/9 (60, Jugears, weedy, skinny, bald, l+th — cunnilingus, 69, hand-start, missionary).

Finished 01:15. FEES: £3. TIPS: 8/3. = £3/8/3

Tonight's I'd only have done for money, too. Full pro!

"And it was the best forty minutes in the week for each one of them!" Jilly said proudly.

They turned the page again but all it said was:

SATURDAY 10th June, 1922

"That's today!" Maxine said.

"So it is!" Véronique responded with kindly sarcasm.

The virgin whiteness of the page was, in its way, as eloquent as any of the detailed jottings on the previous ones. '*Anything* can go here,' it said. Or, more succinctly: 'Anything goes!' Taken with the entries for the previous three days it emphasized as nothing else could have done what Jilly had said about life on the Game: its exciting randomness, its tantalizing unpredictability, its seductive fascination for any girl interested in sex.

"What are all these names — capuchin, pillar, revenge, and so on?" Véronique asked. "Different positions?"

"Yes. Didn't I show you that book? It's in Sherry's library here. It's called *The Geometry of Eros* or something like that. Second shelf down beside the window. See — after a man's picked me but before I take him upstairs he has to pay Madame, so, if I recognize him from before, I've just about got time to take a quick peek at these notes. And then I can pretend I remember vividly all the exciting things we did last time. It may not work but we'll see. It certainly won't if I don't at least give it a try."

"What do the exclamation marks mean?" Maxine asked. "Is each one an actual orgasm?"

"For Wednesday, yes, probably. Roughly, anyway. After that it's just a sign of how much I enjoyed it — sexually, I mean — whether or not I had an actual orgasm. I'm beginning to see a difference between sexual pleasure, which is nice and warm and comfortable and easy, and sexual ecstasy, which is fabulous but exhausting. It's possible to enjoy being fucked — enjoy the contact, enjoy being caressed, enjoy being naked and free — without going to the top of the mountain."

"You got two pounds, twelve-and-threepence in tips," Véronique said before Maxine could make the point. But Maxine, not to be outdone, said, "Fractionally over one-and-tenpence per customer. At Shoolbred's I earned four-tenths of a penny per customer. So a sporting girl is worth about three hundred and fifty times *more* — to *someone* — than a sales girl in a swank store like that."

"Not to some-*one*," Jilly told her. "To some-*thing*. To that tyrant which hangs between men's legs and raises its head a dozen times a day and says, 'Get me a girl!' until the poor fellow gives in."

"You mean it's a tyrant to *them?*" Maxine asked. "Not to us?"

"Certainly not to us," Jilly said firmly.

"How can you say that?" Maxine wanted to argue.

"Because I've seen it happening. Oh, when you *see* a man's prick all stiff and red and throbbing at you, it looks like the most fearsome bully — I grant you that. And it's also true that we have to do what that bully wants for as long as he's paid us to submit. But we are its *paid* servants, remember. The poor man attached to that tyrant-bully is its abject slave. We submit to its desires for forty minutes. He's dominated by it, tyrannized by it, bullied by it, *for life!* When it starts lording over us, it's a fine upstanding ruffian, all swagger and power, but when sweet, gentle, submissive Miss Laycock has finished with it, it hasn't enough strength to lift the skin off warm milk." She stretched out her legs under her dress and, placing both hands over her Venus mound, said, "There's *power* in this little lady. Power you never dreamed of, girls. From the moment we're born, us innocent little females, we're dragooned and lectured and bribed and frightened into never using that power — or just using it to catch and hold the best man available. But we *use* it down there — us girls at Nymphenburg. We sit there in the salon and we watch those poor cunny-haunted men come and go by their hundreds. They *look* arrogant enough. They swagger like peacocks, and throw out their chests — and pull in their tummies! But d'you remember when the boys used to line up for the strap outside the beak's office at elementary school? Did you go to a mixed elementary school? Remember that bravado they put on? It's like that. Underneath it all they know *they* are the real slaves and *we* are the mistresses!" She laughed and fanned her brow. "Whew! Sorry about that, darlings! But I'm glad I got it off my chest at least." She looked from one to the other. "Any more questions?"

"Yes." Véronique licked her lips nervously. "Could we see what Miss Laycock looks like after she's taken the starch out of twenty-eight men in three days?"

"Sure." Jilly started pulling her skirt up again.

"No," Véronique said quickly. "Upstairs."

"Ah!" Jilly let her dress go again and a slow smile spread across her face. "Is Sherry paying us a visit today?"

"He hasn't telephoned."

"Then he isn't. And the boys?"

"Not till tomorrow afternoon."

"Then I've got until two-fifteen with you. The doors down at Nymphenburg open at three on Saturdays." She rose and walked provocatively toward the house. "And you two," she said over her shoulder, "have all night before you!"

Véronique felt Maxine's fingers link with hers. She stared at her in surprise — and delight. "Yes?" she said.

"Yes," Maxine replied.

They raced upstairs to the main bedroom, where Jilly kicked off her shoes and flung herself flat on her back. Like two nurses making a bed, Véronique and Maxine took the hem of her skirt and lifted it up in a most businesslike fashion. Her slim white legs, made pink by the sun, jigged excitedly in anticipation of the frolics to come. She was wearing slack, silky knickers, which Maxine untied and Véronique drew off her. Then she pulled up her knees and let her thighs fall slack, as wide as gravity would pull them.

"No change at all!" Véronique said in a disappointed tone.

"What did you expect?" Jilly laughed. "The men don't carve notches in it — though some of them would like to, I'm sure!"

Excited, vigorous young men

"I thought it would be ... well, you know how a scullery-maid's hands are different from a lady's."

"Yes, but Miss Laycock is *intended* for the use to which I've put her. Besides, we use goosegrease and Vaseline and cocoa-butter lozenges, to make her life easier. And the men's. Can I have a hand-mirror?"

While Maxine went across the room to fetch it, Jilly slipped her fingers among her labia and massaged them gently. "They feel okay now," she said. "They were a bit red and sore after that first night. They were fourteen excited and very *vigorous* young men!" She chuckled as Maxine handed her the mirror and, while she inspected her pussy minutely, said, "I actually counted one of them — how many thrusts he made into me before he shot his load. He must have been about number nine or ten — when it was starting to have no meaning."

"How many?" Maxine asked avidly.

"Four hundred and seventy-three. And I counted one other man, on Thursday night, and that was four hundred and twenty. I'd say four hundred and fifty is about average. Of course, it's not like running — left, right, left, right ... without a pause. They don't do it to a metronome. They'll give you ten slow, lazy thrusts and then they'll change position and give you half-a-dozen more slow ones and then, suddenly, two dozen as fast as they can go. There's every sort of variation ..." Her voice trailed off and she eyed Maxine suspiciously. "What's going on under those gorgeous red locks — as if I didn't know! Go on — tell me the worst!"

Keeping an absolutely straight face, Maxine said, "Twenty-eight men have given Miss Laycock there about twelve and a half thousand thrusts in the last three days."

"Oh my God!" Jilly pulled her skirt up over her head and covered her face with her hands.

Maxine went on: "It works out at about eight hundred and twenty thrusts for a quid. Or ..."

"No!" Jilly shrieked from behind the cloth.

" ... or if you count one, two, three, four, five, six, seven thrusts, you can say to yourself, 'That's another twopence I've just earned'!"

Jilly threw her skirt off her face again and hooted with laughter. "Maxine, darling, you are *priceless!* Tell me if I've got it right. The girls will love this! Seven thrusts for twopence. Or eight hundred and twenty for a quid. Right?"

"In rounded-off figures. If you want it more precisely ..."

"Don't bother!" Jilly laughed again.

"I'll tell you anyway in case one of the other girls quibbles. It's six-point-eight-four thrusts for twopence."

"How d'you do that?" Véronique asked admiringly. "All in your head?"

"I don't know. I just see the numbers in my head and they rearrange themselves. I used to look at my father's congregations and guess the numbers and then count them when they left the church and I was never more than five out. At Shoolbred's I could look at a shelf in the stockroom and see three rows by seventeen boxes with a dozen pairs of gloves in each and say six hundred and twelve gloves, straight away, while Mister Greene was still licking his pencil." She chuckled grimly. "That was my mistake, of course — giving him time to try and wet his *other* pencil!"

"Talking of Mister Greene," Véronique said. "Remember the question Sherry asked you — could you fuck him for money? How d'you answer it now you know you could take a day's wages off him in forty minutes?"

Maxine grinned at the thought. *"Two* days' wages — *and* a little bit more," she replied. "He gets six-bob a day. Yes! I think I could do that — with pleasure."

"But not the kind of pleasure that earns my exclamation marks!" Jilly said.

"Not in a million years." She swallowed heavily. "Can I ask a favour, Jilly?"

"Go ahead, darling."

"Can I look more closely at ... you know — Miss Laycock down there? I've never looked at another girl's pussy before."

For answer Jilly lifted her derrière, stuffed a pillow beneath herself, and spread her thighs as wide as they'd go. "That's the hole where you piss," she said. "That's the hole that earns twopence every seven thrusts. That's Miss Brown, who could make the same boast — more, perhaps, because I've noticed I get bigger tips from the men who use her. And these lips, which are usually closed together, keep Miss Laycock moist and soft. And this little veiled lady up here in her private bower, is a source of such pleasure for us that it's a good thing most men know nothing about her very existence." She broke off and tutted with vexation. *"Now* what are you thinking?"

"I'm remembering something I read in one of Sherry's books — that each time a man ejaculates — not Sherry, mind, because he never waits long enough to build up the stocks again — but a man who's had no sex for three days will ejaculate about three hundred and fifty *million* sperms. I was thinking that in the past three nights almost *ten thousand million* little sperms have been ejaculated up inside here and, if what you say is right, they've all fought each other to death or just died, anyway. Isn't it awesome!"

The two girls stared at each other and burst out laughing again. "Awesome!" Véronique agreed.

"Well, *I* think it's awesome, anyway," Maxine said huffily. "But the thing I really wanted to ask was, what d'you *do* with it all? I mean, when you go back to the salon and sit down —

if you've got no knickers on, does it just ooze out again or what?"

"Yeurk!" Véronique said. "You've got a twisted mind, you know."

"I've got a practical mind. Fourteen fit young naval cadets would have squirted almost a demitasse of sticky into her. And what goes up must come down!"

"Suddenly I wish I hadn't eaten two breakfasts," Jilly said.

"Or drunk all those demitasses of coffee!" Véronique added.

"You mean you just ignore the stuff?" Maxine persisted.

"No, dear." Jilly sighed. "I hope you like gruesome details, because you're about to get them. First of all we have these whirling sprays, which we leap out of bed and push inside us and whirl away most of the sticky into a chamber pot. Then we have these little sponges — vaginal sponges, they call them. They have little strings to let you pull them out again. And we dip them in quinine water and push them up, and the quinine kills any remaining little sperms before they know it's their birthday. The cocoa-butter lozenges we use for lubrication also have loads of quinine in. And we pull the sponges out before we rub in the cocoa-butter for the next gentleman. But, since you are *so* interested in all this, Maxine, let me tell you a little story. One of our girls, called Leone, got stuck in Hamburg once without money and had to work in what they call a first-port-of-call house where sailors come ashore and have a very quick fuck, just to ease off the pressure, before they go on to a more leisurely sporting house. The girls in those quick-fuck houses do a hundred men and more a day ..."

"No!" the other two were horrified.

"I'm telling you — if they took six minutes with a man, they were doing something wrong! Anyway, the point of this

All the girls sat naked • 215

is that they had a half-hour break for a meal around four in the afternoon, and all the girls, half-a-dozen of them, would sit at the table, naked, on two wooden benches. And when they got up to go back to work, Leone told me she turned round for a last look and there, on each of the benches, were three gleaming puddles of sticky that had oozed out of them while they were eating. So, Maxine, I hope you'll sleep tonight after all this!"

"Can I ask a favour now?" Véronique said before a further altercation could develop.

"Gladly!" Jilly replied.

"You remember that double-dildo?"

"Y-e-e-s?" she said in an amused, conspiratorial tone.

"And you remember that we didn't use it for fun at all but for the serious, scientific purpose of discovering what a girl looks like to a man when he fucks her?"

"Y-e-e-s?" She was laughing now.

"Well — at that time you'd only been fucked by three men, so your knowledge was a teeny bit limited. But now, well …" She grinned and let the rest of the idea hang.

Jilly just lay back on the bed and laughed. "Go and get it," she said with imitation weariness. She unbuttoned her blouse.

Maxine leaped ahead of Véronique and returned bearing the dildo just above her brow, like a victor's wreath. Véronique had meanwhile raced out of her own clothes and now stood naked, quivering with anticipation. Her breasts shivered like jellies each time her heart thumped, which was about twice a second. Jilly knelt up on the bed and, taking the device from Maxine's trembling fingers, fitted it carefully into her own hole. As she twisted herself to tighten the strap, she saw Maxine's eyes run up and down her naked body and, feeling she had to say something to break the sudden, charged silence that had fallen, said as casually as she could, "Madame says I'm lucky to be born when I was. Ten years ago a girl with a boyish figure like mine would have been unemployable in a place like Nymphenburg. Of course, girls with figures like you and Véronique would *always* be in high demand there. But long, slender thighs and little bottoms like mine are a new taste among men."

Maxine was too shy to do anything but nod.

"D'you want to stay and watch?" Véronique asked her.

Maxine bit her lip. Her whole attitude was ambiguous.

"You needn't if you don't want to," Jilly assured her.

She swallowed heavily. "Could I stay and ... *not* watch?" A fluttering finger strayed to the top button of her dress.

"Of course!" The other two laughed and flung their arms about her, welcoming her into their sisterhood. Jilly, forgetting the dildo for a moment, poked her rather hard with it in the stomach. Maxine defused all their tension by slapping her playfully on the wrist and crying out, "Impatient girl!"

But when they had undressed her completely, Véronique and Jilly just froze and stared at her, open mouthed.

"What?" a slightly frightened Maxine asked, wrapping her arms self-consciously around her torso.

"But you're *beautiful!*" Véronique whispered, unpeeling her arms again.

"So beautiful it hurts," Jilly said, touching her skin almost reverently.

She had the figure that firms who make lingerie fight to drape their garments upon — full, firm breasts with big, soft nipples; a slender, graceful waist; gracile arms; a willowy back; a pert, curvaceous bottom; a bright red bush up to her navel with a big, juicy cleft down through the heart of it; and long, sleek thighs. But, sensational as all this might be, the most stunning feature of all was her skin itself — smooth, finely textured, and covered from head to toe with freckles of every size. It turned her into a lithe panther-woman.

Véronique went close to her, to touch her as one might touch delicate porcelain, and then sniffed and said, "That's it!" She sniffed again and yet again, putting her nose near Maxine's skin.

"That's what?" Maxine asked nervously.

"Can't you smell it, Jilly? I've noticed this stray perfume in the house all this past week. A bit like cinnamon, with a hint of musk, and overtones of vanilla. *Very* sexy! It's your *skin,* Maxine! Oh God, I could *eat* you, you're so gorgeous."

The girl laughed feebly. "Am I?"

Jilly had meanwhile rubbed Vaseline all over the big knob of the dildo. "Come on!" she said. "Time's flying. We've only got two hours left. Who's first?"

"You!" the other two said to each other simultaneously.

"Véronique first, to break the ice, and then we'll give Maxine the thrill of her lifetime. Have you ever had an orgasm, darling?"

"I'm not sure."

"Well, you soon will be — one way or the other. Come on, then, Véronique. Down on all fours. This one's called bend-and-fill — you bend and I fill. Arch your back after I go in."

Jilly went down on her hands and knees. Jilly thrust her own knee in between them and prised them farther apart quite brusquely. "That's how some of them behave," she said. "Now. They all like to do this — Sherry does it too, so it won't be a surprise."

And she gripped the dildo at the base and moved the knob of it slowly, voluptuously, up and down Véronique's crevice. The girl responded by wagging her tail fast but in only small, trembling movements from side to side.

"Oh, that's good!" Jilly said. "I must remember that. Hollow your back and flash me a little more pussy — yes, that's it! Okay — in I go."

She pushed it in smoothly and swiftly. Véronique gave a gasp and slumped, hollowing her back still further.

"No," Jilly told her. "Arch it upwards, like a hump-back bridge. That's it! You bend and I fill!" And she arched herself forwards, fitting her body to Véronique's humped back and reaching her hands under to fondle the girl's breasts, which, of course, were swinging freely. "There! Is that good? Or is that good!"

"That is g-o-o-o-d!" Véronique managed to blurt out, panting meanwhile with lust.

"And this is the levrette." Jilly knelt upright, her body quite vertical, and, gripping Véronique by the hips, pulled her tightly onto the dildo, thrusting with her buttocks to counteract the movements. "A man with a long prick can touch the top end of your hole that way, so the trick is to tighten your buttocks to stop him doing it twice."

"What's the wurlitzer?" Véronique asked.

"Oh." Jilly pulled out and moved a little away from her. "I don't know if this dildo is flexible enough. You lie on your back and hug your knees to your chest. Okay. Then I get like this." She went on all fours and crawled backwards until her ankles were near Véronique's head and her bottom almost touching the backs of her knees. "No," she said, "this prick won't bend down enough. What the man does, see, is push his prick right down to get the knob into your hole and then he pulls you right onto him. This thing would hurt you if I tried it, but you get the general idea. The man can watch it going in and out, you see. They like that. There are lots of positions where they can watch their gristle slipping in and out of you."

Véronique rolled out from under her. "Maxine now," she said.

Jilly turned to the girl and asked, "Well, darling, in the classic words of the sporting girl down the centuries — 'How do you want me?'"

Maxine breathed deeply. "What you said about Roger coming to you in the small hours?" she said. "And sticking it into you very gently from behind? That sounded nice."

"Is that how you and the choirmaster did it?" Jilly asked innocently.

"Choirmaster?" For a moment she was nonplussed. "Oh no!" She shuddered. "Don't mention *him!*"

Jilly raised two hands to pacify her. "Okay, okay! Just lie down on your right side, then. And bend your left knee a bit — forward. That's it." She lay down behind Maxine and clasped her gently by the hips. "Now, if Véronique will be so kind as to guide the magic wand into your ... That's it."

Véronique was fascinated to see that the two thick, meaty lips of Maxine's pussy were also ornamented with freckles. When she slipped her fingers between them to part them, the bright pink complexity of the oyster they had hidden was startling. An imp urged her to push Jilly away and go down there for a feast herself. Only the knowledge that none of the McLarens was coming today enabled her to curb the impulse. They could make a real night of it, starting early and dining often.

Her imp did not entirely give up, though. After Jilly had slipped the ivory prick all the way in, and out, and in again — a dozen or more times — Maxine relaxed completely, stretched out, fumbled for Jilly's hands, and brought them up to her breasts. She was breathing in huge, shivery gasps and if you shut your eyes, you'd have been hard put to say whether she was in ecstasy or in pain.

When Véronique judged she was so enraptured that she wouldn't really know what was happening to her, she — or that imp — laid gentle hands on her left thigh and lifted it up and back over Jilly's thigh behind her. This, of course, exposed the bright red delta of her Venus mound to Véronique's gaze and, more importantly, to her quivering, slobbering, restless tongue.

When it touched her clittie, Maxine exploded. Her whole body jolted as if Véronique's tongue and Jilly's dildo were two high-voltage probes. She went rigid, stretching out her arms, reaching up with her head, and pointing her toes. This had the effect of pushing both her and Jilly onto their backs, with Jilly still deeply lodged inside her. It also spread her labia wide and invited Véronique's tongue to deeper, wider, more thrilling darts and probes than ever.

And now the poor girl was no longer in touch, or at least in control, of any part of her. She was a helpless prisoner of the kicks and delights, the fires and passions, that raged though her body, shaking her senseless. Her freckles turned bright red. A fine-beaded sweat broke out all over her skin. Her pussy dribbled and glistened with the pouring of her lubrication. And her two merciless companions kept on and on, driving her relentlessly along that plateau of multiple orgasm, where men may assist, observe, wonder, but never partake.

It was so intense that even Véronique, whose pussy was not being caressed or stirred by anything more substantial than her own fantasy, collapsed into an ecstasy of her own. And so at last the three of them lay, naked and panting, side by side, staring with a kind of wonder, deep into one another's eyes.

"Was that an orgasm?" Maxine asked faintly. Her breathing was shallow and rapid.

Véronique struggled up onto one elbow, leaned over, and kissed her tenderly on the mouth. "There's lots more where that came from, darling," she whispered.

"Tonight?" Maxine asked.

"Tonight."

"And have one for me," Jilly said bleakly.

"While you're filling out another page in your little book," Véronique said.

"And earning three hundred and fifty times what I used to get," Maxine added.

"And washing out a demitasse of sticky!" Véronique giggled.

"And trying to decide whether it's th or av ..." Maxine joined her.

"You'll be laughing on the other sides of your faces soon enough," Jilly said heavily. Then, in a more natural tone: "Actually, you shouldn't leave it too long. The Hegels have decided there's going to be a boom in sex — what with skirts getting shorter and chaperons having joined the dodo and hot dance music everywhere. So they've bought the sporting house next door, which was a six-girl house. At the moment they're redecorating and knocking out an archway in the party wall to make one large salon. Also the old Madame's room and sleeping quarters are being turned into workrooms. So, come the end of July, the ten-girl Nymphenburg will become the eighteen-girl Nymphenburg, which will rival the Sphynx or the *Feu d'amour* in Paris. And they'll be looking for eight new girls before that. You two will just walk in over all the others — but only if you go down there and let the Hegels see you."

A sobered Maxine looked glumly at Véronique. "Sherry would let *you* go then, maybe. But if I've just started ..." She shrugged unhappily.

Véronique smiled back at her. "I think," she said quite confidently, "that if you and I can seduce Terence and Rory to the idea of having *two* mistresses each for the next month, Sherry will join them soon enough."

Jilly frowned. "But Sherry doesn't know anything about his sons coming here, too ..." Her voice trailed off when she saw that Véronique's confidence was not shaken. "Surely?" she added.

"I'm equally sure they're all in cahoots," Véronique replied. "And laughing up their sleeves at us."

"But why?"

"Because it makes us feel naughty. It adds spice, from their point of view, if we believe we're deceiving them. Besides, just think back to when he first proposed the arrangement to you — for you to become *his* mistress only. Suppose he'd put all his cards on the table then and there — telling you that *three* men would call in and fuck you just about every day! How would you have taken that? You might have said no — fought shy of it. I would have, I think. Maybe they even tried being honest once — and lost a lot of girls because of it. Anyway, it'll be interesting to see. I think the two of us will seduce the boys but we'll do nothing about Sherry. Just go on pretending I'm his mistress and Maxine's my maid. We'll see how long it is before he caves in — if I'm right."

Jilly licked her lips cautiously.

"It all depends on one thing, though," she warned. "How well you two fillies get on together."

They grinned at each other.

"We're going to discover that tonight," Maxine said.

There was nothing to stay up for. It was a balmy summer's evening with the smell of new-mown grass heavy on the air — too warm for a hot bath so Maxine and Véronique took a warm shower together. They turned off the water, soaped and sponged almost all over, and then just hugged each other, and rubbed their naked, slippery bodies together. But when Maxine wanted to wash her pussy, too, Véronique begged her not to, because she found the musky-cinnamon-vanilla perfume of her sex so powerfully stimulating. She made to wash her own fork but then Maxine stayed her hand, too. "Try anything once," she said with a smile.

"That's the spirit," Véronique said.

They showered off the soap, dried themselves, and stood back from the wide-open window to let the summer breeze finish the job and turn their skins from tacky-damp to silken smooth. Then they slipped their arms around each other's waists and wandered back along the corridor, naked, weak at the knees, and on fire with lust.

"All those nights we've wasted!" Maxine murmured. "Why did I wait a whole week for this?"

"Because you were afraid I'd compare you as a partner with Jilly and find you wanting. And why don't you worry about it now? Because you've seen the Great God Pan at last — and you don't give a damn how you compare with Jilly, just as long as you can have that thrill again."

"And again."

"And again!" They both giggled.

"You're right, of course," Maxine said. "I just have no confidence. I just ..." She tightened her fists to suggest a clamming-up.

Véronique drew a deep breath, "Was it something that choirmaster did? Or said?"

Maxine stopped dead and stared at the wall ahead.

"You don't have to answer if you'd rather not," Véronique hastened to assure her.

After a further agonizing silence, Maxine said, "You're right. I can't *not* talk about it for ever. I said he took my virginity — which he did. But only with his finger. I wasn't going to admit that to Sherry. Not in front of you two. But he did something else to me. I don't know what. Or maybe he didn't. Maybe I just got so nervous and flustered that it happened spontaneously. Anyway, my vagina — is it all right to use that word?"

Véronique stared at her in amazement. "Why ever not?"

Maxine burst out laughing. "Sorry! Feeble joke."

"You!" Simulating anger, Véronique attacked her and started tickling her fiercely.

Maxine shrieked with laughter and fled along the last stretch of the landing to their bedroom. Véronique was hard on her heels. Across the room she raced, with young Véronique's fingers touching her often enough to bring more squeals and laughter.

"Pax!" she gasped, flinging herself on the bed.

Véronique flung herself on top of her ... and the mood changed completely. Panting heavily, they stared into each other's eyes and then Véronique lowered her lips to Maxine's ... and thus began a marathon session of passionate kisses and cuddles, in which fingers and lips and nipples and breasts and tongues and noses all seemed to melt together in one glorious confusion of erotic discovery. It ended with Véronique's head between Maxine's thighs and Maxine's head between hers and each girl staring in a hesitant kind of wonder at the glorious complexities of the other's pussy, shyly opened in welcome.

From somewhere far off, Véronique hear Maxine's voice saying, "He told me the only thing I'd ever be able to get inside me was a propelling-pencil lead. He said I'd never be able to satisfy any man."

For reply Véronique stuck her fingertips just inside those two luscious lips, parted them slightly, and, burying her face in the rich, musky juices of her furrow, extruded her tongue as far as it would go into Maxine's vagina, where she wiggled it around, flattened it, twisted it, furled the tip back and forth, and fluttered it like an aspen leaf.

"How's that for a propelling pencil?" she asked between gasps when she withdrew at last to regain her breath.

"Like this," said a feeble voice from between her thighs. And, a moment later, the whole of her body melted with the most heavenly sensations as Maxine's tongue returned the favour in her vagina.

When they next looked at the clock they found, to their astonishment, that a whole hour had passed — an hour in which their tongues and fingers had played every possible variation on the tricks that two lively, randy, inventive young girls could get up to, buried in each other's forks.

It was Gerty's night off so they rose, grilled a couple of steaks, helped it down with a light salad and plenty of wine, and returned to the bedroom. It was gone nine and the sun had just set. They threw open the curtains to let in some air. A twilight hush invaded the room filling it with suggestions that time was infinite.

Véronique remembered the occasion when Jilly had been looking through binoculars from one of these windows. She went to get them from the library and found a telescope lying beside them in the same drawer. She brought both back to the bedroom, where Maxine was leafing through *The Geometry of Eros,* which Jilly had mentioned earlier.

"The wheel-rim is fantastic," she said, holding the page up. It showed a man curved backwards on his hands and feet, making a semicircle of his body, and a woman riding him astride, firmly lodged on his gristle. "Shall we get out that double-dildo and try some of these?" she suggested.

"Have a look at this first." Véronique trained it on the corner house, where Jilly had said you could sometimes see a couple *in flagrante*. And there they were! Just beginning, by the look of it. A man and his mistress? They both looked about the same age, in their mid-twenties. It was a studio flat, with a big north window, so perhaps he was an artist and she was his model. With the naked eye you couldn't see them in the twilight so they must have thought their privacy was secure.

The girl, a large, florid, Latin beauty, was sitting on a studio couch, dressed in a loose white petticoat and a thin cotton blouse with short, puff sleeves and an elasticated neck and hem. The man, slim and handsome, with a vandyke beard, was naked but for a loose, peasant-style shirt in blue. He was standing behind her with a big, eager-looking erection lying across the backrest of the couch. He was massaging her neck and shoulders. She had her hands on his, guiding them lightly. He had moved the puff sleeves off her shoulders so that the top hem was a straight line across her body, showing the top third of her ample breasts. His hands were straying all over the bare portions of her skin but not dipping inside her blouse. They were smiling at each other.

"That's love," Véronique said with a tinge of envy in her voice.

"Yes," Maxine said after a while.

"It is different somehow. We can't see their eyes nor much of their expressions — just whether they're smiling or not. But you can tell it from their whole attitude."

"They're not doing it for its own sake. Not just for thrills alone."

The woman took her lover by the wrists at last and eased his hands down inside her blouse. At the same time she tilted her head and kissed and licked his erection, which had been there beside her face all this while.

He must have touched some button with his knee for, the next moment the backrest fell against him and he let it, and her, down gently. Then he took off his shirt and climbed on the couch beside her. She moved up to make room.

She just lay there, one big bundle of love, gift-wrapped for him to unclothe and discover. It was such a sweet little scene that the two girls could no longer watch with good conscience.

"D'you think we'll ever be loved like that?" Maxine asked wistfully.

"Jilly seems to have found it — and with her very first customer."

"That's just infatuation," Maxine said. "I know all about *that*, believe me!"

"You're right. Still" — as ever, Véronique looked for the bright side — "you can say one thing: If a man does truly fall in love with a sporting girl, it has to be genuine. Swap me the telescope for a moment. I think it's more powerful than these glasses. I want to see something." She put the telescope to her eye. "Ah! I thought so. They lopped back that tree in Hamilton Gardens and now you can see the whole of that terrace in Little Venice from here. Every house there is a sporting house. There are probably twenty girls being fucked down there at this very minute. Hey! Talk about wasps round a honeypot — look!"

"It's okay. I can see it with these. Jilly didn't say anything about that. Can you make her out?"

"No. She must be *occupied*. One of the twenty."

The pocket-handkerchief gardens in front of the houses were full of girls. The streets were full of men, parading up and down, stopping every now and then to chat with this or that Cyprian beauty, laughing, slapping each other's backs, shoving one another, daring one another, mocking one another, and, eventually, making a choice of this or that girl and going indoors with her, arm-in-arm.

"I suppose the salons get stifling in this heat," Véronique mused. "I wonder what the workrooms are like? Do the men ask the girls to do most of the work?"

She realized that Maxine was swaying gently at her side — not the whole of her body, just her hips.

Maxine became aware that Véronique was watching her, not the distant terrace. She giggled. "I was watching one girl, trying to imagine what was going through her mind as she chatted with the swells, and then when one of them picks her and they walk into the house like that ..." She faltered.

"What? What d'you think goes through her mind then?"

"I don't know. I can imagine that girl is me but I can't imagine I'm her. I mean, I can think of me walking beside a stranger and knowing he's already got that *thing* of his hot and hard inside his trousers and he's going to jab it into me in a minute or two. The physical picture is crystal clear but the mental one's a blank. I honestly don't know how I'd cope with that. Do you?"

Véronique put the telescope down on the chest and went over to sit on the edge of the bed. "I don't know," she replied. "I'm sure I *would* be able to but I can't say how. Did you ever get the strap on your hands at school?"

"A ruler." Maxine grinned as she, too, put the glasses down and joined her. "Why? What perversion are you going to suggest now?"

"No!" Véronique laughed. "Nothing like that. Whenever I was going to get the strap I used to look down at my hands and say, 'Well, dears, it's *you* who are going to suffer this. Not me. You're on your own.' That's how I used to cope. I suppose you could try to distance the whole of your body like that — sort of mentally curl up inside yourself and let your body be jabbed by that hot, hard *thing*."

"I asked a question about five minutes ago," Maxine said archly. "Shall I get it out of the chest?" Without waiting for an answer she suited action to words and, moments later, stood before Véronique, holding the double-dildo. She was panting; her bright eyes, slackly open lips, and wet tongue reminded Véronique of one of those dogs who had nearly bowled them over last Monday.

"Me or you?" Véronique asked.

"Can I decide? What I'd like is for you to wear it and then to lie on top of me — stick it into me, of course ..."

"Are you sure?" Véronique asked solemnly as she picked it up and masturbated the big ivory prick. "It's bigger than even the biggest propelling-pencil lead I ever saw." She ducked to avoid a cheerful swipe of Maxine's hand. Then she stood up to strap it on her. "Okay. I lie on top of you ... what then?"

"Just that. *Cover* me, as animal breeders say. Lips on my lips. Tits on my tits. Tummy on my tummy ... all the way down to feet against my feet." She lay on the bed as she spoke and placed her thighs loosely together. "And instead of poking me like a man, if we just sort of slinked and slithered like this ..." She wriggled her hips in slow motion and see-sawed her body on her shoulder-blades. "I mean ..." She gripped the knob of Véronique's dildo as she straddled her to try this new game. "We needn't pretend you're a man, do we? We don't have to please *this* fellow at all costs, do we! Actually, I don't think this was designed by girls for girls. It's to let a man watch two girls ..." She froze.

"What now?" Véronique asked. She was straddling Maxine and on the point of easing the knob down into the soft folds of her crevice.

"Stop!" Maxine cried excitedly. "I've got an idea. Take that thing off again." She slipped out from under Véronique and tripped across the room to the toy chest.

Véronique was still easing the smaller ivory prick out of her when Maxine returned holding a soft rubber tube, slightly under an inch in diameter, fifteen inches long, and with a furled, rounded ring to make each open end smooth. "God knows what it was *for,*" she said. "Some dubious medico-sexual practice, no doubt. But we can do this with it, see?" And she lay down again on her back, this time with her thighs spread, and invited Véronique to push one end of it into her vagina — with, of course, appropriate sighs and shivers of pleasure as it went in. "Now lie on top of me and slip the other end into you," she said excitedly, reaching one hand around the back of Véronique's thigh to assist.

When it was all the way in she used her thighs to scoop Véronique's tight together and clamp them there. Then — a flash of inspiration, this — she tightened certain muscles down there, which had the effect of squeezing her vagina, gripping her flesh tighter around the tube. This, of course, compressed the air within it, which had the effect of subtly expanding the other end of the tube.

Véronique gasped at the feeling it gave her. "How d'you *do* that?" she asked breathlessly.

Maxine did it again.

Véronique murmured a long, satisfied, "O-o-o-h!"

"It wouldn't give men half as much pleasure to watch *this,* would it!" Maxine said as she took Véronique's head between her hands and brought their lips together. "Put your tongue in my mouth," she whispered.

Soon Véronique discovered the trick of squeezing her vagina, too. Maxine's response was even more ecstatic than hers had been. "I'll bet that would lift a man's scalp," Véronique said. "I must try it on Sherry."

"Can we forget men for this one night?" Maxine complained. "That was the whole point of using this fifteen-inch vagina-tube instead of that monster ivory prick!"

What she had said earlier was true. Any man who had paid to watch would have seen nothing more than two girls lying almost still, one on top of the other, making the smallest writhing movements, and very slowly at that. He would have had to get his jollies at second hand — by watching the sweat break out on their bodies, by seeing Maxine's freckles darken when she was on top, and most of all by listening to the steady outpouring of low moans and stifled gasps as, for the best part of an hour, they kept each other gliding along over the high plateau of the most stupendous pleasure in the universe — the unchained female orgasm.

Loosely entwined, with the 'fifteen-inch vagina-tube' still halfway inside Maxine, they fell asleep at last and only woke up when the cool midnight air gave them gooseflesh. Then they pulled the silk sheet and eiderdown up again and, shunning all mechanical aids, slipped their thighs into each other's groins, and dedicated their fingers to each other's nipples, and warmed themselves up again in no time.

Twice more that night they awakened for a further hour or so of mutual pleasuring. They slept past the communion bell and only awakened when it rang again for matins.

"Must get ready for Rory," Véronique said sleepily, making not the slightest move.

The woke up again at noon, showered, did their morning ablutions, ate a light breakfast, and took a couple of glasses of orange juice back to bed — "We'll just lie down for another fifteen minutes," Véronique said.

They were awakened for the final time when Rory let himself in and shouted, "Only little me!" up the stairs. "Hope you're red-dee?"

"Oh hell, oh hell, oh hell!" Maxine panicked at once. They were both stark naked still.

But Véronique saw it was the answer to every difficulty, the cure for all her friend's fears and anxieties. "No time to worry!" she exclaimed cheerfully. "Get it over with before you know what's happening. Do this."

And she went down on all fours, elbows and knees, pointing her bottom toward the door. She curved the small of her back to make her derrière as pert as possible and her pussy pout at him. Giggling nervously, Maxine followed suit, snuggling close to Véronique so that their hips touched. "Has he got a big one?" she whispered.

"Small but wonderfully satisfying," Véronique assured her. She said nothing as to its satisfying thickness, though. And in this position Maxine wouldn't see it clearly until the deed was done. With luck, it would be over and done with before her vagina could even *think* of going into the sort of spasm that brute of a choirmaster had caused with his insensitive sneers.

"What's *this!*" a delighted Rory exclaimed before he was properly through the door.

"Your special Sunday treat," Véronique said, peering at him under her arm. "Hurry! We're both starving."

Rory went over to the chest, shedding clothes as he went.

"What now?" Véronique complained.

"Can't have one of you going cold while the other goes incandescent," he replied. He came over to the bed holding one of the clockwork dildoes. He trod off his socks as he

Exquisite and fantastic sensations • 233

walked and arrived at the bed naked. "Warm that up for me, there's a pet," he said, slipping it into Véronique's vagina as he waddled on his knees to position himself behind Maxine's inviting derrière. "Maxine!" he exclaimed.

"Yes?" she answered in a shivery, strangulated voice.

"You are fabulously beautiful." He rubbed eager hands all over her bottom. "Why have you kept your charms hidden inside clothes all this week?"

She giggled. He saw her relax. The muscles that had been stretching her labia let go and they collapsed in a thick, juicy invitation. He offered the tip of his prick up to them and massaged her tenderly with it. As he picked up her lubrication he moved a little deeper in, waggling his hips from side to side so that his short, stubby gristle became a prying finger, lifting aside the plush fold of an outer lip to reveal the clean, bright-pink whorls and rilles of her oyster within. It was so richly complex that her actual hole could be hidden anywhere among those wet fleshy pleats and wrinkles. He probed deeper with his knob and found it. He relished the heat of her vestibule as it yielded to let him in.

"Yes! Yes!" she exclaimed, frantic with impatience and still fearful that, at the last minute, her hole would go into spasm again and shrink to propelling-pencil dimensions. She even tried to make it happen — in the pessimistic belief that whatever she *wanted* to do, her cussed body would do the opposite. But even as she tried she felt his *thing* nosing slowly into her, stretching her with the most amazing ease and filling her with utterly exquisite and fantastic sensations.

Véronique, kneeling patiently at her side, with the dead weight of the clockwork dildo now warmed up inside her hole, felt a pang of jealousy. Even at the height of her ecstasy last night, Maxine had never cried out like that. It wasn't the degree of passion that made her jealous; in fact,

Maxine had been even more passionate when it was just the two of them. It was the note of surprise behind her passion — surprise that a man's gristle could feel so fantastic when he slipped it gently in where nature intended it to go.

Rory's special Sunday treat went on for four hours, leaving him and both girls happy and exhausted. Once Maxine discovered her vagina could easily stretch to accommodate a man's gristle, even one as stocky and hard as Rory's, there was no curing her hunger. She wanted him to jab it into her in every position in *The Geometry of Eros,* and — not too grudgingly — Rory obliged her. Obliged them both, in fact. Which explained their utter exhaustion.

"And now we've got to try to seduce Terence, too," Véronique remarked with less enthusiasm than she might normally have shown.

"Oh, didn't I tell you?" Rory said. "Sorry. Something must have distracted me when I came through the door. Poor Terence can't make it this evening. Some church function he can't avoid."

Sherry turned up for his regular weekday fuck at lunchtime the following day. As he and Véronique walked upstairs he kept looking about them. She knew he was looking for Maxine but she said nothing. He laid her on the bed and fucked her only once, a tame but pleasant affair, mostly in the 'missionary' position. Then he lay beside her for a chat. He asked lots of questions about Maxine but all of them merely skirted around the one question he obviously wanted to ask: Was she ready for service?

Her answers skirted a reply to that question, too.

It annoyed him to realize that he was hoist on his own petard — that he could not simply say, 'I hear great things about young Maxine from my son Rory!'

At last, suppressing his exasperation as best he could, he said, "I wonder if she'd like to watch you and me *in flagrante* one lunchtime? Tomorrow, maybe?" And he went on to explain about the voyeurs' room, about which she was supposed to know nothing, of course.

He took her out and showed it to her. She pretended to be surprised and delighted. He told her she was going to make a damn' fine sporting girl; she pretended not to know what he meant.

"Tell her you've discovered the secret door all by yourself," he said. "Lead her to believe I don't know I'm being spied on with you."

Terence must have been talking with his brother, too, for he was not nearly as surprised as he might have been at the sight of two naked girls waiting to pull his wire. He huffed and puffed a little but the sheer beauty of Maxine's body overpowered him and he lay down willingly enough between them at last.

Véronique had practised the proper techniques with Maxine that afternoon, using the most realistic of the dildoes in the toy chest. All the same, as Maxine often remarked about anything and everything to do with sex, theory is one thing, real-life practice is another. Her hands shook slightly as she parked her bare bottom on the bed beside him and reached for that long, gnarled warrior, rearing out of its forest and beating the air above his hairy tummy.

Véronique was not entirely naked. Her single garment was one of those black-gauze bustières with peekaboo holes for her nipples. She now knelt on the bed above Terence's head and lowered her lips to his.

Maxine touched the underneath of that rampant prick with her fingertips — the briefest of touches. She touched it again, in a slightly different place. And again — repeatedly, varying the place each time, trying to avoid a pattern. He moaned a little and reached it toward that teasing hand.

God, it was *huge,* she thought. Would she ever fit anything that long inside her? But she admitted to herself that she'd have had exactly the same doubts about his brother's thick, stubby monster if she'd seen it first, and that reassured her.

When she felt she'd tormented him enough she left her fingertips resting lightly on the spermspouter tube that ran up the middle of its underside. She held the knob fastidiously between the thumb and finger of her left hand and ran her fingers lightly up and down the whole underside. She dipped a fingertip in the jar of skin cream and rubbed it in small circles all around his glans.

She took up a golf tee (this had been Véronique's idea), dipped it in the same cream, and slipped it into the limp, weepy eye at the top of his knob.

"What the …?" he mumbled, trying to get his head around Véronique's to see what this fantastic new sensation might be. But she stifled him with a passionate kiss and he surrendered himself to the unknown again.

The pin of the tee was a mere quarter of an inch inside his knob but that was enough to let it stand upright. Maxine flipped the tee gently with her fingernail. The resulting sharp jabs of pleasure were like electric thrills running all through him. Her next trick was even more dainty. It was something she had read about in one of Sherry's books — something so dangerous that men had died of it. Only the most experienced courtesans, the writer warned, should attempt it. But Véronique said that was just put in to make it more titillating. They had found the carton of rubber rings in the toybox, too — the cornucopia of all their pleasures. They looked like tiny drive belts from a toy vacuum cleaner, made of thick rubber with very little give. They were of various sizes between one and two inches in diameter. The book said to use one just slightly smaller than the prick you were going to pleasure. They had made a small selection to suit Terence's, as Véronique's fingers and lips remembered it.

Maxine took up one of them but found it just a little too tight. Terence struggled to see what she was doing but now Véronique moved forward, hanging her bare nipples over his lips and caressing his pectorals with her tongue and fingers. He collapsed again in a happy stupor as Maxine, taking the next size up, rolled it slowly, tenderly, all the way down to the base of his gristle.

He had not the faintest idea what she was doing; he only knew that it produced the most exquisite sensations and that it left his erection feeling stiffer than ever and, in a curious way, *raw* — peeled to every new stimulus.

And what stimuli!

Maxine was in no hurry. Indeed, the longer she spun it out, the more scope it gave to her invention and the more time to satisfy her curiosity. What the ring did was to allow the high-pressure arterial blood to pump into his gristle, where it became low-pressure venous blood, lacking the force to drain back out again past the tight rubber constriction. As a result, his erection was, indeed, stiffer and more sensitive than it had ever been. Veins that normally lay hidden now bulged like earthworms just beneath the skin. And the skin itself was everywhere stretched and gleaming. The strain even *looked* appalling and if the thing had suddenly started to steam and smoke, neither girl would have been at all surprised.

Maxine ran one dainty fingernail up and down the bulging spermspouter tube until he groaned and begged for mercy.

She smeared her hand with cold cream and massaged it with provocative gentleness, interspersed with short bouts of ferocious tossing. She placed it between the flats of both hands and rolled it as one would try to roll a sausage of plasticine or clay. She gripped the shaft in her left hand and rocked her right palm round and round his knob, pressing its most sensitive glans against the encircling finger and thumb. And she and Véronique between them managed to guess each time when he threatened to rise to an orgasm and so held back until the threat had subsided again. They tormented him thus until his prick started turning an unhealthy looking purple, at which point Maxine slipped off the ring and, with the flush of hot new blood, tormented him to that climax which they had denied him a dozen times or more over the previous half hour.

Again briefed by Véronique, Maxine capped his wildly leaping knob with her fingers, squeezing and letting go in perfect timing with his spurts, and giggling at the hot tickle of his sticky as it poured so copiously from him and made brittle, crackling noises as she continued to massage it to prolonged excitement.

As the intensity of his thrills receded, the pain came through stronger. At last he rolled out of their clutches and sat hunched on the far side of the bed, holding his limp prick in one hand and his head in the other, rocking himself gently, and moaning soft and low. Véronique and Maxine just grinned at each other in triumph.

The remainder of their brief sojourn at that house followed as night the day. Sherry cracked the following lunchtime and demanded that they should give him, too, what Terence had described as the sexual experience of his entire lifetime.

Next day Rory begged for the same.

Encouraged, Véronique and Maxine read wider and deeper in Sherry's library and then practised — one could say perpetrated — upon the three McLarens the fruits of their ever-more bizarre researches. Lunches became longer. The separate evening sessions of the two brothers merged into orgies that left them drained and useless.

Rory crashed a staff car.

Terence fell asleep in court.

Sherry called a Mrs Dillon, 'Mrs Dildo' to her face.

Something had to be done. They all agreed that something had to be done, but none of them was willing to do it. And so each day they dragged their weary bodies and their sex-sated, sex-gorged, sex-glutted pricks to Véronique and Maxine for 'just one more time.'

Relief came one day about a month after the orgies had started. It was July by then and a new hot spell had started. The two girls spent as much time as they could sunning themselves out in the garden. It happened one Saturday morning, while they waited for Jilly to call with her weekly progress report. Last Saturday her book had had three dozen pages filled. She was then up to customer 154, and her bank book showed just short of £90. Maxine was waiting to tell her that male gristle of various sizes had thrust itself in and out of her vagina almost seventy thousand times by then. 'Penile thrusts,' she called them now.

They were lying full length in wicker loungers, soaking up the sun, when both of them heard a little cough from somewhere near by. They opened one eye apiece, looked about them, saw nothing, and closed it again.

The cough repeated itself and a voice said, "Over here!"

They opened both eyes and saw a girl — or, rather, the head of a girl — looking over the fence at them. "May I speak with you?" she asked hesitantly.

They sat up and made welcoming noises. The girl fiddled with two boards in the fence and squeezed between them. She was buxom, with a smooth, waxy-white skin that had seen no sun that summer. She was also rather plain, with a moon face and dark hair, severely plaited. "I'm Elspeth," she said, holding out a hand.

They introduced themselves and invited her to sit down. Jilly arrived at that moment and further introductions followed.

"You're the girl who was here about a month ago," Elspeth said.

"We were all here about a month ago," Véronique told her.

"Yes but Jilly — may I call you Jilly? — Jilly was ... well, I couldn't help overhearing."

"Ah," Jilly said.

"And it's taken you a month ..." Maxine began.

"No. I visit my uncle once a month." She nodded her head at the house next door. "Actually, he's not my uncle — except by courtesy. Which is part of my trouble. He's a friend of my mother's and ..." She floundered and swallowed hard.

"Trouble, you say?" Véronique prompted her. "With the alleged uncle?"

She nodded miserably. "The thing is, we're absolutely broke. Not *him!* He's got oodles of oof. But my mother is."

"And your father?"

She shook her head disconsolately. "And Uncle Cuthbert, as I call him, has suggested a way for me and my mother to earn enough money to keep us in modest circumstances."

Pennies began to drop.

"He wants to put you both in a sporting house?" Jilly guessed.

"No. He wants to put us in *that* house." Again she pointed next door.

"To be his mistress? Or mistresses?"

She nodded. "In fact, my mother already is his mistress. He doesn't pay her but we get our board and lodging. He was offering me forty pounds a year to become his mistress, too. And I was just reconciling myself to the idea when I overheard you talking. And it sounded such fun, the way you described it. So I've not been able to think about anything else all the month!" She smiled feebly. "I was desperate in case you'd all moved on."

The three girls exchanged glances. The problem was, of course, Elspeth's plainness. She had a buxom young figure but her face was nothing to write home about. How could they encourage her to enter a profession where so many pretty girls already crowded the pavements and sporting houses?

"Are you a virgin?" Véronique asked.

She blushed, lowered her eyes and shook her head.

"Who have you done it with?" Jilly put in. "Sorry to be asking these dreadfully personal questions but … ah …"

"The person we would ask to help you would certainly ask us," Véronique explained.

"I was fingered by my cousin," Eslpeth almost whispered. "And …"

"And?"

Now it was a whisper. "This so-called 'uncle' of mine did it. Just once. He was in bed with my mother one afternoon and I didn't know. I went in to ask her something and caught them going at it pretty wildly. They didn't see me, fortunately, so I ran back out. And then I watched them through the chink of the door. I could see his *thing* going in and out of her. And I couldn't tell whether she was in agony or ecstasy but, anyway, she fainted. And he looked about and spotted me and chased me to my bedroom and threw me on the bed and ... well ..."

"Finished off inside you?" Véronique asked.

Again she blushed and nodded.

"And how did you feel about that?" Jilly asked.

Elspeth shrugged. "Nothing, really. I just thought is that it? And what's all the fuss about? I could do *that* without any bother. But then I heard how a girl could earn a lot more than just forty pounds a year. So that's why I'm asking — how could I get to do the same as you?"

"Let's ask Sherry," Véronique suggested. "This is one of his Saturdays. Is your uncle at home? Could you stay and have lunch with us?"

He was not at home and she could stay for lunch.

When Sherry came, Véronique took him aside and explained the situation in a few succinct sentences. "The difficulty is ... well, you'll see for yourself," she concluded. "She is rather plain."

Little did she know!

All Sherry desired by now was a plain, buxom young innocent who wouldn't go reading books and who would think that *doing it* in anything but the good old missionary position was devilishly wicked. If she proved as dull and amenable as Elspeth looked, he might keep her a whole year while he recruited back all his strength. He did not even consult his sons; he knew they'd agree. His only condition was that Elspeth should flee her Uncle Cuthbert's house at once and let herself be put up, temporarily, in a small private hotel in Sussex Gardens, three miles away — and that she should not exchange a single further word with Jilly, with Maxine, or with Véronique. Not now. Not ever — at least while she remained his mistress.

And so it was that, on the morning of Sunday, 9 July, 1922, Véronique and Maxine climbed out of a taxi in Little Venice, each clutching an expensive leather suitcase crammed with even more expensive dresses and lingerie, to say nothing of the perfumes and creams and lotions with which they were going to pamper the bodies that were now their passport and ticket to the good life.

Ten houses of pleasure, built two-by-two, stared sleepily out over the canal on that bright sabbath morning. All the blinds were closed. Behind them, some five or six dozen ladies of pleasure lay deep in the arms of Morpheus, recuperating in mind and body for another afternoon and night of heavy traffic in the arms of sex-starved, sex-driven, sex-obsessed men.

"They're still rather grand," Véronique remarked.

"Though they've surely seen better days," Maxine replied. Her voice shook; indeed, she was shivery all over.

Her friend chuckled. "Now they see better nights instead. For some lucky men — the ones who choose *me!* — it'll be the best nights they'll ever know."

The two girls had no trouble finding Nymphenburg, which they had seen often enough through Sherry's telescope and binoculars. They pushed open the wrought-iron gate and went up the three shallow steps inside to an area paved with flagstones. Véronique set down her suitcase and stared up at the façade. Her feelings were a mixture of excitement and trepidation as she thought of all the things that happened under that roof and behind those now vacant windows every night — things that were now going to happen to her!

"Don't," Maxine said, holding on to her suitcase.

"Don't what?"

"Don't linger out here. People will know we're prostitutes."

"Darling!" Véronique butted her playfully on the shoulder. "In the first place, there *are* no people at this hour. In the second place, they'll know that every time you leave this house from now on. Or are you going to lock yourself in there and never come out? And in the third place, there are dozens of us in this row of houses alone — and dozens more around both corners. We are the majority hereabouts."

Maxine still didn't like it but she said nothing. In a vicar's daughter certain attitudes die hard.

Véronique ran her eyes along the respectable-looking faces of Nymphenburg and the other sporting houses on either side. Again she tried to imagine all the excitement — the stiff pricks, the spreading thighs, the warm, wet, welcoming pussies, the jigajig, the spermspouting — that had been going on for years behind those drawn curtains. Years of it. Hundreds of girls and tens of thousands of men. All that pleasure — surely something of it should linger here? She could not feel it, though.

And she and Maxine were about to become one small part of it all! Again it seemed too vast, too grand a notion to imagine.

"Just think," she said. "In a couple of nights from now, a hundred men or more are going to come walking through that same gate and some of them will pick out you and some will pick out me and …" A little shiver ran through her from head to toe at the thought and a tingle of excited dread fluttered between her legs.

She turned and faced the canal and the houses opposite — or, rather, she faced London and the world in general. "Where are you now?" she murmured. "What are you doing at this moment?"

"Who?" Maxine asked.

"The half-dozen men who are going to walk up this path on Wednesday, still not knowing I exist — much less that I'm going to take them upstairs and let them fuck me. What strange, magical forces are drawing them toward me even now?" She giggled. "Remember what Jilly said — about our pussies giving out some sort of wireless message and all the men's pricks going stiff like wireless aerials to receive the message ... after which they *have* to come down here to find relief between our thighs? Don't you think it's exciting — the mysterious *power* we have over them?"

"Not really," Maxine admitted.

"What, then?"

"I'm just wondering how many penile thrusts are equal to one nice little haberdashery shop!"

Well and truly is it said: It takes all sports to make a world!

A Message from the Publisher

Headline Delta is a unique list of erotic fiction, covering many different styles and periods and appealing to a broad readership. As such, we would be most interested to hear from you.

Did you enjoy this book? Did it turn you on – or off? Did you like the story, the characters, the setting? What did you think of the cover presentation? How did this novel compare with others you have read? In short, what's your opinion? If you care to offer it, please write to:

> The Editor
> Headline Delta
> 338 Euston Road
> London NW1 3BH

Or maybe you think you could write a better erotic novel yourself. We are always looking for new authors. If you'd like to try your hand at writing a book for possible inclusion in the Delta list, here are our basic guidelines: we are looking for novels of approximately 75,000 words whose purpose is to inspire the sexual imagination of the reader. The erotic content should not describe illegal sexual activity (pedophilia, for example). The novel should contain sympathetic and interesting characters, pace, atmosphere and an intriguing storyline.

If you would like to have a go, please submit to the Editor a sample of at least 10,000 words, clearly typed in double-lined spacing on one side of the paper only, together with a short outline of the plot. Should you wish your material returned to you, please include a stamped addressed envelope. If we like it sufficiently, we will offer you a contract for publication.